A LONG WAY FROM HOME

Across the mews, in the shadow of lamplight, I
detected a flicker. Someone stood there, tall, silent,
still. Only the cuffs of his trousers and the tips of his
shoes were visible in the eerie light. I could almost
hear him breathing. I shrank back against the shop,
out of the light and—I hoped—out of his sight. I
wanted to scream; I dared not make a sound. Yet I
could tell from the crunch of his shoe leather on the
cobbled street that he was coming after me.

"I say, my lady." He clamped a hand on my arm
and I jumped in terror. "What are you doing out on a
night like this alone?"

He bent closer, and though I could not see his face,
his breath smelled of liquor while his body smelled of
the best cologne.

"Let me go, sir. I wish to go home."

"Do you? But you're a long way from home, my
lady," he said, inching me up against the wall, his
other hand rising like a claw before my face . . .

JO-ANN POWER

THE MARK OF THE CHADWICKS

ZEBRA BOOKS
KENSINGTON PUBLISHING CORP.

ZEBRA BOOKS

are published by

Kensington Publishing Corp.
475 Park Avenue South
New York, NY 10016

First Printing: February, 1993

Printed in the United States of America

DEDICATION

To Steve—

My rock, my foundation,
my assurance that order complements all chaos
and that, indeed,
one does not exist without the other.

Chapter One

September 1888

I hadn't returned to England for the money. I hadn't!

I squared my jaw and repeated the idea in my mind. Like a mantra from some Eastern religion, my prayer would become my motto. My watchword. My talisman against the frightening memories that England brought to my mind.

No, I was definitely not returning for the money. I knew that was the motivation most would ascribe to me. After all, most had attributed other motives, as diabolical, as absurd. But as my eyes swept the view of Southampton through an icy mist, I grasped my son's pudgy little hand and gathered my courage.

"Mommy, oh Mommy," chirped five-year-old Jeremy with a beaming cherub's grin, "it looks just like New York!"

"Yes, my love it certainly does," I replied as my eyes scanned the swarming docks so similar to the hustle of those Jeremy and I knew so well. I suppressed a geyser of homesickness, then valiantly smiled at him and tugged my darling's hand. "Let's get settled in the hotel first, have a lovely hot luncheon, and then explore, shall we?"

"Yippee!" He jumped up and down while I tried

in vain to keep him dry with my umbrella.

With his child's intuition, he knew I would do anything for him. Anything. Purchase sweet treats from my meager wages. Keep him safe from malicious gossip. Amuse him by riding in an open brougham through an icy mist. Return to England . . .

"Do you suppose"—he leaned against me and batted keen black puppy's eyes at me—"they make peppermint sticks in England?"

Inside I chuckled, but I made round eyes at him. "Hmmm, I do remember they make awful peppermint." His rose-petal lips opened in anticipation because he knew my ploys too well. "But then, of course, that might be because I was always partial to their butterscotch."

He yipped. "Oh, let's go!" He bobbed up and down again.

But the press of passengers down the ramp restrained us from the rampage on which Jeremy would have us.

I laughed aloud now. "My darling, I know you're anxious to leave, but you must contain yourself." I cast about for some amusement to distract him. "Let's see if we can spot your Aunt Helena. She said she'd come down from London to meet us." In fact, she'd probably arrived last night.

"What does she look like again?"

"Like most Chadwicks. Tall, flowing black hair, and dark eyes."

"Like my eyes," Jeremy added as he scanned the crowd.

I nodded and searched for my husband's cousin along the dock. I found no one who vaguely resembled Helena. Neither did Jeremy and again he became restless, the cumulative result of three weeks in second class on this vessel. With compassion, I turned to Jeremy. "I'll search for Aunt Helena while you see how many ships from other ports you can name. Have you noticed that tall ship to our left? I cannot read its name. Where do you suppose she's from?"

He pivoted and stretched up so that his little towhead cleared the rail. "*The China Jade*," he reported. "China. That's what we eat from."

"Yes, my dear, but the country called China gave its name to the porcelain it exports."

"Like Grandfather's company used to ship tobacco."

"Yes," I answered, proud of Jeremy's memory, distressed that he should remind me of my father at this critical time. Oh, that my father still lived, still shipped tobacco and brandy and tea . . . If he were alive, Jeremy and I would not be here in this predicament. I hung my head and then raised it to seek diversion for both my son and myself. "What is the name of the lovely ship there to our other side?"

He pivoted once again and squinted into the finest of rains. "*The Black Pearl*. Black pearls? Are there really such things?"

I grinned at him and felt relief as we took a few more steps down the gangway. "Yes, absolutely. They are very rare, very costly."

"They must be very big, too, to need a big ship to carry them."

I smiled at Jeremy's insight. He never ceased to amaze me, this intelligent child of my heart. "My dear, shipping companies name their frigates almost anything. Remember Grandfather's stories of his fleet?"

"Yes, yes, I do." His onyx eyes gleamed. "I like *The Red Devil* and *Golden Daughter* best."

"Named after his best friend—"

"And you."

"Yes, and me. If you own a ship, you can name her almost anything that suits you."

"Someday I'll own one hundred ships to sail the seven seas, just like Grandfather did."

9

He turned, so serious that I brushed his pale hair beneath his broad sailor's hat. My gloved hand covered his crown like a minister giving benediction. "I hope you do, my love."

"I will," he vowed with an intensity born of the past year of upheaval and uncertainty. "I will, Mother. You wait and see. Then I will name each one whatever I like." He grinned and I could tell the imp searched the gangplank before he ventured forth with his ideas.

He grinned at me. "What do you say to 'The Long Plank'?"

I nodded with satisfaction at his quick wit, then watched his gaze land on the bustle of the lady in front of us.

"'The Green Bustle'?"

I frowned at his improvisation, but he was not dissuaded.

"Or, um . . ."—his eyes searched the crowd waiting on the cobblestone dock—"'The Blond Giant'?"

I began to smile when my eyes found the figure his words denoted.

My heart dashed widly about my chest. I fought for breath, squeezing my eyes shut and opening them again to the sight of the man I had spent years banishing from my mind. Yes, my eyes confirmed my worst fears. It was Graham come to meet us. Come to see us in spite of my expectation to meet him at Darnley Castle. Come in ironical notice that as the last person to see me leave the country five and a half years ago, he should also be the first to see me return. Damn, damn, why did this man always surprise me? Why was I always at his mercy?

I raised my eyes to the bruised sky, and with a will I inherited from my Dutch grandmother, I captured my fear. Leashed it like the feral animal it could become and yanked it into the dark closet where it must remain, out of sight, out of mind, while I did what I must here in England.

10

I would show Graham the calm, deliberate woman I had become. I would show him the young American debutante who had learned to live with disillusionment and poverty.

With that resolve, I allowed my gaze to find him. He stood to one side of the gangway, a towering, muscular, exquisite specimen of man. He wore a cobalt-blue tweed inverness coat, whose cape flapped like two bat wings in the off-shore breeze. In like frenzy, his luxuriant bronze hair whipped wildly about his furrowed brow. He stood, umbrella hoisted high, one foot before the other, the picture of leisurely intent. The picture of the gentleman.

My caged fear beat at the door of reality. I could not let the beast out to roam. Not before this man. No, Graham Chadwick was a man to whom I must not display fear. Courage only.

I gathered serenity around me like an armored cloak. "That Blond Giant, young man, is your Uncle Graham," I offered, all the while watching my brother-in-law as he found us, waved solemnly, and waited.

"Really?"

"Yes, he is the Chadwick you most resemble. Let's see if you notice it when you meet," I offered too gaily. My eyes were still on Graham's, while I felt my son withdraw inside himself as he always did these days when about to meet strangers. Hurt, yes. Jeremy was hurt by the whispers, the gossip that surrounded us in New York. Young though he was, he knew people stopped to stare and talk about his mother and his grandfather. Somehow, he felt the gossip spread its filth to him and understood no reason for it. My heart writhed in the torment given to so small a child over the indelicacies of a brutal society. Graham Chadwick's presence was to Jeremy that of another stranger, someone new to hurt Mommy and, inscrutably, his innocent self.

Now, *now!*, when I needed the crush of passengers to take their merry time descending the ramp, they seemed to fall away with rapidity. My steps took me toward Graham even as my mind was ravaged by the sight of my only living male relative.

I crossed the cobbled street, a formal smile painted along my mouth. I stood before him at last, and when my eyes had swept up his imposing figure, I met his eyes—his obsidian eyes—and could not hold the pose. My facade shattered like fine crystal in an iron vise.

Just in the nick of time to save my self-respect, I felt his hands travel my arms, sweep my shoulders, encircle my back and embrace me. My breath left my body. His warmth thrilled me as I never thought to be warmed again. His was more human kindness than I had felt from anyone in over a year. More welcome than I had had from friends in years. More manly concern than I knew how to receive. I pulled away, not wishing to meet Graham's eyes yet knowing I must.

Brazen, breathtakingly black, his eyes met mine with none of the warmth his body had shown. Unemotional, I thought, as when we had first met years ago. Yet, the years had altered other characteristics that I had assumed would never change. Silver streaked along the golden hair at his temples, fine lines etched the full, firm lips that in response reminded me of molded marble. He was how old?—all of thirty? thirty-one?—and appeared another decade wiser. Yet, other things remained the same. His skin was still burnished from his days of tending to his ships at dock or sea. His body was still firm, unyieldingly erect. Formidable. His untimely aging had only made him more magnetic.

I recovered by falling back on my manners. "You are in good health, Graham."

For my cool courtesy, he gave fervent kindness. "But you have grown quite stunning, Vanessa." He examined me with an intensity that had me looking at his cravat. He could still frighten me with the

12

probing power of his black eyes. Eyes that exhumed every truth, every passion, good and evil. Eyes that could delight so like my son's . . . Eyes that could condemn so like my dead husband's . . .

He touched the point of my chin with one finger and lifted my face to his view. I felt his examination as one would a doctor's, impersonal and piercing.

"I swear no English rose can match the vibrance of you American women. It was true when I first saw you; it's truer now." He flowed nearer. Our umbrellas collided and tangled.

I stepped back. "I'd say it was the weather."

He cocked a brow. "We *could* declare it was the atmosphere. Yet, I know as well as you no sturdy flowers grow in the dark." He tore his eyes from mine to find a fidgeting Jeremy. "This, I presume, is Jeremy." Graham extended his hand. "How do you do, young man?"

Jeremy met Graham with a cold cheer he gave any stranger. He thrust his hand into his uncle's and performed with a polite generosity taught him by my father. "How do you do, sir? It's nice to meet you."

Graham squatted before his nephew and threw me an inquisitive glance. "So your mother has told you much of us, has she?"

"Yes, sir." Jeremy checked my eyes before continuing. "She has said that you are my father's youngest brother. That you are a cousin to the Queen and very famous."

I stood still as stone.

Graham's unfathomable eyes traveled to mine as he spoke to Jeremy. "Did she tell you that you, as well, are cousin to the Queen?" Graham's voice grew raspy. "And very famous?"

I gaped at Graham. How could he raise this subject now . . . and to Jeremy, no less?! What was he doing?

Jeremy shook his head. "No, sir." Jeremy tilted his face up to me. "Is that true, Mommy?" he asked, delighted at the idea and unaware of the fury that this

13

pointed question caused me.

How dare Graham do this to me! How dare he open the subject that could destroy my son here on the dock, bare minutes after our arrival. That caged animal called Fear, whom I'd locked away, tore at the door to be released. I stepped forward and put a hand to Jeremy's shoulder.

Jeremy's clean brow wrinkled. He knew my protection for what it was.

"Yes, my darling," my eyes blazed into Graham's, "because you are a Chadwick, you are also a cousin to Queen Victoria."

Beneath my hands, I felt Jeremy's body suffuse with joy. "And famous, *too?*" he almost pleaded.

My eyes never left Graham's. "Fame is a prize to be won by good deeds, my darling. I think you must learn life's ways before you earn its rewards."

Jeremy sagged a bit. He hadn't understood my words, which were, of course, meant more for his uncle Graham than for him.

Graham flexed his jaw and stood. His face looked serene, but I could see what the facade cost him. I read it in his eyes.

They burned. He turned away from me and searched the crowded dock, then raised a hand and gestured to someone near the line of carriages.

From the throng, a rotund fellow dressed in black servant's serge approached. He carried a huge black umbrella such as valets use to assist their employers. I remembered all the servants in the Chadwicks' employ and this man was new.

Graham turned back to me, his eyes now free of the fires in his mind. "Shall we take ourselves on to better conditions? In the expectation that you would not wish to travel immediately after disembarking, I have booked rooms for us at the Hotel Warwick."

I filled with resentment. "It *is* where I intended to spend a day or two before venturing on to Darnley. However, Graham—"

14

"Good. Then we'll go now."

Graham's man had reached our side by this time and stood waiting as his master and I stared at each other.

I stood my ground. "You assumed I would come quietly," I said simply.

Graham appraised my stoicism with its equal. "Quietly. Quickly."

"Expediently?"

"Vanessa, please. I asked if you had no objections."

"I was not under the impression what you said was a question."

His lower lip twitched. "Perhaps it should have been."

"It *definitely* should have been."

He fought to control his gentlemanly demeanor. No Englishman worth his crust discussed such delicacies in front of children and servants.

But I didn't care. Graham was the one who had come here unexpectedly. Let him deal with the consequences.

"Helena is to meet us. I asked her to come and she eagerly agreed. I will not leave without her."

"She's not coming, Vanessa."

"Not coming? But why? Is she ill?" I feared for my lovely friend, Graham's cousin.

"No, not ill. MacCarthy, please see to my sister-in-law's luggage. Perhaps Master Jeremy would like to come with you, eh?" He winked at Jeremy, who nodded more out of adult's expectation than of joy. But when he turned to MacCarthy, and Jeremy and the two of them wound their way through the crowd, Graham offered his arm to me. "Vanessa, shall we retire to the carriage while MacCarthy talks to the steward?"

I moved not one muscle. "Helena, Graham. Tell me about Helena."

"I asked her to remain in London. I wished to

meet you myself."

"Why?" I whispered, anguished. "Why? I wish no rumors, no scandal. Helena should have come to meet us. You and I cannot travel unescorted! People will have a bonanza. Too many remember—"

"I have provided for the social proprieties, Vanessa. I have hired a traveling companion . . . an educated woman who can also serve as governess to Jeremy."

"I will not risk it. No companion or governess or MacCarthy, for that matter, can wipe the stain from my reputation."

"Perhaps not. That is a bigger task, requiring more than chaperones, Vanessa."

I waved a hand. "It does not matter."

"But it does," he bit out. "It matters to me. This is my family's reputation we speak of as well. And this matter will be put to rest, by God." His anger ebbed. "Now you will listen to me . . . We have MacCarthy and Jeremy and Miss Simpson. Furthermore, I reserved a suite with four separate bedrooms at the Warwick. I persuaded Helena to let me come alone because we need this time. You and I have much to discuss before my father's will is read."

"You are wrong, Graham. We have nothing to say. Too many people said too many things . . . ridiculous things . . . years ago."

"The time has come to bury the past."

"That's impossible, Graham."

"I believe opportunities abound."

"I have come only for the reading of the will and the possibility of a decent income placed there for me."

"And for your son."

I arched a brow in derision. "Perhaps placed there to clear some family conscience."

"Yes, perhaps. But to clear our names, you must come with me, Vanessa. No scenes, no scandals . . . Just a brother-in-law escorting his dead brother's wife to a local hotel and on to London and Yorkshire."

"You make it sound so simple."

"It is, Vanessa."

His logic seemed undeniable. Peevish, I replied, "Do I have a choice, Graham?"

"Yes, Vanessa. Today you have choices."

Tears sprang to my eyes and I spun from him. Very well. "Which is your carriage, Graham?"

Chapter Two

The Hotel Warwick was the grandame of temporary residences in the thriving port of Southampton. Although not as stupendous as the Grand Hotel in New York, the Warwick served the same function: She must provide every amenity to the itinerant idle, the politically prominent, and the financially adroit traversing the British byroads of the world. As such, the Warwick claimed sumptuous suites, with yards of cream lace and mauve satin at the windows, pink brocades upon the settees, and ferns, ferns, *ferns!* at every window and in every dark corner. The staff was obsequious, the service gilded. Furthermore, the formal dining room offered cuisine from one's flightiest fantasies.

I remembered so well. I had enjoyed the Warwick's pleasures once, years ago, in another lifetime, when I was young and gay and terribly in love with my husband. We had spent two nights here on our way to the coast for summer air. Ensconced in one fabulous suite, I had waited for my errant husband to return from one extremely lengthy afternoon's business meeting. I had paced the floor, ignoring the opportunities to read or play solitaire. So today, I was not surprised when I realized that in all the Warwick's two hundred rooms and assorted amenities, not one entertainment existed for an adult, much less for an intelligent child.

Jeremy had grown bored long before I had finished unpacking one trunk. I sat in indecorous display upon the Persian carpeted floor as I rummaged through the small drawer in the door at the bottom of the upright steamer trunk. "They're not here, Jeremy. Are you sure you put them in this particular trunk last night?"

"Yes, ma'am."

Heavy footfalls heralded the arrival of Miss Simpson from the bedroom designated as mine. "And the cards are definitely not in the other steamer, Mrs. Chadwick," boomed the woman Graham had engaged as chaperone and governess in one. Her stentorian voice bombarded one's eardrums. Indeed, her fire-plug body, with heaving bosom and rolling hips, overpowered all of one's senses.

"Thank you, Miss Simpson" I smiled at her stoic expression. Through all my troubles, I had not lost my belief that one catches more flies with honey than vinegar. However, from the instant I had met Simpson a few minutes ago, I detected her attitude toward life was of the sour variety. "If we do not find the cards, we will play chess then."

"I know where that is!" Simpson affirmed with pressed lips, pivoting about to return from whence she'd come.

A knock sounded at the connecting door. Jeremy hesitated, but when I nodded permission, he rose to open it.

Graham, attired in a navy day suit, perfunctorily smiled at Jeremy and walked to my side. He towered over me, then peered down, mouth taut with disapproval, and extended a hand.

"Vanessa, whatever are you doing? They have maids here to unpack. And Simpson is engaged for that purpose."

"I'm aware of that, Graham. I was anxious to find Jeremy's deck of cards and couldn't wait for the maids."

19

· "Come, come," Graham grasped my hand and helped me up. "I'm here to take care of Jeremy." With his other hand beneath my other elbow, he pulled me much too close, and because I was unsteady, my torso brushed his. The tingling of my breasts against his corded chest belied my strict exterior control. His large hands steadied me. I drew back and smoothed my taffeta skirt.

He stood before me and I felt his eyes rake over me. Did he know how my body reacted to his? Could he feel through the layers of chemise and corset and gown how he unsettled me?

"Vanessa," his voice broke and he cleared his throat, "I think it best if I give you an opportunity to rest. This has been a harrowing trip for you."

He could see that? I looked up at him, surprised, grateful, aware how indifferent Jeremy might be to the idea of spending the afternoon with a stranger, albeit his uncle. "I don't think that Jeremy—"

Graham placed his index finger before my lips but snatched it away before he touched me. "Vanessa," he breathed laboriously, "I will do this."

I fought the urge to close my eyes and rest just once in mellow companionship with him. But so many years divided us, transforming us from friends to acquaintances. The way back might not exist. I hid my fresh sorrow in bravado.

"Again, Graham, do I have a choice? It seems you have things in order. Even to dissuading Helena from meeting me at the dock."

"You *will* have this argument, won't you? I asked her to wait to see you in London because I wanted to meet you first, alone."

"I dislike being manipulated, Graham."

"I know that well! I meant you no harm. Please . . ." His eyes shifted to indicate Jeremy. "Let us discuss it this evening. There is so much we need to say, and Jeremy is in need of some sarsaparilla and cake, and perhaps a tour of my shipyards to romp and shake off the doldrums of your voyage."

How *could* one man change from tormentor to protector in a few seconds? I feared I did not know, but had to agree that Jeremy needed more attention than I, in my fatigue, could offer at the moment. "Jeremy, my dear, it seems your uncle knows the way to your heart."

Jeremy eyed his uncle, hungering with a child's appetite to feast on the joy Graham offered, debating if he could taste the fruit and trust the man.

Graham cocked his head to one side. "No place for gentlemen, I would say, young man, when women wish to wile away the afternoon in a tub of hot water and bubbles."

When Jeremy saw me nod, he perked up a bit. His clearing joy at the way the day was unfolding affected Graham and they smiled at each other, forming a truce for their initial outing.

I went to the corner bedroom door and called for Miss Simpson.

With help from me and his governess, Jeremy was deftly dressed against the day. In a few minutes he and Graham left, with MacCarthy close in attendance. Simpson suddenly declared a migraine headache and retired to her room "for a few moments of solitude before Master Jeremy returned to share it with her."

I arched one brow at her. Such ingratitude appalled me. She was a servant and had more than many, yet begrudged her solitude to a child. I watched her go and wondered how long she would remain with any employer. Indeed, I wondered how she had endeared herself to Graham.

A knock came upon the hall door and I gave up my speculation for the time being. When I opened it, one petite maid entered with delicacies for tea, and another followed with preparations of lavender oil and lavish terrycloths for my bath.

Their preparations sent them scurrying about the

suite, and when they were done and the door closed behind them, I walked toward the tea table, laden with a silver service fit for Queen Victoria herself. Scones and biscuits sat beside soft apple and bosc pear butters; blueberry tea cakes towered high beside oranges and pineapples that someone had shipped from the tropics.

Who could speed such cargo here?

I smiled as the answer came to me. Graham, of course. He had done this for me—for my comfort. Down to my favored Devonshire cream for the fruit. I poured myself a cup of tea from the heavy silver pot, laced the brew with milk, stirred, and sipped. The aromatic brew was from the Ch'ing Emperor's Szechuan province. Graham, again, had remembered my preference for it. I smiled and sipped again. Its ripe flavor only resurrected memories of how Graham had become so solicitous to my needs, even when my husband and the rest of the Chadwicks had not. I found myself famished and sat to eat my fill of Graham's repast. Sated, I pushed the cup away and sighed.

Graham, Graham, how much we have changed! You, now the heir, and me, *me!* the tarnished woman whose dowry made your inheritance worth something once again. I shut my eyes to the ghoulish fickleness of fortune and made for my bedchamber.

Suddenly suffocated, I tore at the buttons of my jacket. I stripped off the traveling suit and jabot and layers of undergarments, freeing myself of bodily constraints. Plucking out my hairpins, I freed myself of my last outward trappings of society. I combed my fingers through my waving hair and massaged my scalp.

I stepped into the lion-footed brass tub and sank up to my hairline in clouds of steaming lavender bubbles, reveling in the sumptuous caress. As I submerged myself into the soothing pool, I soaped the mass of my hair. I lifted one leg, then assayed my

22

body through the ripples of water. At twenty-four I still looked firm, with taut thighs and midriff. My full breasts, which I had so rued as a girl, still stood erect. That aspect of my figure alone had always made men turn to look at me, especially in summer frocks or evening clothes with sweeping décolletage. At five-feet-four, I had a prominent bosom that could work for good or ill. When a coquette, I had used my figure as any other would. Now as a mature woman, I dressed with discretion, wishing to attract no man ever again.

Roiled by my memories, I rose from the tub on a whoosh of turbulent waters. Perfunctorily, I wrapped a giant towel around me and coiled another in my hair. Perhaps more tea would soothe my nerves. I entered the bedchamber and reached for my amethyst silk dressing robe, the one my father had given me two years ago as a birthday present.

"My darling girl," he had smiled at me over the beribboned box from Bonwit Teller's, "you must always wear purples, particularly in the privacy of your boudoir. The color makes your eyes rich purple." My eyes, he had continued, that would see another husband, a worthier husband.

I had turned from my father then, even as I turned from the thought now. The tension gnawed at me. The tension of remembering my father's words, the tension of seeing Graham again. Graham, who could do such violent things to my emotions. Who could make my mind a seesaw of moods: surprise, anger, suspicion, sensuality.

Ahhh! Why had he come? When I had asked him inside his hired carriage, he had turned his face toward the window and claimed he owed me that courtesy. Courtesy. Yes, I needed that. And he was right, I needed it from him. Especially from him. Now. Today.

Oh, had I only had courtesy from him and his family six years ago when I needed it! But that was when Charles had been alive. And blood ran thicker than water ... The Chadwicks had believed Charles. Charles ...

Charles, whom I met at one of Mrs. Astor's subscription balls one summer evening after my coming out. Charles, whom I found enchanting, charming. Prince Charming, my friends dubbed him, and almost a prince he was, too. Charles Albert Jeremy Chadwick, Viscount Chadwick, heir to the tenth Earl of Darnley. Charles, my first love, my first lover, my joy ...

And my agony.

I raked my fingers through my hair, then combed it straight to my waist. As the silk mass dried, curls fell around my face and form. I paced the room. Remembering, remembering. Good heavens, it was so hideous to remember. ...

How I had loved him! From the first moment I had seen him, I, too, thought him Prince Charming. With raven's hair and eyes, Charles appeared to be a young girl's dream of love. And adept dance partner, he swept me into his strong arms and onto the ballroom floor in a Strauss waltz meant to beguile. A witty conversationalist, he led me into his circle of globe-trotting friends and into his whirlwind society, introducing me to artists and actors, even to his notorious friend—that voluptuary Oscar Wilde. Within two weeks, Charles courted me, kissed me, and asked me to become his wife. My father, my farsighted father, had peered over his pince-nez at my suitor and drummed his fingers on his office desktop.

"Vanessa, my dear," said my father without taking his eyes from Charles, "I assume you have considered all the implications of this. How you will leave your mother and me to live in England. How your painting will become more—more European in flavor and technique."

Yes, said I, I had considered those two most important issues.

"And you, Viscount Darnley, you are prepared to deal with these concerns?"

"Yes, sir," replied my handsome nobleman as he calmly sat, one leg crossed, top hat in his hand, before my father. "I feel as though I have known and loved Vanessa for centuries. We are very attuned."

My father raised both winged brows. "Are you attuned to my daughter's spontaneity, sir? Her gaiety? Frankly, I myself find English society more attuned to sluggishness. My daughter is a sprite, sir, and has not one sluggish bone in her body."

"Daddy," I whispered in reproof.

My father put up one meaty palm in vast objection. "I know, my dear, I know. But I must say these things. The man wants to whisk you off and yet he set sight on you only two weeks ago. I've never closed a momentous business deal in my life in less than a month, and *this* man—this man comes along and wants your hand in marriage in less than half that! I don't understand it."

As for me, I thought there was little to understand. I loved and that was all I knew. Everything else, I assumed, would fall before the power of that love.

So I had married. Wisely, I thought, and extremely well. I, who claimed descent from two hundred years of wily Dutch merchants in New York City. I, who remained the only living offspring of my father's famous Vandergraf family. Vandergraf. The family responsible for the opening of the Erie Canal, the financing of railroads across the Plains, and the operation of the fastest clippers to open trade with China, Japan, and India. The family whose money built America and whose ravenous rivals gobbled her millions whole. Rivals, who ate my father's business like sharks in fast waters, leaving my mother to grieve to her grave, my father to fight to a fruitless end. And me. Me, sullied as I was, to walk alone with only my fatherless child through the devastation.

A knock that reverberated from the hall door

dragged me from my reverie. I sniffled and straightened my dressing gown, put on my slippers, and gave shaking attempts at fixing the tendrils of hair about my face. To no great avail were my reparations and, finally, rather than be rude, I made for the door. I asked who was there. No one answered. I asked again. Finally in frustration, I flung it open, only to find no one.

I frowned, then took a few steps into the hall. Glancing both ways, I saw no one who might have knocked. But as I stepped back into my suite, my foot tread on crackling paper.

I stepped aside and noticed the translucent ivory envelope now marked by the impression of my slipper. Bending to pick it up, I felt its fine linen quality. No name addressed its contents to me, yet logic said it was meant for me. I tore it open and found old newspaper clippings, ragged at the edges, yellowed with the years. American papers—The New York *Times*, the Washington *Star* . . . A clipping of my engagement announcement to Charles; another of my wedding portrait; a third of my father's loss of his railroad to his former friends of Wall Street, that Morgan man and Gould, and that Tammany crowd, corrupt as sin and salacious to boot.

I crushed the infernal clippings between my hands. Who would have done this? Wildly, I looked up and down the hall, and disregarding my dishabille, I pursued its length toward the grand staircase. But all was silent. I returned to my room and slammed the door.

I stalked the length of the sitting room.

What evil-minded fiend had saved these things? And for more than six years? Why? I gazed at my hands that held the poisonous pieces, then gave a laugh which soon became a sob. How could the perpetrator know I needn't see these pages again to recall every word of the content, every line in the photographs?

I knew what heartache they resurrected. I sank to the floor and let the sob transform to tear-filled misery.

Moments, minutes, perhaps hours later, Jeremy burst through the door. "Mommy! Mommy!"

My maternal instinct had me covering my wet face.

Another's hands captured the points of my shoulders and drew me to warm solace. "Vanessa, Vanessa," Graham stroked my hair and drew me to his chest. "You look so frightened." He lifted my face to his gaze. "Please calm yourself. What's happened to make you cry so?"

I shook my head, trying desperately to recover my dignity.

He bent, and through my sorrow-blurred vision, I saw his expression harden as he realized what I held. "What the blazes—?" He extracted the papers from my hand.

"What is it, Mommy?" Jeremy gathered close.

I tried to recapture the clippings, but Graham was swifter, stronger.

"Old newspaper clippings, Jeremy. About your grandfather. It makes your mother sad. Perhaps you should go to your room, Jeremy, and dress for dinner."

"Mommy?" Jeremy awaited my agreement. I nodded, and he reluctantly left his uncle and me alone.

I brushed away my tears and moved toward the window overlooking the park. Clouds hung low across the barren expanse of gaslights and benches. People beneath huge umbrellas scurried in the now-driving rain. Dusk changed relentlessly to night. Then I heard Graham step across the carpet. He was so near that his human heat permeated the delicate silk of my dressing gown. My eyes fell closed.

"Vanessa, tell me how these got here."

In the barest of facts and tones, I recounted how I had found the clippings.

He flowed nearer, his voice caressing me like

brushed velvet. "No wonder you were frightened! I hope you're not considering taking the advice?"

I turned. He was so near that my breasts grazed his waistcoat. Involuntarily, I shivered, looked up, and examined his face. His face, so bold, so severe, that to paint it would require the liberal application of greys to sculpt the hollows at his chin and cheeks and eyes. "What are you talking about? What advice?"

His eyes drilled into mine as he raised one hand with a clipping. "This. Didn't you see it?"

His fingers opened and I placed one hand upon a crumpled column. In large script were inscribed the words, "Go home."

Chapter Three

I stared at the script. My mind raced, stuck, then churned in a mire made of the unanswered question: Who was my enemy?

I think I must have babbled something, because Graham led me to the settee. He put his hand to my brow and then to my cheek. "You're awfully pale. You aren't going to faint, I hope?"

I stared at him, at the ridiculous idea that I might succumb physically in that vapid way, then shook off his hand with a nonchalance totally foreign to my nature. "I have never fainted in my life."

"You are so right. No feigned fragility from you." His black eyes grew even more troubled. "You do not recognize the handwriting, then?"

"No. I doubt the person who wrote it wanted me to."

"Absolutely right." He frowned. "But I can't imagine who would do such a thing."

"Graham, I can think of many who would wish 'that Chadwick woman' out of England."

"Vanessa, time heals—"

"Time?" I choked on the memories time had made only more vivid, more vile. "Time has healed nothing here, Graham, because *someone* remembers. Someone who has something to gain from my absence."

"Absurd! I can think of no one. No one with a motive for such viciousness."

"No one?" I rose from the settee and walked toward the tea tray. With measured purpose, I poured two cups of tea, added milk to mine and nothing to Graham's, then calmly turned, walked across the carpet, and handed him his. "There were many who resented me when I first arrived in England more than six years ago. I came bearing all those stigmas the English aristocracy had come to despise . . ."

Graham placed his tea aside. "That's an exaggeration . . ."

"Is it? First, least important, there were Charles's friends. School chums from Eton and Oxford and his regiment of the Grenadiers. Men who had been taught from the cradle to marry well-brought-up ladies of their own set. They saw me as uncouth." My eyes drifted down to my teacup. "A woman who didn't know that it was perfectly correct to add milk to tea after it was poured but milk to coffee *before*.

"Minor points, Vanessa."

"Yes, to Americans perhaps. But there were other issues which are more important ones here. The matrons of society saw them: I was dreadfuly young. Eighteen. Certainly a marriageable age, but then, of course, I had spent those years in New York and never even been to the Continent. What did I know of polite society? Culture? Did I speak French? No? What a pity! A smattering of Dutch? How unfortunate. Did I perchance play the piano? I did? Wonderful! Could I give a rendition of one of Liszt's shorter works? When I did, it was too good. They concluded I would show up their daughters. Then when they learned that, in addition, I could paint, I merited their acceptance. Painting mitigated some of their concerns, but when they learned I perferred oils to watercolors, I was again déclassé."

"You are hurt, Vanessa, but in all honesty, I must say that their snobbery never seemed to bother you then."

"No, you are right. My bitterness came after my disillusionment. I knew those slights and took them with a pinch of salt. I was *in love*, Graham. *In love*, and it didn't matter to me what the rest of the world thought as long as Charles valued me. It was after I discovered Charles's treachery that other people's view became more hurtful, shameful."

"The shame should have been all Charles's."

I swallowed. "It should have been, but as his wife, I felt the taint. I thought his dalliances were my fault."

"He had liaisons before you both were married. . . ."

"Yes, most men do, don't they? Certainly, even an American girl knows that! But the liaisons are supposed to end at the altar. Or so I believed." I bit my lower lip in remembered jealousies. "That brings us to another group who would wish me ill—those ladies of good and ill repute who had fond hopes of continuing their relationships with Charles. You can't deny the existence of, at the very least, two mistresses—one in London and another in York."

Graham nodded curtly.

"And then there were those young ladies of substance and of the blood who fancied themselves as the next Countess of Darnley. Women like Ann Windemere and that lovely black-haired Irish girl, poor thing. Charles laughed over her one night. Laughed over her moonstruck adoration of him. I listened in horror. Me, not three months married and lying there warm from our lo—" I swallowed at the delicacy of the subject I had just touched, memory almost having drowned my sense of propriety.

I went on, other memories indiscreetly rising to my mind. "Charles criticized her for adoring him. 'She's part of the Ascendancy,' he told me, and chuckled as he toasted the girl's silliness by downing another gulp of wine. 'What makes her think I'd want her for a wife?'" Suddenly, I remembered his bored expression as he leaned over me and tried to kiss me. To

31

seduce me with his ways once again.

I jumped from the settee to pace the room, kneading my hands.

Graham's voice broke into my troubled visions of that night so long ago. "Marriages are arranged more for advancement or security than for love. Surely, even in America among the upper classes, it's so. It's been true here, indeed almost everywhere in the world, since the dawn of time. I do not excuse my brother's bad behavior, but in his marital views, he was a child of his parents."

"As we all are, Graham."

He nodded.

"Which brings us to the point where I dare name my most vital, my most vocal opponent." I met him squarely, eye to eye. "You."

Silence reigned for untold moments.

Into the void burst a gleeful Jeremy. He came to a skidding halt at the sight of two adults at an impasse.

Graham broke our stare first and tried for a smile at Jeremy. "I presume, young man, you are hungry and eager for supper. Shall we dine now, early?" His eyes slid from an agreeable Jeremy to me.

I nodded. "Certainly," I said, taking the clippings and turning for my bedroom.

Even the fact that Graham had invited Jeremy to dine with us, instead of leaving him in the suite with MacCarthy and the governess, did nothing to assuage my turmoil of emotions at that moment. Fraught with anxiety, I managed in less than twenty minutes to wind my hair quickly into a large, simple bun and to array myself in my finest mourning dress. Returning to the sitting room, I waited for Graham and Jeremy, who had disappeared, I surmised, into his uncle's room.

I stood before the cheval glass, pinning my mourning brooch against my high collar and assessing my gown. The garment of solemn black silk with lace overlay was lifeless now, having lost its sheen in the two years since I'd purchased it. I had used it so often. Too often. For my mother and my father and now . . .

"Turn around," Graham instructed, and I spun about.

We were alone. Graham advanced, and his eyes ran up my gown to define my breasts, my shoulders, my vulnerable throat adorned by the clinging lace and mere brooch. His eyes showed no emotion, but I could see he understood my lack of real jewels spoke of my newfound poverty. He shook his head slightly. "Vanessa, I thank you. I did not expect that you would dress in mourning for my father."

"Graham, I will not lie and tell you I loved him. I felt no daughterly affection for your father. He felt no paternal affection for me. To him I simply represented a good bargain, an arrangement to save his heritage and his good name. I bore him no emotion, but I respected him until the day he supported Charles by believing his accusations. I would not fail to mourn the man for one misjudgment of character. We each make similiar miscalculations. I can only hope they remain limited in number and severity."

Graham stared at me. "You realize people may assume you wear the mourning for Charles."

I bristled. "I am aware of that, yes. I have learned to disregard the gossips. They will say anything. Shall we go, please? I'll get Jeremy."

The maitre d' was expecting us and immediately fluttered about, fussing over us like a hen. In the dimly lit room aglow with sconced gas lamps, we waited as he asked a waiter to make one last preparation at our table before seating us. I scanned those dining.

One elderly gentleman ate alone. Two other men attacked a saddle of lamb with great glee. Toward the center of the room was the largest party, two men and two women. Something about one of the women made my eyes return to examine her. Dark-haired, elaborately coiffed, lithely formed, she was pale. Delicate. Most unique. Most . . . Irish.

My body froze as my mind declared who this lovely creature had to be. Margaret Hamilton-Fyfe. The striking Irish girl who had loved Charles. The one whom he had laughed at that night in our boudoir. The one who had created such a scene by declaring in public that she adored Charles and no other.

The maitre d' obstructed my view of Margaret and now offered to show us to our seats. Stricken, I followed, hoping against hope we would not need to pass her table on the way to ours. But there was no such grace.

Margaret rose, and by her action made ignoring her and her party impossible. We paused. Other members of Margaret's party rose; the men shook hands. Her blue eyes bored into my body like twin pokers. I forced myself to stand more erect. She was taller than I but not as big as Graham who, for interminable moments, made all the polite conversation necessary. Then Graham turned to me and placed his hand on my elbow.

"Vanessa, you remember Lady Margaret Hamilton-Fyfe, who is now Contessa D'Monteforno." We nodded, she and I, feigning politeness with a shake of cool fingers. Meanwhile, Graham continued with conversation my befuddled mind couldn't follow. I shook hands with Margaret's husband. He was a swarthy Italian count of short stature and darting eyes, which wandered to my décolletage as he kissed my hand too leisurely.

When we said our goodbyes, I paused to put Jeremy in front of me. Margaret had eyed him too much these last moments. I feared for my boy. When we finally were seated at our table and I noticed how the potted plants almost obscured Margaret's view of us, I sighed in relief. Graham began a conversation with Jeremy about the delights of the menu and the

34

game of cards the three of us would have after supper. I sat, eyes fixed on the menu. Confused. Confounded.

What was Margaret doing here? In Southampton? Without thinking about his reaction, I asked Graham.

He looked at me. "You weren't listening, then."

I swallowed audibly. "No, I guess not."

"They are returning to Palermo to the count's villa." Graham then turned and squinted at his menu.

My thoughts coiled in agony. "Oh, Graham, she was once so lovely. Now she seems so hard."

"I think you would be, too, if you were married to the most notorious rake on the Continent."

I stared at Graham. I *had* been married to the most notorious rake in the British Isles! Only I had never known until the end. Until it was too late.

Graham blinked and looked at the array of crystal goblets before him. "Word has it, the marriage was most necessary." He glanced at Jeremy, who sat toying with his silverware, uninterested in the adults' conversation.

"They have children?"

"No, none. She has lost all three . . . or is it four? I can't say."

"But Margaret loved Char—" I broke off my words as my train of thought crashed at the sight of Jeremy across the table. His cherub's face tilted up at me in question. I returned to study my menu.

Margaret had loved Charles desperately. Enough to make a spectacle of herself in public. Not only once, but twice. That first time was just three months after Charles's and my marriage. We had gone to the theater in Drury Lane one evening, and at intermission I went to the ladies' salon. When I emerged and looked for Charles, I had to travel the length of the corridor before I heard his voice drifting from an alcove.

"Margaret, my dearest, you must return to your

party," Charles instructed her.

"Not until you tell me," she insisted.

"Tell you what, my pet?"

"That you love me," she had retorted. "You told me." Her voice fell to a whisper. "You showed me. Remember? No man would make love—"

"My dear girl! You are young, very innocent, and very lovely. Very lovely, my girl, but mad. And I really don't want you to ruin your reputation."

"I don't care about my reputation! I care only that we—"

"Margaret, Margaret, you must accept the fact that I am married, well and finally. It will do you no good to go mooning about when a woman of your bounteous charms can attract any man."

I broke into their conversation by suddenly rounding the corner. "Ah, Charles, here you are. I was looking everywhere for you."

Suavely, Charles introduced us, and as he did I saw the delicate features of the lovely woman harden with hate. Like a portrait transforming before my very eyes, Margaret went from waif to witch in one moment. Then she turned on her heel and left us alone.

Later that night, after Charles rose from our bed and poured himself a hefty draught of Madeira, he laughed about her. Laughed at her lineage and her lack of fortune. Laughed at her innocence, at her boldness to think . . . to even dare think he might find her acceptable as a wife.

His criticism led me to examine my own innocence and boldness . . . and to wonder, albeit only for a moment, if he had ever laughed at me. I shook it off and prided myself that he wouldn't. After all, I was his wife. His chosen wife.

But I was as wrong about that as I was about so much else.

Now I glanced up from my menu and turned in Margaret's direction. She had changed seats! Her eyes

riveted on me with a demon's stare, sh
nostrils, stretched her lips across her teeth
imitation of a smile, and then returned to
Her lips moved, but I would have wag
month's salary from Bigelow's that the w
mouthed bore absolutely no resemblance ω the
dinner fare. Indeed, they probably read like a recipe
for destruction. Mine. She had neither forgotten nor
forgiven.

Could I blame her? Hardly. She and I were so alike.
I had not forgiven or forgotten either. I squirmed in
my chair and returned to the menu.

The printed words suddenly brought to mind
those others that had been thrust into an envelope
and shoved beneath my door. I froze in my chair.
Merciful heavens, could she have been responsible?

She hated me enough, God knew. But how would
she have acquired them?

As anyone else could. From friends for favors. Or
from detectives for money. Oh, yes, it was possible for
Margaret to have acquired them as anyone else would
who hated as she did me.

"Vanessa?" Graham intruded in my thoughts.
"Vanessa, do please choose something. Our waiter is
coming."

I ordered. Lost in my reverie, I ate silently. Only as
we came to the end of the repast did I notice Graham
and Jeremy. My son, famished but pampered with
his favorite foods, had devoured his dinner. What's
more, he'd done it with manners befitting a prince. I
was proud and relieved that I hadn't had to reprimand him in such a public place. I would hate
to think Margaret or her husband could find any
fault with Jeremy or me. Grateful they couldn't, I
finished my coffee and looked to Graham to see if he,
too, was finished. He nodded and I rose.

Exhausted but head held high, I led the way out of
the dining room and through the lavish lobby to the
wire caged elevator. As we entered our suite, Jeremy

off with Simpson to change into his bedclothes. at Graham placed a hand to my elbow. I faced him reluctantly, eager to be alone with my suspicions.

"Graham, I am weary."

"I can see that. But—"

"No more talk, please."

"You won't play a game of cards with us?"

"No." I turned and my hand was on the knob of my bedroom door when I stopped at Graham's next words.

"She's not capable, you know."

"What? Who?"

"Margaret. I don't believe she's the one who delivered those clippings to your door this afternoon. That's what has troubled you during supper."

I faced him.

"What opportunity would she have to clip those papers? Possess them? She—like the rest of us here in England—knew nothing of Charles's courtship of you until it was accomplished. You came here to England as a bride, legally wedded and morally bound. What good would it do for her to seek newspaper clippings weeks old from across the ocean? And from whom?"

"Friends, Graham. We all have friends. Perhaps someone who knew Margaret's interest in Charles found the articles and sent them to her."

"You trust no one, do you?"

His question jolted me, but I answered forthrightly. "Would you if you were me?"

"No," he sighed. "Betrayal binds the heart's abilities."

He spoke with such weariness that I assayed him a moment, then took up my argument. "She has motive. Margaret made a scandal with her public display of jealousy after Charles and I were married. I caught her one evening at the theater proclaiming her undying affection for him. He turned her away discreetly and then, as I told you, he criticized her

38

later for her proclamation. But then there was that other time . . . at the British Museum when she would not be deterred. He tried to quiet her. She lost her temper and railed at him."

"Yes. That was most distasteful. Too many overheard her that day, but she paid for her own foolishness. She was not welcome in many drawing rooms after her outburst at him there. Not long afterward, her parents sent her to Italy on 'an extended tour.'"

"Perhaps she met her husband then."

"I daresay that has not been a saving grace."

"No, she still carries a torch for Charles, I'd say."

"You have no idea, do you?" Graham examined my eyes. "No, I see you don't. The woman went to Italy to rid herself of a child. Yes, it is well known in the best circles."

"Oh, you can't mean that—that Charles—?"

"Charles."

I felt as if someone had knocked the breath from me. I clutched my chest. "And I thought I was finished listening to the litany of his perversions."

Graham reached for me. Not wanting his pity, I broke away, tears welling in me.

In the solitude of my room, I sat in one large chair and wept soft tears, not for myself nor my son, but for Margaret. Margaret, who clung to her love for a man who could never have comprehended such devotion. Margaret, who had her life destroyed by one man's whim.

I dabbed my cheeks and began to divest myself of my dinner dress and finery. Then I took my ablutions without assistance from Simpson. Intimidating as she was, I would rather do without her than suffer her superiority. So when she came in, I quickly bid her good night. I found myself sitting before the dressing table, brushing the same strands of hair over and over. Poor Margaret, I thought, poor woman. I could only hope that one day she learned of Charles's true nature so that she might live a fuller life. I rose from my chair.

Outside my door, in the sitting room, I heard no sounds of Graham and Jeremy gaming and thought they must have retired. Presently, I heard what had to have been Graham's adjoining door open and close. His footsteps took him to the table where the hotel maid had placed the brandy and a tray of glasses.

My mind drifted to our conversation of the afternoon. I continued to brush the hair that wended its way to my left breast. The same breast whose swell Graham had once bathed with gentle strokes of his tongue. I closed my eyes and remembered that one wild afternoon when Graham had tried to comfort me in my tears over Charles's betrayal. How Graham had picked me up from the floor, rocked me like a father, consoled me like a brother, and suddenly—madly, passionately—kissed me like a man. How he had smoothed the hair from my brow, the tears from my cheeks, and murmured how I mustn't let Charles hurt me. I remembered how shocked I had been at Graham's concern, at his perception, at his ardor. Equally, I remembered how shocked I had been at my acceptance, at my trust of him, at my desire for him.

We had kissed as he caressed my back and then my breast. Transported, we moaned and yanked apart, startled at the power of our emotion. He had apologized. I had demurred. He had fled the room, and later that day, he had fled the castle. He then returned to London or so he wrote his father. And I didn't see him again for months. Not until the day I left England. Then, as I departed in disgrace, Graham came to meet me at the docks. He said little, so little, I wondered why he had come. Then he slipped a fat envelope into my hands. I watched him go and I cried. As the ship cast off, I opened the envelope to find my divorce papers. The tears I cried after that were sobs of betrayed anger. I had never been so surprised by someone before unless, of course, I counted how surprised I was to learn of my husband's true rakish character. What could I deduce? They were blood brothers.

But years had added strength to my character and I was not so surprised by feckless people anymore. I rose from my chaise and went toward the door. When I opened it, the gaslights of Southampton cast iridescent rays about our sitting room.

I found him amid the shadows. He sat in one overstuffed wing chair, with the dancing fire lighting the hollows and planes of his manly face. Minus his waistcoat and cravat, he wore his white shirt open at the throat. His hair gleamed silver and gold in the glow of blazing flame. His brooding eyes, which had been riveted on my bedroom door, remained stoic at my appearance and my approach. Yet they roamed over my body from toe to crown. With a nod of approval, he raised the snifter of brandy to his lips, drank, and licked his lower lip.

I went to the table and poured myself a generous draught into a snifter. Its heady aroma thrilled my tangled nerves. I would sleep tonight.

I went to the window, seeing none of the city, feeling only his eyes upon me.

His voice, his rich bass voice, gloved by brandy and cloaked by darkness, bathed me.

"You obsess me, Vanessa."

Waves of excitement washed my every cell. My eyes fell closed. His voice returned to stimulate each nerve.

"I have tried for years to rid my mind of you. You remain, against my will."

I faced him. "Is that why you asked me to return?"

"Partially." He placed the snifter on the wine table.

"Tell me then. I've been the victim of so many partial statements. I would hear all of yours."

"So you shall. I will begin with *brave*. You always were so brave. And *strong*. Stronger than anyone

41

gave you credit for."

"I seek no credit. No fine reputation. Such things are dreams beyond me now."

"Vanessa, it's distressing to hear you so jaded. You were so unsullied."

"That was long ago."

"No, a person's inner nature does not change like that."

I drank my brandy. The burning liquid fortified me. I whispered in reply, "Mine did."

"I doubt it."

"Don't."

"I can prove it to you."

"Don't waste your time."

With one lithe lunge, he pulled me to him. One iron-sinewed arm encircled my waist while the fingers of his other hand crept up inside the sleeve of my robe, caressing my upper arm and shoulder. His torso pressing to mine sent hot shivers through my body. He fixed my curves against his hard planes as his mouth, sweet with the vapors of brandy, hot with the essence of need, came to rest at the corner of mine. His lips spoke against my skin.

"Soft . . . I remember how soft your skin was, how yielding your mouth." He pressed a feather-light kiss against my lower lip.

I reeled, mesmerized.

"You were and are delicious," he murmured. Then in one swoop, his mouth crushed mine. I'd never known how a kiss could luxuriate and demand. I'd never known how a kiss could pulse to my breasts and my groin.

I must have pulled away.

"Now—" he released me so quickly I almost fell backward—"you see, if you were truly hardened, you would have predicted that little advance. And, if truly jaded, you would have lingered in the kiss."

I bristled at his intimate knowledge.

"Know this, Vanessa." His eyes bore into mine. "I

invited you here to hear my father's will because you are named in it. And even if you weren't, I'd ask you to return to witness its reading because as my brother's widow, you should be here for propriety's sake. Yes, I want you here, Vanessa. For many reasons. Not the least of which is to exorcise you from my mind."

Rapaciously recovering my dignity, I glared at him. "A nice speech, but you, too, have reason to be rid of me."

"I invited you here to solve many mysteries, but I would not have you go anywhere until the past is resolved. You cannot believe I would seek to frighten you. This is me . . . Graham . . . the brother of your nemesis. Don't confuse us, my sweet."

"Confuse you?" I gave a laugh of indignation. "This"—I waved a hand—"this swaggering behavior of yours is more like Charles than the Graham I knew. The Graham I knew touched me only once . . ."

"So you do remember."

"Yes, I remember! I could not forget"—oh, what could I term it?—"one of the few kind occurrences I knew while in England?"

His face was obscured by the conflux of shadows. "Is that really how you remember our encounter—as kindness?"

"No! As passion! Let's call it by name!"

"Indeed. Label it as truth now. I could barely name it then. But now—" His hands sought to pull me into his embrace.

And I resisted. "No, Graham, no. You know as well as I that passion though it was, I will not fall into your arms."

"I see you will never be able to trust any other man after what he did to you."

"Trust? Trust! It's not a word I've used in years. I've had so many obstacles to overcome since I left England. My return to New York when I was six months along with child. The birth of my son, in disgrace without any recognition from Charles. The decline of my father's business. The scandals at home. The death of my mother and then my father . . ."

"Vanessa . . ." He was beseeching me, dragging me into his arms.

"No!" I thrust my palm against his chest. "Graham, think! What would English society say of 'that Chadwick woman' if they could link her to her husband's brother? They'd say she was a schemer, just as her husband declared her to be. They'd say— no, they would have proof of the most sordid kind!— that she was precisely what her husband declared her to be . . ."

"Many now know about Charles . . . how he died and of what disease. Society has so many examples of his perfidy."

"Do they? It doesn't mean they'll accept me in polite society. I wear the label still, Graham. It clings like the dirt, the unclean thing it is. To them 'that Chadwick woman' will forever wear the name her husband branded her with . . ."

"No!"

"Yes, they remember it, even if they don't believe it or use it in polite society. 'That Chadwick woman,' they'll nudge each other when I pass. 'You remember. She's that American girl, the adulteress!'"

Chapter Four

We never spoke of it again.

Ha. Speak? I could not bear to even look at him. I was angry, as I always was, when I recalled my former husband's actions against me and the label I still wore because of them. Heaven knows, I had tried to forgive, but I could not. When I could excuse myself for such a lack, I knew it was because I could not forget. How could I forget when I still suffered from Charles's maliciousness? When people—my former so-called friends—passed me on the street and turned their eyes away, snubbing me with the cut direct, denying me and my son the barest niceties of social conduct. To live unforgiving, I knew, consumed any joy in life. So now when I had occasion to bend my head in prayer, I asked that one day I might find forgiveness in my heart. That day had not yet arrived.

"Come, Vanessa," Graham looked up at me and scowled.

He had alighted, so too had the others—MacCarthy, Simpson, and Jeremy. Meanwhile, I had sat alone in one corner of the coach amidst my self-turmoil. The coach, which MacCarthy had hailed for us at Victoria Station, had evidently come to a stop before the Chadwick family's townhouse.

I glanced out. Expecting to see the Chadwick family townhouse on Park Lane that I knew so well, the view that confronted me was another. I frowned. Another longer look assured me that, indeed, I had been right the first time. This certainly was not Chadwick House—that elegant white Regency with the circular staircase and wide portico in the finest section of London. This was a red brick Georgian. . . .

"My new townhouse," Graham confirmed as he beckoned me boldly with his large hand. "Come, come, Vanessa. I have a meeting in less than an hour with two business partners. I must prepare."

I grasped his hand and stepped onto the running board and out into the midday London chill. The weather here was an improvement over that in Southampton. When we had boarded our train early this morning, our clothes had been soaked by the steady downpour. In fact, Simpson and Jeremy had gotten quite the worst of it and sat shivering through the first of the trip. Now, an erratic drizzle distinguished London's precipitation. I pulled my cape about my shoulders and took a precarious step downward to the pebble sidewalk.

I turned to see MacCarthy grappling with hand luggage given down from the roof by the coach's driver. As one by one the traveling bags filled up the sidewalk, the hackney's tempo quickened. His pace became a staccato; his sharp commands punctuated the rhythm of the bags as they hit the ground. He seemed to be enjoying this as he drew the attention of passersby.

But Graham turned and glanced up at the man as he reached for another bag. I could tell by the furrows lining Graham's forehead that he was not pleased and meant to give the man a what-for.

Just then the driver shouted, "'Ere go, Guvner!" and sent a valise airborne over his shoulder—straight in the direction of Jeremy.

I shrieked.

But Graham was quicker. He snatched Jeremy up by his coat collar and yanked him back just in time to miss the valise as it thudded to the ground.

"Take care, man!" Graham barked at the driver. "You almost killed the child."

I ran to Jeremy and let my eyes and hands assure me of his safety. But Graham had pulled him well clear. Jeremy and I glared up at the driver, while Graham scalded the man with burning words I had not ever heard in polite society.

My ears rang with Graham's reprimand; my memory recorded yet another threat on me and mine. I clutched Jeremy closer to my side.

But the driver seemed so unperturbed. He listened politely enough to Graham, then paused long enough to smack his lips and twitch his head. "Sorry, sir, ma'am. I meant it fer yer man, I did." He grinned a toothless apology at Jeremy. "Wouldn't 'it the little fella, I wou'nt. Not ole Jack. I likes kids, meself."

Graham nodded toward MacCarthy. "See that the rest of the baggage is properly cared for, MacCarthy. I'll send out the footman to help you in with it. Jeremy, you come with me and your mother. Vanessa?" Graham crooked his elbow toward me.

I took Graham's arm and Jeremy's hand, lifted my skirt, and mounted the wide red brick stairs of this strange house.

Curiosity got the best of me, and I swallowed some of my anger and my fear. "I suppose I have to ask why we are here and not at Chadwick House."

He did not deign to look at me. "Because this is *my* house. Smaller, more modest than Chadwick House. But mine. You will be comfortable and, I daresay, courteously cared for."

"I never doubted it," I whispered as we approached the massive front door. "I merely inquired as to why—"

Graham disengaged his arm from mine, opened the door with a twist to the ornate brass handpull, and pushed it open to stand aside for Jeremy and me to precede him. As Jeremy scampered past us into the foyer, Graham surveyed his domain but continued to address me.

"*Why?* I answered you. We're here because this is my house. Many speculate if I am lord over my father's estate—"

I blushed, knowing one of those who speculated had been me.

"—but I have no doubts who is lord *here*. And here we shall stay." He closed the door as two uniformed domestics, an older woman and a youthful housemaid, scurried before us.

"Good afternoon, Lord Darnley, ma'am."

The dark-haired woman curtsied and pulled herself up to a full height of perhaps five feet.

She was the oddest-looking creature I had ever seen. Oh, her face was not ugly. No. Except for one disastrous set of features, she might have been quite fetching. Her face was very round but drew up to such a high-pointed tiny nose and slash of a mouth that one wondered how her eyes could get the view beyond that snout.

If the snout offended, it was her body that struck one more. She had more length between bosom and hip than any human I'd ever encountered. Long and lean there, she appeared disproportioned. What came to mind was a mongoose. That frenetic ferret which feasted on snakes, that's what she looked like. A brown-haired mongoose. With eyes that snapped and saw everything in a second's flash.

The housekeeper.

I noted how opposite the maid was. Sixteen perhaps. Quite plump and plain. Plain brown hair, caught to her skull in a net, and plain brown eyes, caught now in fear of her employer. Despite her girth, she was perfectly kempt in her long dove-grey uniform, which did little for what was her only remarkable feature—her tea-rose-pink complexion.

"May I 'ave your wraps, Lord Darnley, miss?" the maid offered, hurriedly taking her eyes from my face to some proper level around my throat. She had been taught—and most recently at that—by some severe soul. I suppressed a smile, nodded, and began to unbutton my cape.

Graham, too, removed his coat and faced the housekeeper. "Mrs. Atherton, where have you been?" Graham narrowed his eyes at her.

She twitched. "Sorry, sir. We had no idea exactly when you were coming, sir."

"Not excusable, Mrs. Atherton. I told you it would be the noon train. That it was the three o'clock is no excuse for your not meeting us at the front door."

Atherton blinked. "Yes, sir."

Reprimanded, Atherton stared straight ahead. She did not, as many a servant would, hang her head. I wondered why. What was more to me was that her manner, for a servant whom I deduced was as new to her position as supposedly the house was, was extraordinarily lax. No servant, new or old, would miss receiving the man of the house, here or in New York. Where had she come from? And who, in God's name, were her references? Most puzzling was the fact that it was not like Graham, whose meticulous dedication to detail had rebuilt the one-hundred-twenty-two-year-old shipping company, Darnley and Sons, into a profitable commercial firm, to hire someone who failed—and so quickly, too—to perform to standard.

But it was not for me to ask, and certainly, under the current conditions between us, Graham would not offer the information willingly. I filed the troubling question away with a growing list of others.

"Vanessa, this is Mrs. Atherton, the housekeeper, and Luddie, the maid. Mrs. Chadwick," Graham said tonelessly as he removed his inverness and handed it across Luddie's outstretched arms. I politely smiled at the two servants.

I didn't know whether to be thankful or offended by Graham's declaration of my status. While I might have the social right to still be called "Mrs. Chadwick," I did not expect it of him. I noted he did not say "Viscountess," which, of course, had been my title while Charles and I were married. Nor did he refer to me as "Miss Vandergraf," which truly would have insulted my sensibilities, especially in front of Jeremy. Nor, certainly, was I "Countess of Darnley." Or would I ever be. Indeed, the most I would ever be would be "Mrs. Chadwick." Even if Jeremy were named the rightful heir to the old earl's title and estate, I would have no right to be the dowager countess. I was, after all, a divorced woman with no rights to my former husband's names or property.

Instantly, I remembered Graham's statement of a few days ago that he wanted me here for many reasons—not the least of which was the removal of scandal from his family's name. If assuming the title of "Mrs. Chadwick" served his purpose and saved my respectability, who was I to dissuade him?

Graham's eyes flowed everywhere about the manly mahogany paneled foyer as if he were assessing it, reviewing it for future reference. "Mrs. Atherton, where is Peters? Send him out to MacCarthy to help with the luggage."

"He'll be right up, sir. He went to the cellar a few minutes ago to let the wine merchant in with the delivery."

"I see. Very well. We'd like some refreshment." He turned to Jeremy and for the first time in many hours, I saw Graham truly smile. "We would like some hot tea and scones and biscuits with jam and . . . anything else, Jeremy?"

"Peppermint sticks!"

I laughed, shocked. "No, Jeremy, I don't—"

Graham, whom I caught eyeing me with glee, quickly dropped the gaiety for a more severe tone. "Yes, as Mrs. Chadwick says, Atherton. Tell me, is Mrs. Chadwick's bedroom finished?"

"Yes, sir. It is. They finished hanging the draperies

and the canopy this morning. And the little boy's is done, too, sir."

Graham was frowning, headed for the hall table and the silver bowl, where those who called left their cards. He picked up a handful and faced the housekeeper. "Good. Glad to hear it." He searched the foyer for a moment and found Jeremy, who stood gaping before the goliath battle standard hung with the Chadwick coat of arms upon the far wall. "The little boy is Master Jeremy," Graham corrected Atherton, and Jeremy turned to give them both a grin.

Atherton and Luddie curtsied once more, then the housekeeper continued her litany. "I'm sorry to say the other bedroom for the gov'ness is not white-washed yet, my lord, but it is neat and clean. I think she'll find it to her liking."

Simpson, who had hung back from us, took this in with what, in her class and station, passed for approval—an indrawn breath that raised and lowered the bosom.

"Miss Simpson," Graham turned to the governess, "please take Master Jeremy upstairs. Luddie, show them up to the third floor. Mrs. Atherton"—his eyes ran to the hall clock directly in front of us— "I expect Baron Rothschild and Monsieur Piccard in less than half an hour. When they arrive, please show them in, as I need MacCarthy to run an errand for me. Also, see that Mrs. Chadwick is comfortably settled in her room and then acquaint her with the house."

Atherton was clearly flabbergasted by so many immediate demands. Her flickering eyes raced from Simpson to MacCarthy to me and then to her employer.

Atherton would need training. In the meantime, what she needed now was to do Graham's bidding in priority order. If she didn't have an idea what that order was, I did. I turned to Graham.

"If I may, Graham, I will acquaint myself with the

51

drawing room, while Mrs. Atherton attends to the preparations for your guests. If you will just point me in the right direction, please."

Graham, already preoccupied with his meeting and one calling card he had separated from the rest, cast me a relieved look. "Certainly. Make yourself at home, Vanessa. The drawing room is to your left."

Atherton was already moving toward the handsomely carved double doors. "Please, Mrs. Chadwick"—she had recovered some of her dignity and her direction—"follow me." She put her hands to the brass insets and slid the doors wide for me. I followed her into a truly startling room.

Its brilliance took my breath away. Never, not at Chadwick House or at Darnley Castle, had I seen such loveliness. Oh, true to Graham's words, this house might be smaller. Some might even call it more modest than the splendor of Chadwick House, with its Louis XIV appointments and its Rococo frivolities of plastered scrollwork and lacy embellishments on every nook and cranny. But this—*this* radiance delighted the eye. My eye.

Graham had selected some of the most graceful pieces of furniture and ornaments ever created and assembled together by man. The walls were a pale peach, the crown molding and floor molding ivory. The floor's burnished marquetry framed the delicate peach and jade and soulful whites of the thick-piled, boldly wrought Chinese carpet. Two alabaster Empire settees beseeched the visitor to pause and ponder the glories of the art upon the walls and tables. Each item had been placed, it seemed, with a perfect understanding of its power to interest and then to please.

I glided into the room, mesmerized.

"Thank you, Mrs. Atherton. I am fine. Go prepare for the guests. I'll ring if I need you."

I heard her slide the doors closed and, now alone, I inhaled deeply of the room's atmosphere. Roses. I closed my eyes and spun around to inhale the perfume. When I opened my eyes, I noticed Atherton had placed dried rose petals about the room in various porcelains. And what porcelains! Here, there, everywhere upon the side and end tables, they lay. I recognized them immediately as the green and white Ming design cast for one of the first Chinese emperors of that dynasty over five hundred years ago. But even they were minor beauties in this wonderland.

I found bright brasses from India, and jade carvings from Korea. Upon one wall, a long scroll pictured a Japanese geisha, dressed in a morning kimono of subtle beige, walking home from the vegetable market with a basket of fresh delicacies for her repast. Within one corner stood a glorious silk screen that told of daily life in a Chinese lord's household whose confines bulged with wives and concubines, offspring and servants. Two other walls bore gold candle sconces and occasional miniatures of Chadwick men and women. Each wall held delicate gas lamps to light this room to peak brightness for any viewer seeking diversity or solace here.

I walked forward into the center of the room. Before me was the focal point of the room: a four-foot-tall white marble, green-veined fireplace. Doric in its simplicity, it heralded the main feature of the room: a watercolor of springtime in Darnley Meadow, the castle's village in Yorkshire. A picture of serenity and glorious life. A picture of spring, with its gentle green grasses and willful wildflowers cropping up about the cottages of villagers, tenants of the lords of Darnley Castle since William the Conqueror seized the land and gave it to one loyal vassal, an ancestor of the noble house of Chadwick. A picture conceived in newly wedded joy. By me. More than five years ago.

Graham had saved it. My God! And placed it here for all to view. I thought it long destroyed, along with my dreams and my good name.

Tears came to my eyes, obscuring my vision. I reached for the back of one settee and circled it to sit. I found a handkerchief in my reticule and dabbed my eyes.

Amid this serene room, Graham had placed my watercolor. My eyes rose and fresh memories of its creation filled my sight. The day I began it was only a week or two after I had arrived at Darnley Castle in a coach and four, to the cheers and applause of the entire staff and villagers alike. After the twenty-two servants of Darnley had welcomed me with a small reception in the hall, the village elders had sent Charles an invitation to a spring dance and fireworks on the Green. Day was dying as we arrived to see the red-tinged sunset cast a glow over the white-thatched cottages and their jovial inhabitants. The next afternoon, I had gone again to pay my respects to the vicar and had seen the beauty of spring in every scene. Days later, when finally my artist's wares had arrived at the castle, I set to work to reflect on paper what I'd felt those first days. But what I'd felt soon passed— within months, as one by one I saw my fantasies destroyed.

If Graham found joy in this painting, he could keep it. I certainly didn't wish to set eyes on it ever again.

My vehemence had me heading for the doors. I thrust them wide and landed directly in Graham's arms.

He put his hands to my elbows and held me away. "Vanessa, you are still here? I thought you had gone upstairs long ago."

I gazed up at him. Then suddenly I realized, he was not alone. Beside him stood two gentlemen. His visitors, I concluded and tensed. I focused on the wall beyond Graham and tried to contain my runaway heart.

Oh, God, it was one thing to travel here on ships

and trains where anonymity could be maintained. It was even possible to hold one's head up sufficiently to be introduced to the servants of the house. But society was so different. Proper men and women needn't curtsy to me or say good morning. They needn't smile or pretend they didn't remember. These two gentlemen were part of that society, dedicated to that order that denied recognition to the errant. They could just as easily snub me as the others did! I was so eager to disappear that I pulled at Graham's grasp. He squeezed my elbows and dropped his hands. I shifted my gaze to his. He grit his teeth but turned a serene face to his guests.

"Gentlemen, my sister-in-law."

I glanced at him, but he went on with the introductions, unperturbed by his reference to my status. And as for me, I presented the best public face I could muster. I did my duty, taught me long ago by an adoring mother: I received them cheerfully.

But, of course, I was glad I did; I knew them both from years before. The Baron Rothschild, London's foremost financier and the British Empire's first peer of the Jewish faith, took my hand.

I held my breath. Never, *never!* had I expected any kind of decent reception by any peer of the Realm, let alone a man of his standing.

"My dear," Nathan said, shaking my hand so vigorously that my fingers hurt. "I am delighted to see you again." His large, benevolent eyes sparkled at me and I returned the kindness. He had grown older, with more grey in his thinning hair and elegantly barbered beard than when I had last seen him.

"Thank you, sir." I groped for fine language, some remark I could make that would be appropriate. Something I could say that would relieve Nathan of what must be to him the embarrassing necessity of confronting a woman of ill repute.

Graham relieved me of the responsibility. He seemed not to pause when he turned to his other guest and said to me, "And, of course, you remember Monsieur Piccard."

"Yes, certainly."

Who could forget Piccard? A dashing black-haired, monocled French merchant of immense wealth, great charm, and an equally great addiction to the gaming table. It was to Piccard that my husband had lost thousands of pounds on too many occasions.

Today, he bent over my hand with the flourish of the French and brought it to his wet lips. "Madam," he breathed, and rose as his eyes searched mine, "I am thrilled that such a beauty has returned to brighten the English landscape."

I pulled my hand away. "Thank you, monsieur."

I could not reply that I was happy to be there. In truth, I was choking with regret. What could Graham possibly have to do with a scoundrel such as Piccard? Indeed, the mix of Nathan and Piccard had me dumbfounded. What interests Nathan Rothschild had were legitimate, but Piccard was quite another kettle of fish. Piccard had been implicated in more scandalous affairs than the Prince of Wales. It was said he kept more than one mistress in high style in Paris. His wife of many years followed his suit. But worse, three years ago my father had told me it was rumored that Rene Piccard had cheated the French Republic on taxes from his large Asian export-import concerns. While none of it had ever been proven, the tarnish remained. To look at him now, he seemed not to care.

"I understand," he said in English tinged with a flowing French accent, "that you have come for the reading of the old earl's will."

"Yes, I—"

Graham interceded. "Yes, Rene, she came at my insistence."

Nathan was pleased. "I hope you find your stay serene, my dear."

56

"Thank you, Nathan. I hope so, too." I looked at Piccard and Nathan, then over to Graham. "If you will excuse me, please."

Graham nodded. "As you wish. I was just showing Nathan and Rene the house. Gentlemen, shall we take a quick look at the drawing room before we go into my study?"

I made my way to the broad carpeted staircase. My footfalls made no sound against the lush forest-green runner. I reached the landing where three more paintings hung. These startled the senses as much as the main piece in the drawing room. But for a different reason. These were no ordinary stairway embellishments. No portraits of the family's famous. These were textured oils of primary colors that vibrated with life against the rich mahogany walls. Scenes of Paris and the French countryside, from the new French artists who called themselves "Impressionists." I smiled to myself. Graham had chosen well.

I glanced down the hall to where the sitting room and private dining room would be located. Then I pivoted to take the next flight of stairs. Less broad, less ornate, this set of stairs no doubt led to the private bedrooms.

At this landing, I heard noises from the far end, which gave me indications that Jeremy and Miss Simpson discussed his arrangements. I passed one set of closed doors and knew from their size alone that they led to the master bedroom. I passed another more modest door; it, too, was closed. I found the next door open.

I paused before the portal. Inside, Mrs. Atherton fingered one of my brooches and, seemingly dissatisfied, gave a nod of her brown head and returned it to the jewelry case inside one tiny drawer of my smaller streamer trunk. With speed, she opened another drawer, extracting gloves—white, lace, long, short, it didn't seem to matter. She slammed that drawer shut and reached for the knob of another.

This room, then, was mine. And what she searched for—that was mine also?

"Thank you, Mrs. Atherton." I moved not an eyelash. "You needn't trouble yourself to unpack those gowns. I won't be needing them here. Lord Darnley tells me we are to travel on to York tomorrow."

She fell back as if doused with hot coals, then struggled to her feet. Her eyes darted over my features like a mongoose facing a testy rattler.

"Yes, ma'am. As you wish, ma'am. Of course, Mrs. Chadwick. I am so used to working in a solitary state"—she put a palm to her chest as if in surprise—"I didn't hear you coming."

I bet you didn't! I stood my ground. Let her crawl out of this if she could.

She stood back from the bed. "If I can't press your clothes for you, can I order your other clothes for you? Or fix a nice hot bath?"

"Yes. Both, please."

"Lord Darnley says Luddie's to act as lady's maid to you while you're here. That's really the order of things, isn't it, Mrs. Chadwick? Even though Miss Simpson was to fill in on the trip—as companion and governess, I mean."

"Luddie's fine as maid, Mrs. Atherton. Whatever Lord Darnley wants. Where *is* Luddie?"

"Miss Simpson needed her to help with Master Jeremy, so I thought I would help you, ma'am." Still feigning friendliness, she kneaded her hands.

"I see. Well, do carry on, Mrs. Atherton."

She forced her thin lips to an imitation of a smile. As I took in the room, with its huge four-poster draped in watered yellow damask and floor-length windows swathed in yards of the same bright material, she hastened to her duties. In less time than it would take me to decide where to arrange even my smallclothes in so bounteously furnished a boudoir, she had slid away, only to return moments later to announce the completion of her work.

"If you don't have any other requests, Mrs. Chadwick, I'll see to the cook's final preparation for supper."

"You do that, Mrs. Atherton."

She turned to go.

"Mrs. Atherton?

"Yes, ma'am?"

"I'll have Luddie do all my packing and unpacking from now on."

"Yes, Mrs. Chadwick. Thank you, Mrs. Chadwick.'

If she walked any faster toward the door, she would have been running.

I closed the door against her and eyed my trunk.

Now, *what* had she been looking for and *why?*

Chapter Five

What had she been looking for?

Gloves? Not likely.

Jewels? Why? To admire? To steal? Perhaps to pawn?

I had none. I had sold the last months ago to pay the rent in the rooms I occupied on Tenth Street near the antique shop where I worked. But Atherton didn't know that.

Or did she?

Word traveled here in England. I, most of all, should know that. What didn't go by word of mouth certainly went by printed word in such daring newspapers as the *Morning Star* or the *Tatler*. They'd tattle all they could. Good, bad, anything that stood for gossip. The editors had no scruples, and from what I understood, each year the reporting grew more titillating. Why, I understood they now made a regular practice of showing photographs of the celebrated, particularly of the American heiresses who came to "husband hunt."

Photographs. Oh, my God. Had Atherton come to search for the clippings? The clippings that had been delivered to me yesterday?

I sat down in one giant wing chair and forced myself to be logical.

Why would she want them?

Was she the person who had sent them? Not likely. I did not know her. Furthermore, she was not the sort of woman Charles would have taken up with. She had no motive. No vendetta. Or, she had not *that* motive. Still, there was another possibility. . . .

She might be connected to the person who had sent the clippings. *That* was a possibility.

Atherton might know Margaret Hamilton-Fyfe.

Or the actress whom Charles had taken up with—whose name I had never known. Yes, Atherton could know her.

But then, how could I trace someone whose name I didn't know?

But Margaret was still a vital person. I had no idea if she was even in London or carried a grudge or even cared about the lost loves of the late, infamous Viscount Darnley.

But how to discover *who* that person might be who had sent the clippings? I was back to the beginning.

If I knew more about Atherton's background, I might have a better starting point. But she would not reveal anything, that much was certain.

Graham would not tell me. In fact, he was barely civil to me since last night's confrontation. I had rebuffed his advances, hurt his pride. He was not likely to do more for me now than he had to. Besides, even if I would approach him, he was ensconced with Nathan and Piccard.

I knew so little about any of these mysteries. And until Helena arrived, whenever that would be, I would probably remain ignorant of much.

I sighed and leaned back in the chair.

My reverie was interrupted when Jeremy cried out in protest not once, but twice. And never having known him to be so wicked, I knew I had to inspect.

When I reached his doorway, Simpson was pulling at his traveling clothes one way and he was pulling the other.

"What seems to be the problem here, Miss Simpson? Jeremy?"

Both spoke at once.

I lifted my hand to silence Jeremy and motioned for Simpson to speak.

"He is sneezing, ma'am. Catching his death from that rainstorm this morning and probably yesterday's too. I'm putting him to bed with a hot water bottle and some porridge."

I put my hand to his brow. He did feel a bit warm. "I think you're right, Miss Simpson."

"Ohh, no, Mommy, I—"

"I'll tell you what, Master Jeremy . . . " Luddie came up behind us. "If you get all warm in your bed, I'll have Cook send up some ginger cookies she made this afternoon."

I smiled at the girl in gratitude. Jeremy took the bait, of course, and yelped how he'd love to have a whole plateful.

Simpson opened her mouth to object but I cast her a negative look before she could do so.

"Why, Luddie, thank you. I think that's a wonderful remedy for the sneezes, don't you, Miss Simpson?"

Simpson mumbled her agreement and tried once more to remove Jeremy's shirt. This time he let her, but I could see it would be slow going. I stepped forward.

"Miss Simpson, in my small steamer trunk I have some wonderful liniment which I have always used in a poultice for Master Jeremy whenever he is ill. I do believe it is in one of the drawers with my other medicinals. Could you go retrieve it for me, please? And I will see he gets into his nightclothes."

She left, none too happy, but when she was gone, I was happy. I worked at disrobing Jeremy while I eyed Luddie.

Industrious child, she worked at folding and smoothing and sorting his clothes to put them away

62

in the drawers.

"Have you worked here long, Luddie?"

"Oh, no, ma'am. Just two weeks now."

"Do you like it here?"

"Well, yes, ma'am. There's not much to like yet, not many people until you came to visit. I mean, beg your pardon, ma'am, but it's a new 'ouse and such. And the master ain't 'ere much. Not yet, anyways." She forced a smile and returned to her sorting.

"It is a lovely house, though. I'm sure when Lord Darnley settles his affairs and creates a regular schedule, the house will become more lively. And of course, he knows so many people. Like Baron Rothschild."

"Oh, yes, ma'am. Last week, the Marquess of Kinsdale was here for a meeting. Good-looking, he is. Young and very rich, they say."

"It's so exciting to see so many nice people, isn't that right?"

"That's right, ma'am. In my last place, I was the scullery maid. I couldn't even go above stairs. Now, I'm right 'appy and I 'ave a chance to show 'ow good I am. I am to be yer maid. An' if I don't do sumpthin' just right, I 'ope you'll tell me. I learned, I did, from the maid at my last position. I'm a quick learner. An' I want to do well. I always wanted to be a lady's maid. Now that I got a promotion, I want to do right."

"I'm sure you will, Luddie. And yes, of course, I will help you along. I'd be happy to." I reached for Jeremy's hairbrush. "Who was your employer previously, Luddie?"

"Lord and Lady Rathbone. Their townhouse is on Upper Brooke Street in Mayfair. Do you know them?"

"Yes, as a matter of fact, I do. A charming couple. I suppose that's where Mrs. Atherton was employed also."

"Oh, no, ma'am. She came from someplace else, she did."

"Oh, and where might that have been, Luddie?" I tried to sound nonchalant.

"I'm not sure, ma'am. She doesn't tell me much, me bein' just the maid an' all. I do know she learned of this position through an agency."

"An agency?"

"Yes, ma'am. Over on Piccadilly. The Gwynns, it was."

The Gwynns. I had heard of them. They were the best of private placement agencies for respectable servants. But never had I expected that Graham would take to an agency. But then, never had I expected he would open his own house and leave Chadwick House empty.

Yet another mystery with no solution.

I finished brushing Jeremy's hair, kissed his crown, and nodded to him to crawl under the covers.

"You be a good boy now, my dear. I'll have Miss Simpson read to you, and Luddie will see to those cookies, won't you, Luddie?"

When Luddie agreed, I tucked Jeremy in and returned to my own room.

I closed my door and walked toward the window. The rain had stopped just enough to cause clouds to part, permitting rays of golden sun to touch the tops of homes and sidewalks. The slender windows of other homes across the street shone like sparkling crystals in the brilliant reflection. I yearned to feel that sun upon my face. To walk vigorously without countering the pitch of a ship. To walk a few solid city blocks—and to do it alone.

I smiled.

It was just the remedy I needed.

I picked up my reticule and stuck my head out the door. The hall was clear. I moved quickly, sound-lessly, down the two flights of stairs. No one seemed about. I reached into the front hall closet and carefully removed my cape. Still no one appeared, and when I turned the front doorknob and slipped out, no one came to inquire where I might be going or when I might return.

Out on the sidewalk, I paused only long enough to note the number of Graham's house. Thirty-two. Thirty-two Raleigh Street. And then I scurried to the corner.

I eyed the houses. This part of town was one I'd never seen. Nice houses. Clean, bright, smaller than the Palladian and Gothic expanses of the mansions in Mayfair. Modest, middle-class houses.

At the corner, I looked up at the lamppost. I was now on Marylebone. A surprise, too, because as I looked around, I knew I had never been in this particular spot before. But I also knew that if I was to reach my destination, I'd need a carriage.

A curricle passed with two ostrich-plumed ladies hurrying home from their afternoon jaunts, their liveried driver dour in his perch. A barouche went by, a young dandy inside.

I began to walk east and then south on Portland Place, putting my cares at bay for a few minutes. It was indeed a pleasant part of town and I enjoyed the exercise. At the next corner, I stopped to survey my surroundings and suddenly smiled.

A bank stood in the middle of the next block. I didn't have much money. But to go where I was going, I'd need a cab, and to hire one, I would definitely need British currency. In no time I was in and out, five American dollars exchanged for its equivalent in pounds and shillings now in my possession. A cab could not be far behind.

I was right. Within two blocks, I had found and hailed one. He took me to my destination within minutes. I alighted in front of Gwynns Services on Piccadilly, paid the driver, and marched into the glass-front shop, where a doorbell announced my arrival.

A few solid chairs invited guests to sit and wait for the three clerks who manned great desks behind a massive wooden railing. Each of the three clerks, two

65

women and a man were busy with customers. Judging by the ladies who were Gwynns' clientele, the business seemed reputable. Indeed, if tone of voice alone indicated class, the clerks spoke in hallowed ones meant for Westminster Abbey.

Just as I was about to sit, one of the ladies sailed past me and out the front door. I turned and was confronted by a gaunt moustachioed gentleman with serious blue eyes.

"Good afternoon, ma'am. May I help you? I am Norald Gwynn, the owner of the establishment."

"Yes, sir, you may help me. I am,"—God heavens, I hadn't thought this far ahead!—"Mrs. Dunsmore." My mother's family name. "I have heard of your service, Mr. Gwynn, and wished to have a preliminary discussion."

"Certainly, Mrs. Dunsmore. I'd be happy to assist you. If you would please come this way . . ." Gerald Gwynn stood aside while holding open the swinging wooden gate. He took me to his desk and indicated a chair for me.

He sat before me, his elbows on the desk, his hands steepled in front of his mouth. "You have recently arrived in London from America?"

I nodded. "My husband is in the export-import business and we will be opening a house here soon."

Gwynn's eyes never left my face. "Export-import? Really? How interesting."

I began to worry suddenly about my appearance. Did I not look the part of a businessman's wife?

"Yes, my husband and I arrived in Southampton only yesterday, and I am in quite a rush to order my household."

"I see, and where is that?"

"On Upper Brooke Street."

"I see." At the prestigious address, he sat more erect and pushed his spectacles up his hooked nose. "If you will please describe your needs to me, Mrs. Dunsmore, I will be able to help you quickly and efficiently."

I could not tell whether he totally believed me or not, so I hurried on. "My household consists of my husband, myself, and our five-year-old son. I have brought my personal maid with me, but as you know, I will need staff for an entire household. My husband has business associates here in London, but of course, I do not know their wives well enough to ask for recommendations. And I certainly do not want to be perceived as someone who is inquiring simply to snatch their good servants away. Nor do I have the time or the desire to interview and hire them myself, without proper screening, you understand."

"I certainly do, Mrs. Dunsmore." He gave me a curt smile.

He believed me. I breathed more easily but held my carriage as stiff as before.

He picked up a pen and began to write on a sheet of paper. "I assume, then, we are speaking of a housekeeper and a butler."

"To start, yes. But before we discuss particulars, I would like to understand how Gwynns does its— shall we say?—selection?"

"Gwynns, I daresay, Mrs. Dunsmore, has achieved a fine reputation because of the very discreet way in which we do operate. For ladies such as you, who find themselves cast abroad in this new world of ours, we offer assurances that our people are honest, upright men and women who seek to find satisfying positions in stable households. Many times staff who, for one reason or another, are desirous of a new position come to us, present their credentials, and ask us to add them to our list of possible employees."

"And references?"

"We do a complete check of their backgrounds, ma'am."

"How so, Mr. Gwynn?"

"We ask our applicants to bring us three letters of reference."

"Do you ever interview the previous employers?"

"Not usually, no. Our people come from the very best houses, and we find that their stationery and their seals are sufficient. Why do you ask?"

"Well, my husband has a friend who did hire one of your people and . . . well, I have heard word he is not happy."

This made Norald Gwynn squint. "Really? That is extraordinary. Unheard of, really. May I—yes, yes, I must inquire who your husband's friend might be?"

"I really do decline to say, Mr. Gwynn. You see, my husband says the gentleman would really like to give the woman a chance to prove herself."

"My, my." He shook his head and frowned. "I have never heard negative remarks before. This could ruin me. I never have heard complaints." Beads of perspiration popped from his forehead. "I really must insist you tell me who it is, Mrs. Dunsmore. Perhaps you are mistaken and the woman did not come from us at all. There are others, you know, who try to perform the same quality service but who lack our thoroughness."

I pressed my lips. "I was most positive they said Gwynns."

"Mrs. Dunsmore, please. I assure you, your words will be kept in strictest confidence."

I cast my gaze down to my lap and kneaded my hands. "Honestly, Mr. Gwynn, if you're quite sure . . . ?"

"I give you my word, Mrs. Dunsmore. None of this conversation will pass my lips again. Who is the disgruntled gentleman your husband knows?"

"Darnley. Lord Darnley. Heir to the Chadwick estate."

"The only remaining son of the old earl?" Gwynn fell back in his chair. "Oh, my! Oh, my! I am distressed to hear that. I sent him a woman most recently who came with very good references."

I shook my head and tsked. "It is a shame."

He searched his memory. "I remember the case. I

do believe the woman came with a reference from his own family. . . ." He rose from his chair, went to a large secretary, and opened one of the drawers. He rifled through files and extracted one small card. He pushed his glasses once more up his nose. "Yes, yes. Here it is." He returned to sit before me. "Atherton. From Craven in Yorkshire. Been employed as staff all her life. First, a lady's maid and cook in the home of Lord and Lady Reginald Stafford of York, then cook here in London for the Hamilton-Fyfes." He put the card on the table. "The Hamilton-Fyfes are a very good family, Mrs. Dunsmore. Very reputable. Irish. But British, if you know what I mean."

I nodded. It was all I could do. Margaret. Margaret! I sat forward. "But you said the woman was referred by one of the gentleman's own family. Isn't that rather odd? I mean, why would he come here merely to find a person he could have been referred to personally?"

He shook his head vigorously. "I have no idea, Mrs. Dunsmore. Frankly, at the time, it appeared to be a mere coincidence."

"I see. They are not close, then—Graham Chadwick and this relative?"

"I daresay they are, Mrs. Dunsmore. It was his cousin who had good words to say of Mrs. Atherton to the future earl. Miss Helena Chadwick, now of Chelsea."

How I'd gotten out of there with a shred of my sanity left was beyond me. I sat alone in a tearoom, off to one corner, with my thoughts, my hopes, my good intentions churned to a pulp.

Yesterday, someone had wished me so much ill that they had sent me a virulent message on six-year-old newspaper clippings. Last night, one of the people in this world who had much to resent me for had appeared in the same hotel as I. Today, a valise almost hit Jeremy, and minutes later, a new house-keeper went through my belongings like a thief in the night.

And this afternoon, I learned that that same housekeeper had once been employed in that very person's house.

Coincidence? Or logical, preplanned malice?

I could not tell. Certainly not until I saw Helena. Helena knew of Atherton's character, perhaps even of her intentions. Helena knew everything.

I wondered if she knew that Atherton had once been employed by the Hamilton-Fyfes. Or that she had once worked in Yorkshire.

It didn't really matter what Helena knew of Atherton or how she knew it. I poured another draught of tea for myself and stirred milk in slowly. No, it didn't really matter. Because—I sniffled and put my handkerchief to my nose to cover my sudden tears—because I was now afraid.

Afraid of Margaret.

Rich, rabid, and vengeful, Margaret could carry her cause too far. She could do more than send me old clippings or write me hateful messages. She could speak against me in society. If—considering her own downcast status—she kept any society at all anymore. Or, she could try to harm my physically. But what joy would that bring? Charles was dead. Hurting me would never change the fact that he had married me and that Jeremy was our offspring.

That was it! She was trying to get me to go home so that Jeremy would not remain in England to hear the reading of the old earl's will.

To prevent Jeremy from winning the place of honor. Was that what she wished to see?

I closed my eyes and breathed deeply.

"Would you care for more tea, madam?" the waitress asked as she had twice before.

I shook my head. "Thank you, no."

"We're closing, madam. In about fifteen minutes,

madam. Could I ask you to pay now?" She tried to look tolerant, but I noticed impatience in her dry smile.

"Yes, certainly, I am sorry." I dug in my reticule for my money purse. "Is it really that late?" I asked myself more than the waitress.

"Yes, madam."

I dug out my change purse and gave her the exact amount for my tea. I gazed at the money I had left. Two shillings. Two shillings would certainly not buy me a cab ride back to Graham's house. In my haste to search for clues to Atherton's behavior, I had failed to provide for myself adequately.

Angry at myself, I rose hastily and thanked the waitress. If I were to get home—hopefully before dinner and without anyone knowing I'd been gone— I would have to hurry. I knew I had far to walk.

I pushed through the revolving door out to the street and came to a full stop. It was dark. I searched the local buildings for a clock tower. I spied one whose turret was almost obscured from me at this angle. I hurried down the gas-lit street and peered up at the medieval spire. And then gasped at the sight of the hour. Seven-fifteen!

They were sure to miss me at Graham's. Graham's . . .

I turned back for the tearoom. But when I got there, the revolving door had been locked. I knocked upon the window glass, but my waitress and the proprietor scowled and bade me leave with a wave of the back of their hands. My waitress, perturbed, I assume, because she had gotten no gratuity for her service, told the proprietor something that made him glare at me and shoo me away once more. I backed off.

Not remembering too clearly the route I'd taken from Gwynns to this side street, I couldn't get my sense of direction to work for me. I hesitated to walk in the wrong direction, so I stood trying to determine if there was anything at all—any landmark—I possibly recognized. There was none.

In desperation, I began to walk. I'd find a bobby soon, I told myself.

But I didn't.

The night grew blacker. The fog grew denser.

And, as one block became another, I grew more fearful of ever finding a policeman. All the shops—for this was a shopping area—were closed up tight. No one traversed these corridors. At least after dark. And I alone seemed to walk among the stores repeatedly, as if in a maze. I could not find my way out. Finally, I paused in front of one bakery to rest and think.

Across the mews, in the shadow of the lamplight, I detected a flicker. Someone stood there, tall, silent, still. Only the cuffs of his trousers and the tips of his shoes were visible in the eerie light. I could almost hear him breathing. I shrank back against the shop, out of the light and—I dared to hope—out of his sight. I edged along the shop's wall, my back to the brick that scraped and tore at my cape. I wanted to scream; I dared not make a sound. I could tell from the crunch of his shoe leather on the cobbled street that he followed me.

I came to the end of the shops and had a choice: to run across the street and into the light, or to duck into what seemed to be an alley. The lighted way meant he could see me, chase me easily, but the alley . . . Who knew what that meant or where it led? My assailant might know that alley better than I ever could.

"I say, my lady . . ." He clamped a hand on my arm and I jumped in terror. "What are you doing out on a night like this alone?"

He came closer, and though I could not see his face, his breath reeked of liquor and cigars, while his body smelled of the best cologne.

"Let me go, sir."

"Why?" He leaned closer and now I could see he had overbright bold eyes. They traveled greedily over me—over my eyes, my hair, my mouth, my throat. "I knew you were lovely." He inched me up against the wall. "I've heard you were, you know."

"Sir, please . . ." I was trying to keep my wits about me as he now pressed his whole body against mine.

"Please what?" He was laughing.

"I wish to go home."

"Do you? But you're a long way from home, my lady."

"Yes, I am. And I think perhaps you have some mistaken idea that I . . ."

His long dark brows winged up in stark surprise. "That you are not a lady of the night when indeed you wander the streets alone?"

"I . . . yes!"

Who was this man? So educated. So intimidating. So frightening.

He pressed even closer.

"Sir, you will let me go."

"No, my lady, you will come with me!"

His other hand rose like a claw before my face. He closed a strong hand about my throat, encircling my waist and dragging me back by my hair with his other arm. I struggled mightily. My reticule dropped. And then I began to scream.

He had not dragged me ten paces when I heard footsteps—running footsteps and men shouting. I struggled all the harder. Help was at hand!

My attacker cursed and tried to muzzle me with one hand. I bit into his palm and tasted only fine leather. He laughed once more. I kicked at him and got one shin. He growled and lowered me to the pavement, arching me backward, backward, over his arm. I moaned and beat at him with my one free hand. In the dark and confusion, he lost his grip on my hair, and I lurched away from him and screamed once more. He lunged at me and cursed. I scurried away. It was then I saw what had frightened me when first I spied him.

A long knife . . . shining brightly in the gaslight.

"You are such a pretty lady. Now we shall see, my pretty lady, how pretty you will be! No more men will so freely want you!"

I backed into a stack of crates and sent some crashing to the ground. One fell on my foot and I cried out in pain as well as fright. Who was this madman and how could he know who I was?

I retreated one step after another, realizing too late that this was a hell-dark corner. There was no way out. My last refuge was none. I flattened myself against the wall and began to scream. If I were to die, I would do it protesting.

The sounds of men—many men—drew closer.

My assailant paused, turned in the moonlight, then glanced at me. For the first time, I saw him clearly. Broadly built, black-haired, bearded. Liquid eyes. A powerful face. Handsome. Devilishly handsome. And he sneered at me, then raised the knife beside his chin. "Tonight," he grinned sardonically, "you survive."

And then he was gone.

I remained half standing, half propped against the wall, stunned. The bobbies came, a few men, I never knew how many. I allowed them to comfort me; to find my reticule; to take me to the local station and feed me strong, hot tea.

When the police were replaced by a keen blue-eyed Inspector Curtis, I knew they had decided I was at least honest if not lucid. After the inspector scratched his grizzled red beard and declined to ask the same questions for yet a third time, I begged him to take me back to Graham's. Out in front of the precinct, two bobbies came round with one of their plain black municipal carriages and placed me inside, with a woolen blanket for my lap and a hot brick to warm my feet, while Inspector Curtis plopped down opposite me. He asked no further questions of me, but of himself he obviously asked many as he squinted out the window and chewed at the inside of his mouth, ruminating indigestible fodder.

Chapter Six

Inspector Curtis supported me all the way up to the front door of Graham's. He lifted the giant knocker and let it bang against the wooden door. I leaned into him. My mind dazed, my body bruised, I barely understood much other than that we had arrived and I was safe. Or, at any rate, safer than I had been alone on the London streets.

Inspector Curtis lifted his hand to knock once more, when MacCarthy tore open the door.

"My God! Mrs. Chadwick! We've been worried sick about you."

Curtis presented his card to MacCarthy. "Inspector Curtis of the Yard. I'd like a word with Lord Darnley."

MacCarthy took one look at the card, checked the appearance of the natty man in the grey worsted suit before him, then fell back to let Curtis in with me. "Come with me, Inspector, come with me. This way to the drawing room." He hastened ahead of us to slide open the double doors.

My eyes found Graham first. Head hung, thumbs hooked in his trouser pockets, he paced the floor like a caged lion. In front of him stood two bobbies. At my appearance, Graham halted in mid-stride, went white as a shroud, and came straight for me.

"Vanessa! Dear God!"

The bobbies, burly fellows in black with their tall-bowled hats and chin straps that crushed their pudgy jaws, turned to gape at me and Inspector Curtis.

"Vanessa . . ." This was the voice of someone dear to me, someone who drew near and placed a tender kiss upon my brow. "Hello, my dear."

I looked up into the smiling countenance of Helena, grasping her hand and breaking into copious tears at the same time. She led me to the settee, knelt beside me, and stroked my straggly hair from my face.

"It's all right now, my dear," she crooned. "You are home."

I heard Curtis introduce himself to Graham and Helena and the two policemen who were from this precinct.

Graham's voice pierced the air. "What's happened, Inspector? We've been out of our minds wondering where my sister-in-law could be."

I felt Graham draw near me and place one trembling hand upon my shoulder.

"Well, sir," Curtis said, "Mrs. Chadwick has had quite a shock. She's not recovered yet and she seems to be logical, but she is still very frightened. She should be, too. She met up with quite a brute, I'd say, sir. Quite a brute."

"What do you mean, Inspector?" Graham asked.

"Yes, Inspector," Helena patted my hand and inquired of the man, "please tell us what evil Mrs. Chadwick has encountered this evening to look as if she's been dragged through the streets?"

"I am distressed to tell you, ma'am, that that is exactly what happened to her."

Helena froze. "Oh, my! No, Inspector. Such things—"

"—Do happen, madam. I'm sorry to say, they do. Here in London. Probably more so these days, what with Jack the Ripper out."

"Inspector," Graham boomed, "please don't frighten Vanessa any more than she already has been."

The red-haired inspector frowned. "My lord, I beg your pardon. I don't mean to frighten anyone, but from what we've heard from Mrs. Chadwick, we think she might have been Jack's next victim."

The two bobbies muttered to each other and grimaced.

"Inspector, really!" Helena was appalled. "Such histrionics are not necessary. You people from the Yard needn't come round scaring the respectables of the city with that—that ridiculous story. Why, the *Star* has it all about that it is women of ill repute who have been murdered lately. In Whitechapel and Spitalfields, not in our part of town. What a tale! Really, Inspector!"

"Beg your pardon, madam, but this is not a tale. It's the truth. And we have had quite a few unsolved crimes lately—some with very nice, respectable ladies attacked by those who'd like to get a name like the Ripper's for their own use. I'm looking at every case, ma'am. Every one. And sorry to say, this one sounds very familiar to what we've been seeing with some of the ladies of the night, so to speak—begging your pardon, Mrs. Chadwick, Miss Chadwick, my lord. We're just going by what we heard from Mrs. Chadwick. And she was attacked by a man that fits the description of Jack. Tall and dark. Nicely dressed. Fine speech. Right, Mrs. Chadwick?"

I swiped at the last of my tears and nodded. "He wore expensive cologne as well."

Graham stared at me. "You remember that?"

"Yes." My head fell back against the chair and I stared into Graham's stormy black eyes. "Leather gloves, too. Nice white stock. Freshly laundered, I would guess. And a long, shiny knife."

Helena sucked in her breath and pressed my hand. "Oh, my dearest, you have had such a terrible experience. How will you ever overcome it?" She stroked my hand. "Not to worry, pet. We'll put you back together, shan't we, Graham?"

"Yes. Yes, of course, we will." Graham turned to the inspector and demanded an explanation.

Inspector Curtis reached into his coat pocket and extracted a notebook, which he flipped open. I knew that notebook. He'd copied long, almost verbatim notes during our conversation. In slow, methodical detail, Curtis recounted my evening. Graham and Helena listened stoically. The two bobbies themselves now took notes. When Curtis finally flipped his book closed and gazed at Graham and Helena, they murmured their thanks.

"Frankly, Lord Darnley," Curtis said, "I'd like to return tomorrow—if that's all right with you and your sister-in-law. I'd like to see if we can make any more sense of this when she has recovered from the shock a bit. Is that permissible, sir?"

"Absolutely. Whatever you need to catch the culprit, Inspector, I'd be eager to assist."

"Thank you, my lord. I appreciate that."

Graham politely smiled at Curtis. "I'll see you out, Inspector. What time do you think you'll return tomorrow?"

"Say, ten o'clock? Give Mrs. Chadwick a chance to get some sleep."

"Ten it is, Inspector."

Curtis looked at the policemen. "Come along, Sergeants. We have much to discuss."

The officers said their goodbyes to us all. Graham nodded to the inspector and preceded him out the door to the foyer.

"Tea?" Helena offered me. "Would you like some tea, my pet? Or cocoa? I'll fetch Mrs. Atherton." She stepped away to the bellpull by the drapes, then quickly returned to hold my hand and pick and fuss over my wild, unbound hair, my scratched face, and my torn attire.

I sat, exhausted, listening as remnants of the conversation between Graham and the inspector drifted in from the foyer. I heard abhorrent words like "almost raped" and "madman" and "mistaken for a harlot." Then I heard the front door open and close.

Graham returned to stand before me. In his eyes I saw fear and anger. I recoiled that he should be so distressed by my behavior.

Atherton arrived with a tray and sat it on the end table beside me. I felt her eyes skitter over me. I did not return the look but stared at Helena, who smiled serenely at me.

"When did you arrive?" I asked her as she poured hot cocoa into a china cup.

She offered me the cup and saucer. "Sip some of this first, dear."

My hands shook and the cup would have fallen if Helena hadn't reached out to assist me. I whispered my thanks and fervently prayed Atherton would leave. I did not wish my condition to be a source for her gloating. She must have read my thoughts, because she opened her mouth and asked if there was anything else we needed. Thankfully, Helena waved her away.

When Atherton closed the door behind her, Helena answered me. "I came round immediately when Graham sent MacCarthy to me at five o'clock or so." Her dark eyes filled with tears, which trickled onto her thick black lashes.

Graham cleared his throat. "I assumed you had gone to visit Helena."

Helena swiped at her tears and reached into a pocket for a handkerchief. "But, of course, you hadn't. We were so frightened. It was so awful for you to leave without telling anyone where you were going or why. We were mad with worry. We had no idea where to look. I, of course, returned with MacCarthy. Then Graham had no choice but to send for the local police. Those two men came and asked a lot of questions, but we had no answers. They put out a search here in the neighborhood. But Abercrombie Mews?"

"Yes, Vanessa," Graham insisted, "I want to know how in the world you got down into that neighborhood."

"I have no other explanation than to tell you I got lost. I needed to walk. I'd been so cooped up on that ship, I was frantic to stretch my legs. And the weather suddenly broke and it was so pleasant."

I was being honest but I was also acting. The tension of playing this part made me knead my hands.

Graham snorted. "For hours?"

"Yes, I passed a few shops and walked in a park. Then I decided I wanted some tea and exchanged a few dollars for pounds. But it wasn't nearly enough. I'd forgotten how much things cost. So when I went to pay the bill in the tearoom, I had just enough. When I went outside, it was dark. The banks were closed. I knew I had to walk, because I had no money to hire a carriage." I ran a hand across my brow. "Please, no more, no more. How is Jeremy?"

Graham frowned. "His cold is worse, and he was very worried where you were until I told him you had gone to visit a friend and would be home later. Aside from that, he is fine. I tucked him into bed over an hour ago. Simpson says he sleeps well, considering his physical condition."

"Thank goodness. I could not bear for him to know about tonight. You must not tell him. He has suffered so much these last few years. He is sensitive and I do not want him frightened."

"Rest assured, Vanessa, I will tell him naught of what's passed here tonight," Graham vowed.

"Of course not, my pet." Helena stood up. "None of us will breathe a word. But now we must get you into your bed."

I stood up but the room weaved before me. I floundered. Strong arms scooped me up and pressed me against solid comfort.

"I'll take her up, Helena. Please ring for Luddie

and send her upstairs to have her help Vanessa into bed. Good night," he nodded once, then turned away.

Graham walked slowly through the drawing room and into the foyer. Before he began to climb the stairs, he paused and settled me more securely to his chest. "Have you the strength to put your arms around my neck?"

I nodded and did as I was told, then let my head find its natural repose beneath his chin. I breathed in the subtle sandalwood and spice of his cologne. So soothing to the senses. So unlike that other man who'd held me in his arms tonight. I cuddled closer. Graham suffered from a frisson of some sort.

He took the stairs with measured strides. Not once did he falter with the burden of my weight. But with each step I grew more grateful for his special care, more desirous of his solace, so that when he shouldered open my bedroom door and bent to place me gently on the spread, my arms ached as he left them.

He let his hands slide down my arms to clasp my hands. His eyes spoke of a thousand unspeakable emotions. Then he raised my fingers to his lips, rubbed his mouth against my knuckles, and whispered hoarsely, "Promise me you won't leave me ever again without a word of your intentions?"

What could I answer?

I adored the sentiment but abhorred the restriction.

Anger surfaced amid those volcanic emotions in his eyes. "Promise me!"

"I . . . can't."

Fury erupted on his face. He clamped his jaw and labored at self-restraint. He stood erect, staring at me while the lava of his emotions spilled over his countenance, raging through his body with a virulence that shook its might and then went uncommonly still. With great deliberateness, he put my hands firmly against my chest and pivoted for the door.

In abject misery, I watched him go, then curled into my pillows and wept fresh tears.

When Inspector Curtis arrived the next morning, I was waiting for him in the second-floor sitting room. I had had a dreamless night, probably a blessing granted me in my exhaustion. I felt mentally fit, even though I knew I still looked rather battered and wan. I sat now in a modest lavender day dress. Across my lap Helena had arranged a knitted afghan and in my hand she'd placed a cup of jasmine tea.

Helena had taken up a seat opposite me, perching herself on the edge of an overstuffed chair with the jitters of a fussing mother bird attending her chick. Graham—who had bid me good morning with all the civility of a stranger—stood, one elbow on the mantel, one hand across his mouth.

The two of them listened as once more Inspector Curtis took out his pen and notebook and began the discussion that drew me into my encounter with the mysterious gentleman in Abercrombie Mews.

"I am very pleased, Mrs. Chadwick, that you were able to see me this morning. This case disturbs us greatly at the Yard. And last night, I called in a friend of mine from the Third Precinct to talk about some similarities of this case to two other cases."

Graham dropped his hand from his mouth. "Really, Inspector. I wish you would leave off with these references to those notorious cases with this man the *Star* calls 'The Ripper.'"

"Lord Darnley, I'm sorry to say this case bears too many similarities to two others we've listed recently. Both of those, we think, were perpetrated by the same gentleman."

"Gentleman?" Graham's eyes went round.

"Gentleman," Curtis confirmed. "The man in question is well-dressed, well-spoken, and seems drawn to ladies who walk alone."

"In Abercrombie Mews?" From the tone of Graham's voice, he found the whole idea preposterous.

"No, not in the Mews. But close by, my lord. Close by." Inspector Curtis looked at me. "And he carries a knife. He has killed the other two ladies in the most appalling fashion. I am glad to say, Mrs. Chadwick, you escaped the man. Because if, indeed, he is the same one, you are most fortunate. Most fortunate."

Helena was incredulous. "Here, here, Inspector! We all know that women of a certain calling have been abused, maimed, disappeared, dropped into the Thames, drowned, and killed for centuries, centuries! Just because there seems to be the latest uproar—"

"Vigilance committees and town meetings are prudent measures, ma'am—"

"Prudent, Inspector, but really not warranted in our section of town. Why, here no 'Ripper' is possible. This 'Jack' is probably just someone's newest term for a mad person. . . ."

"Yes, ma'am, that's exactly what this man appears to be." Curtis looked at Graham. "I don't want to put the cart before the horse, sir, but all the facts point to the same thing. Until I conclude otherwise. So, we must go over the facts of your sister-in-law's case until we are quite sure what they mean. Quite sure."

Graham nodded in agreement. Helena huffed.

I scarcely knew if I still breathed, my heart beat such a violent tattoo.

Inspector Curtis tapped his pen against his mouth. "Now, Mrs. Chadwick, I would like to discuss your conclusion about his education. You seem convinced he was well-schooled."

"Yes." I licked my lips and found some remnant of sanity. "Very. I remember asking myself why such a man would find it necessary to . . . well, take up with women in the street when . . . he can find . . . shall we say, companionship in many quarters. But that was before I saw the knife again and understood his true intentions."

"Saw the knife again?"

"Yes. I saw it when first I knew someone watched me from across the street. I should say I saw its gleam in the lamplight. But I had no idea what it was. That was before he spoke or threatened me."

"Can you describe this knife?"

"Well, sir, I am no expert on knives. I saw it clearly only for one moment. You might say it resembled service cutlery. One that a cook might use to slice meat. Large, perhaps ten inches long, with a triangular blade. I am sorry, that's all I remember."

"Hmm. Let us return to the matter of his education. Let us try to determine how you concluded that."

"His speech."

I frowned and felt fear raise the hair at the back of my neck. I closed my eyes to remember. What was it about his speech that frightened me *now?*

I squeezed my eyes tightly and opened them. "He spoke in clear sentences. No cockney. No Scots or Irish or Welsh lilt to the words. Crisp English. He'd been to a proper school that taught the queen's aristocracy to speak."

"I beg your pardon, ma'am," Curtis broke in, "but you are an American lady. How do you know the British so well?"

"I told you, Inspector, that I was married to a peer of the Realm for a year and a half and lived here during that time. I know what I'm saying. That man had fine speech." I closed my eyes again and once more heard the timbre of my attacker's voice. "He had a deep voice. Bass. Resonant. When he laughed, it went to the marrow of your bones." I shivered. "Such a chilling sound. And he spoke with full verbs. No contractions. No *don'ts* or *won'ts* and certainly no *ain'ts*. A gentleman of the highest class."

My mind's eye filled with the vision of his handsome face. "Large eyes. Light-colored. Blue or light hazel perhaps. But more likely blue. Pale liquid blue. Black hair. Jet-black, perfectly groomed. He sees his barber often. And perfectly shaped winged brows. Wide-set, a perfect frame for those uncommon blue eyes. He wondered why I was on the street. Asked me why I was out alone. Taking me for a doxy . . . saying I . . . Oh, God . . ."

I sat forward. It didn't matter. I still saw him. I still heard him. His telling words.

"He knew me."

Graham cursed.

Helena gasped.

Inspector Curtis leaned forward into my line of vision. "How did he know you?"

"I . . . I'm not sure. I mean, I don't recall ever meeting him. But he . . . what did he say?"

I raked my hair and stood up. The afghan fell to my feet. Graham was suddenly at my side with a hand to my arm to steady me. I stared past him to the window. Outside, the sunlight streamed in glorious abandon. I saw only the black of last night and my menace.

"He said . . . he called me 'my lady.' Said I was a long way from home. Did he say I shouldn't be alone? I don't remember!" I put one palm across my eyes and shook my head. Graham patted my arm. I saw the man's face once more. "Bearded. He had a muttonchop beard. Odd for a young man to have an old man's beard. But he was handsome, anyway. 'You are a long way from home,' he said. How did he know that? How?" My hand fell from my eyes. "And then he said . . . he said I was a pretty lady, and he flashed the knife and grinned in that sinister way. He said he would make sure that no more men wanted me. Oh, no, no." I could barely utter the words. "He knows me." I glanced up into Graham's sorrowing eyes. "Oh, Gray, what am I to do? He knows me!"

Graham stroked my hair.

"Lord Darnley—"

I felt Graham lift a hand to ward off any more inquiries from Curtis. "Helena, get MacCarthy immediately. Tell him I want paper—lots of paper from my desk—and pens, pencils, and a large, sturdy book."

Helena turned on her heel and left the room.

I looked at Graham as he slowly smiled at me.

"Inspector, Vanessa is about to do you a great service. She will deliver you clues to your culprit within moments."

Curtis stepped forward. "I don't understand."

I did.

Graham nodded at me. "You know best how to help the inspector."

I nodded in gratitude and, with Graham's help, returned to my chair.

In the doorway, MacCarthy appeared with Graham's items, and I sat forward as the portly fellow placed them all regally in my lap as if he were displaying gifts for royalty. Helena stood to one side and Graham stood before me, while the inspector resumed his seat.

I situated the book in my lap, then took up the black fountain pen and one grey sheet of writing paper, obviously Graham's personal stationery, with his silver embossed initials at the top.

I sat poised, pen in midair. I checked Graham's confident expression. "I haven't done this in so long that I—"

"Do it. You can."

I rolled the fat Waterman pen between my fingers. Ink had never been a favorite medium of mine. Not from a brush. Certainly not from a fountain pen. But I had no choice tonight. I looked at Graham. *Do it. You can.*

I began. A stroke here, one there, another. The dimensions were all wrong. I crushed the paper and put it aside. I hesitated. What had he looked like?

I tried once more. A few lines here and there, and

suddenly the outline of his oval face appeared. Perspectives there and there. His eyes, wide-set. His mouth.

I paused and closed my eyes. His mouth in repose. What would that look like? I tried and could not imagine him in any other way than as he appeared to me—sardonically displaying his perfect white teeth. I opened my eyes and drew him as I'd seen him. The mouth was not pretty.

His hair I sketched in. It had been parted down the middle. Softly waving. Gleaming. And black. Black as onyx stones.

The nose. I could not remember it. His nose was not a prominent feature, so outdone was it by the symmetry of his other graces.

I faltered and could not go on.

Graham came round to stand behind my chair. "His beard, you said, was mutton-chopped. Draw it in."

I did. When I finished, I could remember the nose as straight, plain, Roman. Unnoticeable. I drew it quickly.

I held up the portrait and examined it. The eyes needed definition. Those incandescent eyes of blue. Pale blue.

Graham put a hand to my shoulder and squeezed it almost painfully. "Oh, my sweet God, Vanessa! Do you know who you've drawn?"

I spun around to look up at him. "No! Who?"

"You're quite sure? You've never met this man?"

"No. Only last night in that alley. Who is it, Graham?"

Curtis stood up. "Yes, Lord Darnley, who is this man?"

"Except for the beard . . . the eyes, the nose, the wave of the hair . . . My God!, Vanessa, I would say you have just sketched the best portrait I have ever seen of His Royal Highness, the Duke of Clarence!"

Everyone in the room murmured disbelief.

I shook my head. "But, Graham, that's absurd. The Duke of Clarence! Ridiculous." I stared at my sketch. "Impossible. I drew what I saw. I did. I know I saw *this* man."

"And *this* man is Clarence, I tell you," Graham insisted.

"But, Graham, I have never met Clarence!"

Curtis harrumphed. "Yes, how could she draw someone she's never met?"

"But I did meet this man!"

Graham shook his head. "And this man is Clarence. Eddy. The man is my second cousin, for God's sake. I know a man who is my relative, especially one so distinctive as that."

"No." I stood up and put my pen and paper on the table beside my chair. I walked to the window. Outraged. Confused. "I have never met Clarence."

"Think, Vanessa. When you and Charles came to London for the season, you might have met him. Danced with him."

"No. The only member of the royal family I ever met was Bertie. Prince Albert. At a weekend party, a fox hunt at the Marlboroughs."

Curtis was intrigued. "So, you've met His Royal Highness, the Prince of Wales, Albert Edward. Who bears many resemblances to his son—his eldest son—the Duke of Clarence."

"Inspector Curtis, I tell you, I have met the prince. And perhaps the father and son do resemble each other, but I have no firsthand knowledge of that. But never in my dreams would I portray Bertie—who is a kind soul known to me as jovial and witty—as the type of man who could do what this man did . . . say what he did. Never."

"Well, Mrs. Chadwick"—he put both hands behind his back and swayed forward on his toes—"have you ever had any fantasies, delusions—"

Helena stepped in front of the inspector. "Really, sir! This is preposterous! That you should be so rude as to suggest that our Vanessa might have imagined this perversion. Our Vanessa has suffered enough castigations. We will not allow any more!"

Curtis eyed Helena. "I am sorry, ma'am, to do this, but my job is to find out what really happened last night. If that means asking difficult questions to get difficult answers, then I must. And I will."

"But she has answered that she did not know him."

The inspector smacked his lips in impatience. "Ah, yes, but her original statement was and the question before us remains: Did he know her?"

"She says he did."

"Precisely. Then how?"

Oh, I knew. I knew so well.

Graham intervened. "Vanessa is well-known."

Helena almost whispered. "Graham, you can't—"

"Can't what, Lord Darnley?"

Graham frowned at Helena yet spoke to the inspector. "But I *can* tell you, Inspector, how Clarence or anyone knows Vanessa."

I groaned.

"Vanessa was one of the first American beauties to grace our shores and marry a nobleman. As such, her fame spread before she even arrived. The *Tatler* and the *Star* recounted her life's history and interviewed friends of her family. Even her lineage was printed, discussed. . . ."

"Lord Darnley, that still does not explain—"

"Just a minute, Inspector. When she arrived here in London as a bride, one young society photographer persuaded her to pose for him."

I stared now at Graham. I had forgotten this most vital piece of information!

Graham returned my look and went on. "She posed with roses in her hair and in her hand. The portrait was a most unique composition; a marvel of symmetry; a study of a stunning American woman who quickly became the toast of our society. In their haste to discuss Vanessa, the other smaller newspapers

89

published the photograph as well. Other photographers imitated the style. Shopkeepers somehow got hold of copies of the portrait and sold them by the hundreds. Along with Jennie Churchill, Vanessa became renowned as the first of the 'professional beauties,' Inspector. Her portrait—I know because I have seen it in countless homes—still graces many a table in many drawing rooms across our land. So you see, Inspector, many people could easily recognize Vanessa. The man next door . . . the local constable . . . the Duke of Clarence. Why, Her Majesty herself could know this lady."

Relieved, I sank into the nearest slipper chair and ran a hand across my brow.

The inspector came to stand before me. "Did this man call you by name?"

"No."

"Say where you lived?"

"No."

"Name your relatives, your son?"

"No."

"Declare where he had seen you or how?"

"No."

"Well then, Mrs. Chadwick, I am at a loss as to how you can say the man knows you." He crouched down to enter my line of vision. "You have a startling recollection of faces, Mrs. Chadwick, and I understand your perception given your talent as an artist. But what I need you to do is rake your memory, ma'am. Why do you conclude he knew you?"

I looked at him. A kind man, funny-faced, with all that coiled red hair and beard to match. Those small all-seeing blue eyes. That pensive mouth.

Why had I concluded my attacker knew me?

I turned to the window, then rose to look out onto the street.

What had he done?

What had he said?

" 'Tonight you survive,' he told me as he turned on

his heels to run. He's coming back to get me, you see. 'Tonight you survive.' He showed me the blade and smiled fiendishly, ear to ear with that handsome mouth. 'You are such a pretty lady,' he said, and moved closer to me. 'We'll see how pretty you are after this. No more men will want you!' Oh, yes. That's what he said: 'No more men will want you!'"

I faced the inspector. My hands trembled. "He knows me, all right."

Curtis frowned. "I am afraid I still don't understand, Mrs. Chadwick. That statement is not an extraordinary thing to say, particularly to a lovely woman."

I shook my head furiously. "It is to me, Inspector. It is to me!"

"You'll have to explain that, Mrs. Chadwick."

I was choking with my pain and fear. "I can't." How could I reveal the pain of my husband's accusation? To an investigator? I swallowed back the bile of disgust. I was trapped.

"I—I really can't go on. I—I must lie down. I—"

Graham spoke up. "Please, Inspector, I know what you want. I can explain from here. Please. I insist my sister-in-law be allowed to return to her room. These events have been such a shock."

"Yes, certainly, sir. I can see Mrs. Chadwick needs a rest. She and I can continue this another day."

It took MacCarthy plus the footman to get me upstairs to my room, while Graham related to Inspector Curtis what I in my misery knew was the whole of my sordid past.

Chapter Seven

The next morning, I had barely finished my coffee when the post delivered a letter that had me staring, standing, spilling liquid and letter upon the carpet.

I caught my cup before it shattered. I could not, however, do myself the same justice. I stooped to pick up the letter. With shaking hands, I opened the parchment and read once more words that made my heart stop.

"The other night's encounter should show you adulteresses are not welcome in England. Now go home!"

I could not breathe. Tearing at the neck of my negligee, I rushed to the window and tried to open it.

"Ma'am! Mrs. Chadwick!?"

I stared at Luddie.

"Oooo, Mrs. Chadwick, what's the matter?!"

I tried to speak.

Luddie bolted for the door.

I worked against the window latch. It stuck. I pried at it with my fingers, cursing it roundly, pushing at it, cutting a finger against sharp metal.

Then my hands were covered by another's.

"Vanessa. Vanessa, don't." Graham's arms surrounded me as he engulfed my fingers and stilled them. "Thank you, Luddie. You may go. I will take care of Mrs. Chadwick."

He worried the window latch and threw open the casement. Cool autumn air rushed at me. I sagged but could not stop the tremors of my body. I felt his arms once more capture me, enfold me, press me to his warm, hard torso. I felt his lips ruffle my hair as he whispered in my ear, "Sweet, no one can hurt you here. Calm yourself. You are safe."

I shook my head violently. "No, no. That's not true."

He clasped me harder to him.

I writhed to be free. "Let me go, let me go."

He turned me to him, thrusting one hand into my hair to steady me and make me look up at him. "No. Never. You have taken all these shocks in great stride." His black eyes examined me relentlessly. "Why, Vanessa? Tell me why you have broken this morning?"

I raised one hand, and his gaze traveled to the cream parchment I had crushed into a ball. His eyes grew round. His arms released me.

I stepped back against the window. A breeze swept through my silken gown and wrap.

"Another message which came in the morning mail, Graham."

"My God, Vanessa! Let me see it."

I sidestepped his advance. "No. This message is for me alone. It is in handwriting that resembles that of the first message."

"Let me see it, Vanessa."

I shook my head. "Why? Don't you believe me? Am I now considered insane, making up threatening messages to send to myself?"

"Don't be absurd, Vanessa. These events have snapped you—"

"I'm a lunatic, is that right? Well, don't ask me to show it to you. It's mine. Meant for me. Please do me the courtesy of sending a message to Inspector Curtis. He'll need to see this."

"Vanessa, be reasonable. If you show that to him,

he'll return again and again. He'll want to sample the handwriting to compare it to Clarence's. As I told you last night after he left, Curtis doubts the assailant could be Clarence, simply because my cousin has no mutton-chop beard. But people have devised disguises before. Curtis is bright and not easily put off the scent of a track. If you show him this letter, you must tell him of the first one, and he'll demand you show it to him. Then you'll be describing other elements, other events which might bring painful memories."

Lucidity claimed my mind. "Do you mean to imply that you did not tell him every detail of my past?"

Graham nodded. "I told him only the barest facts."

I waited.

"I told him that your marriage ended when circumstances led my brother to accuse you of sharing your affections elsewhere. Unable to counter his circumstantial evidence, you were divorced by my brother. The story became fodder for the gossips. The result is that many people now know about the former Viscountess of Darnley and how she was disgraced."

I eyed him. "Is that all you said?"

"Yes. I think the rest explains itself. Your portrait giving you exposure to the world might mean anyone could recognize you."

"You related to Curtis nothing of Charles's perfidy?"

"What good would it do?"

"To show him what a den of iniquity I lived in."

"Guilt by association? Of what redeeming grace is that? We want Curtis to focus on capturing the ruffian in the Mews. . . ."

"You believe that man is the one who has been sending these notes?"

Graham raked his hair. "God's blood, Vanessa! How in hell do I know? It seems logical to me. You arrive here in England and suddenly you receive

94

threatening notes. Then one night you are attacked by someone you yourself say knows you!"

"Suppose the man of the Mews is not my man of mysteries?"

"It is possible. Possible, but not probable. The incident, piled on these others, is enough for me to declare we will leave for Darnley Castle tomorrow morning."

"You do not want the police to investigate the Chadwicks at all, do you?"

He stepped back, braced his feet apart, and crossed his arms. He had his overcoat on, and had evidently been ready to leave and launch his business day when Luddie had caught him and brought him to me.

He scowled at me. "No, I would not like the police involved, if that's what you're getting at, Vanessa. I do not want them mucking about in my private matters. The newspapers these days pick up on such items and—"

"And suddenly you're the talk of the town."

"Precisely."

"And the Chadwicks have already had enough of that."

"Absolutely."

"Don't you think *I* have had enough as well?"

"I know you have. That's why I told Curtis only the facts he needs to assist him in his search for the man of the Abercrombie Mews. Now you are breaking under the strain. In all these events, you have been quite resilient, quite brave—"

I chortled. *"You* are quite mad."

"You are quite maddening!"

"I am not here to please you."

"Of that, I am all too painfully aware."

"Then also be aware of this: Since I have set foot in England, I have received nothing but threats and malice and bodily harm. I do not normally live like this. On the contrary. I live a quiet, simple life with few friends. I am not given to enduring pain. I had enough the year and a half I spent with Charles. I want an end to these threats. I want an end to my torment, none of which was ever my doing. So if I wish to run to Curtis with what evidence I have, you will forgive my haste."

"I can't allow you to do it, Vanessa." Graham paced the floor.

"In America, we hold our policemen in high esteem. We don't consider them snoops or ill-bred bunglers."

He halted before me. "Let me investigate this, Vanessa."

I narrowed my eyes at him. "How?"

"I have my ways."

"Through your friends, I suppose. The subtle English way."

"It works."

I sighed. Yes. I knew he was right. There was no substitute for the way the English aristocracy filed behind one of its own in time of crisis. Or in time of possible scandal. For when it came, if it came, scandal was anathema to them. But instinct told me Graham had other reasons for keeping the investigation private. "Why are you doing this?"

"I have my reasons."

"Which are?"

He bit his lower lip, looked at the floor, and shook his head. "Family honor. My own and yours. Justice. For us both."

"Both? What do you mean?"

He spun from me. "I cannot discuss it. I will not. You must take the reasons I give you. Honor and justice *are* two good reasons."

I eyed him, wary of his diversionary tactics. "We've had this discussion. I told you then, neither are obtainable for me."

"Oh? And I suppose Nathan and Rene cut you the other day?"

"No, surprisingly they didn't. But they are men,

96

both of whom have traversed society's rules. But women control the access to society, Graham. And I am a woman subject to their dictates. Nathan's and Rene's wives, good, bad, or indifferent, would have given me the cut direct without a second's thought."

"How do you know?"

"If I were a gambler, I could bet money on it. But since I'm not, I'll stand by the record of countless women who have breached society's dictates and suffered at the hands of their more auspicious sisters. In any case, I'll never test your theory."

"No? Why not?" He folded his arms and peered at me. "You're not afraid of them?"

Now my body shook, not from fear but from fury. "I never was a coward, Graham. Anyhow, the point is moot. They'll never have the chance to cut me."

"What if I told you they will?"

"What? Why?"

"Business and pleasure. Nathan and his wife are to join us in Darnley the day after the reading of the will."

A hand went to my throat. "Oh, Graham, how could you!?"

"I had few choices."

Choices. Hadn't Graham himself told me that today I had choices. "I will not be present when you receive them, that's all."

"Oh, but I need you. I doubt Nathan's wife would come so far if she knew she were to enter a house where no womanly amenities might greet her."

"Helena can hostess. She'll be there for the will and she would love to stay on, I'm sure. She knows the house because she used to live at Darnley."

"But she was never mistress there. You know how to run the place."

"So does your housekeeper there. I assume Mrs. Bellweather is still alive and in good health."

"Yes, she is, God save her, but she has not entertained a lady and gentleman in years and—"

"And neither have I."

"The crux of the matter *is*, Vanessa, that I need the very best in preparation and entertainment for my guests. I also dearly need this business agreement to be finalized to my benefit, Vanessa. You cannot refuse me in this."

"What else have you devised for me to do?"

"Only to act as hostess for me, just this once."

I glanced at the note in my hand. "And I can repay you for the honor of reintroducing me into society by forgoing the opportunity of telling Inspector Curtis about this note and the other?"

"If you do tell him, the opportunity to be reintroduced to society, as you put it, may end before it begins."

"Why should I care?"

He seemed to stop breathing as his eyes gazed into mine. "Oh, but you do."

I turned from him and the truth.

"You care because you are innocent and always have been. You were cruelly abused and maligned, and if there is anything in God's great world I can do to rectify what my brother and my father did to you, I give you my solemn promise I will."

"I do not hold you responsible."

"No, perhaps not. But my worthiness is questionable because I bear the same name, the same blood. And I have my own reasons. I cannot see injustice done . . . cruelty go unpunished."

I turned and the sight of him ravished my senses. He had tears in his eyes and his marvelous mouth bit back agony.

"You see, I saw firsthand what obscenities Charles could commit. Yes, I saw them long before you came to us. Long before I saw you brought here. Long before I came to know you. You who were so bright, so gay, so charming and innocent. Ah, God help us all, you were so innocent. Just like Iselton."

"Iselton? Your brother?"

"Yes, my older brother . . . older by four years. Sweet, funny Izzy, who at the tender age of nine wandered in one day on Charles in the farrier's shack. Izzy came and told me he had caught Charles with a playmate, both of them naked as the day they were born. The friend escaped with just a departing show of bare buttocks, but Charles presented himself before Izzy, hands on his hips, bold as brass in his all-together. Totally nonplussed. Fourteen-years-old and impressed with his status as heir to the great earldom of Darnley. Hah! What rubbish! Impressed by our father that to be earl of his domain was a license to do almost anything. And he had. Drowning a kitten who'd scratched him; threatening to sack a groom who'd been rude; later being sent down from school for gaming in the dormitory. Charles tried to dominate everyone, everything.

"Then when Izzy discovered Charles and his playmate at their naked cavorting, Charles tried to intimidate Izzy, but Izzy thought the world was created just for enjoyment. He took no malice from Charles's threats. Neither did I. I was just five. Izzy and I thought the whole event an occasion for great giggling.

"But Charles took great exception. He had threatened Izzy with a beating if he told our father. That's when Izzy and I knew there was nothing to laugh at in this episode. I told Izzy he had to tell father or, if he couldn't face him himself, to confide in our governess. But Izzy wouldn't, of course. To tattle would be against his code of honor, and by that time, Izzy had already been treated to a sample of Charles's wrath—a few strokes with a cat-o'-nine-tails. So Izzy decided to keep his own counsel on this.

"But, of course, he discovered Charles at it again and again. He told me that Charles often went into that old wayfarer's cottage beneath the cliff of Darnley Castle. Izzy even took me down there one day and we hid behind the trees. But one day Izzy went alone and was not too careful. Charles saw Izzy in the window, ran out of the cottage, and seized him. Pinned him down. Beat him brutally. Broke a rib, I think. In any case, Izzy never really recovered well. Trying to keep it from my father, Izzy never saw a doctor, never had the thing set right. Ever after, he was hunched over, out of breath. Father, absorbed as he was in his women and racehorses, never seemed to care enough to do anything about it. Izzy could never run again. Or laugh. And Izzy was always so full of fun and laughter. I miss him to this day."

Graham straightened and looked about him. "Forgive me. I rattle on."

I stepped closer and gazed into his eyes. "Did Izzy ever tell your father?"

"Never. Izzy died just before his fourteenth birthday, weakened from that broken rib and a case of pneumonia as bad as I've ever seen. He'd been out riding, when his horse fell on top of him and pinned him beneath with a broken leg. It was days before we found him. By then, he'd been lying about in mud from a two-day downpour and he could barely talk, much less breathe. He died the next day. A wonderful chap. You would have liked ol' Izzy."

"If you loved him, I would have, too."

"Thank you for that."

I glanced at the threatening note in my hand. "I can see you're had many tragedies in this family."

"What happened to you was the greatest tragedy. Let me correct that. I seek to. Let me restore you to your rightful respectability. I know I haven't been very successful thus far at keeping you from harm's way, but I promise you I will do my damnedest to keep you safe. Let us leave London. I feel things will be better at Darnley. That man who attacked you, whoever he is, cannot, *would* not follow us so far. Margaret can't either, without us knowing about it readily and easily. I will keep you and Jeremy safe. After all, I feel responsible for you. It was my

100

personal entreaty that made you come, wasn't it?"

"Yes. And I confess it was not for the money alone that I came."

I looked up at him, and his eyes flashed with some strange emotion I could have called expectation.

"Why *did* you come, Vanessa?"

I swallowed hard. Some errant thought, some wild longing swept through my conscious mind. But so fleeting, so outlandish was the premise that I might find ecstasy with—no, no, that was impossible. I shook my head.

"I came for the very gift you offer—to be restored, if only in some small measure." I slipped the note into my pocket and told myself to remember to file it away between the pages of my locked diary, just like the other one. "I won't need you to send a message to Inspector Curtis. Let us leave London quickly, Graham. Let us leave all these people behind and move forward."

The coach rounded the bend and paused. I remembered this necessity from countless times before when I had approached this particular hollow in the Darnley road. The Chadwick horses, four matching chestnuts, were given slight pause as they rested for the last climb of the day—the pinnacle of Darnley, Darnley Castle.

Curiosity bade me refresh my memory of the home of my husband's ancestors; the house of my mirth and my sorrow; the abode of my misery; the place of my abandonment.

Castle Darnley. She was as majestic, as specious as ever. That blunt Norman monolith, made of mottled rough-hewn stones carved from the cliffs near the sea and dragged up this mountain climb by peasants who did their new masters' bidding or got the whip.

Castle of the Arnleighs. Abode of the Norman knight known as The Falcon, who had befriended the conquering William when both were children. The Arnleigh Falcon, who fought the native Saxons and Vikings for this wild northern frontier, crossed the moat and captured the eighth-century tower, killed the local lord, then took to wife his daughter. The Falcon's descendants, the fierce Arnleighs, who endured four hundred years of strife to Anglicize their name along with their culture. To maintain their hegemony over this land despite the Plantagenet intrigues and the Scottish raids across the northern marches.

Finally, when the Arnleighs embraced the Yorkist cause in the War of the Roses, the family's fate hung in peril when the heir presumptive was one brash young maiden who was given the choice of hanging for her treason against the Lancastrian Henry Tudor or of taking to husband a loyal supporter of Henry's. Clifford Chadwick, known as the Shadow for his bravery as a spy for Henry, took the young Yorkist sympathizer Eliza Darnley to wife and—as the family Bible in the old library eloquently recounted—lived out his remaining twenty-two years with his loving wife and six strapping sons.

Thenceforth, Clifford and his Eliza, whom Henry dubbed the first Earl and Countess of Darnley, begat a line of earls who had supplied the family with many a male heir and an ever-growing fortune. Until the eighteenth century, when that fortune dwindled and they sought another way to shore up the family name and treasury. Then they married into a merchant family whose only remaining daughter brought them a shipping business rich from Indian spices and cottons.

Darnley and Sons was what the earls renamed the commercial fleet that the merchant's daughter brought with her as dower. Darnley and the next set of sons then proceeded to run the fleet almost aground with bad management.

So once more, the Darnleys had been compelled to

search for a means to rebuild their fortunes and sought salvation from a woman. An only daughter with a suitable inheritance. A sizable dowry. Mine.

Suddenly, the coach lurched and I was thrown to my left against Jeremy, who slid against Helena. He yelped.

"I am sorry, my dear. The horses need to rest before they climb this hill." I glanced at the others—Graham and Helena, Simpson and MacCarthy—all discomfited by the rough ride yet silently enduring it.

The carriage bounced as the Chadwick coachman and groom yelled instructions to the horses. I reached for the handgrip above me. We idled a moment, then felt the surge of power as the mighty mares yanked us from some mire.

Jeremy swung his legs about. "When will we get there, Mommy?"

"Soon, my dear, soon."

Jeremy, still suffering from a cold, had felt the strain of the last few days and had grown peevish, restless with the confinement of yet another train trip, another long coach ride.

I could not blame him. I was so tired of it all myself.

I pursed my lips as the coach rumbled on. Why should I be surprised at the condition of this road?

When I had arrived here as a bride more than six years ago, the road had felt as ancient. Now, I took it as proof that the noble Chadwicks had fallen on hard times once more, enough to let this road—this most important main road from Darnley through the village to the sea—lie potholed and treacherous once more.

I glanced at Graham. His eyes slid away from mine, his thoughts shrouded against my intrusion. My eyes went to the road as I pondered the illogic of purchasing a new London townhouse while keeping this road in such a state of disrepair. The villagers—those hardworking men and women who grew

103

wheat, raised chickens and pigs, and went to service every Sunday morning—deserved the repair of this road if for no other reason than to make the journey an easier one. Anger swelled in my breast that Graham had not tended to this most vital matter.

The rash of red and golden autumnal flowers on the hillside invaded my consciousness with their splendor. I closed my eyes as I remembered this scene from the first day I had sat in this coach beside Charles and viewed the beauty of Darnley, the beauty that had inspired me to paint that pastoral which now dominated Graham's drawing room on Raleigh Street. I remembered the villagers coming out to meet us, lining this road, waving their hands and hats, hoisting their children upon their shoulders to catch a glimpse of the new viscountess. I remembered how Charles had encouraged me to return their waves and how I had pressed myself against one window of the coach and done so with great enthusiasm.

I had never been sorry. Among these simple, industrious people, I had found great happiness, great rewards. They had benefited from the road's repair and had known the money that paid for it had come from my sizable, much-publicized dowry. They had shown their gratitude by inviting me to their parish suppers and their harvest festivals. I had gone, at first with a reluctant Charles and later without him. I had gone and learned their names, their family histories, their maladies, their day-to-day joys and sorrows. They gave me their friendship, tutored me in the local folklore, and confided their secrets.

In return, I gave them a representative of their interests with Charles and, through him, his father the earl. I cannot say I had great influence. I did take some personal credit that after I had spoken of the sad condition of this road, it had been repaired. And I took some pride in the fact that when I attended church, many parishioners would smile broadly at me while they performed the obligatory doffing of their hat and curtsying to their lord and master, the earl and his son the viscount. I took great pride when they lined up to thank me for my involvement in getting a doctor from York to visit twice a week to care for their children and their elderly. Ah, yes, I took great pride.

Now, I took none. Had none.

Today, no one lined this road to meet me. No smiling faces or waving hands greeted me. No fireworks would go off this night as that first night more than six years ago. No feast in the castle's main hall. No. Today, none of that.

Six years ago, "the American beauty" had arrived. Today, "that Chadwick Woman" came. This time, she came bearing not money to improve their lot but scandal to char the brilliance of their heritage. Indeed, she was not worth a greeting, no matter what she'd once done to help them. Because in the end, all those good works meant naught compared to the shame her immoral actions had cast on the village.

I hung my head and squeezed my eyes shut. Somewhere, I had to find new courage for this hour.

I could tell by the sound of the horses' hooves that they crossed the stone bridge over what had once been the moat. A hollow sound of the hooves meant they passed beneath the Gothic arches, erected by some medieval Darnley lord. Then, the shrill reverberations of the horses' hooves denoted their path toward the Saxon great hall, the entrance to this sprawling residence the Darnleys called home.

The horses came to a dead stop, and the coach rolled forward and back as it settled into the centuries-old cobbles. Graham preceded me from the coach and, as he had these past few days, turned and offered me his assistance.

Avoiding his eyes, I grasped his hand, lifted my skirts, and descended to Chadwick land. I glanced about me. Two footmen and the head butler began the work of getting the luggage down and sorted. Of

105

course, I knew all three of these servants, whose families had lived in the village long before the Normans seized it. They cast surreptitious glances at me. Oh, yes, they remembered me, too.

I swallowed back my nervousness and focused my attention on the wide stone steps that led to the castle's great hall. Now that I was here, I was filled with trepidation.

Was this really a haven from the horrors that had confronted me in London and in Southampton? I stood immobile on those stones, raising my eyes and reacquainting myself with its round towers, its arrow slits and murder holes, where Darnley defenders had once poured boiling water and caustic brews on their attackers. Once, I had not feared these ancient apertures. But in my recent nightmarish memories of Darnley Castle, these ghoulish slits personified my enemies who, with black, narrowed eyes, had once sought to destroy my marriage, my reputation, my son and, yes, perhaps even my sanity.

I almost quaked with cold fear. I pulled my cape about me. Was it possible that I had left London for Darnley Castle and, thereby, traded one set of threats to my safety for another set to my serenity?

Graham took my arm and, by his firm, insistent gesture, urged me forward. He said not a word. The others followed, seeming to me to spill out of the coach with an almost audible sigh of relief. I knew what faced me.

That great hall lay before me. The hall, which had housed the last Saxon lord Rolfe and his daughter Rowina, and had once been invaded by William's loyal retainer, the falconer Geoffrey. The hall, which had once seen Eliza Darnley raise a knife to the throat of her mortal enemy Clifford and yet on the next day marry him. The hall, where to the left The Falcon's blue and white battle standard hung side by side with the threadbare glory of Rolfe's blood-red one. The hall, where nine centuries of Darnley

106

escutcheons lined the wall to illustrate how Rolfe's and Rowina's red had been halved by The Falcon's blue, then adorned with a falcon whose hood Clifford had added to denote his role as spy.

I surveyed the wall and shivered. It was still deadly cold in this castle.

The array of servants who lined up to greet their new lord and his guests brought no great warmth into the hall with them. Indeed, they eyed me as they were presented to me and the others. I remembered them all, all humble for themselves but proud of their stations. All hardworking men and women of whom even the disdainful, vain Charles had been proud. We stood facing each other, the travelers and the staff, for brief moments, as Graham said a few perfunctory words, merely performing the function of a lord returning to his domain and his chattel with his relatives and two new servants.

I stood there, nodding and smiling slightly as each one was reintroduced to me by Graham.

"Vanessa, I know you remember the footmen, John and Todd Surrey, Tim Rogers, and Henry Wilson. The upstairs maids, Teresa and Lucile. The downstairs maids, Ida and Mary. Lucile will be your maid, Vanessa. And here is Forbisher."

I smiled more broadly at the butler. He'd once been my friend when Charles was alive. But I could tell from his sullenness that the old man was not happy to see me. And as his eyes went to Jeremy, I saw fear and jealousy there. So here was another person who distrusted me and feared me. Would the list never end? Yet, Forbisher, ever mindful of his manners, muttered a greeting before he turned his baleful eyes on one of the two new servants in our retinue, MacCarthy. Forbisher now had three people to mistrust.

Inwardly, I sighed and turned my attention to Graham, who continued his introductions down the line. "And of course, Vanessa, I know you remember

107

Mrs. Bellweather."

Only Mrs. Bellweather, the housekeeper, displayed any great joy at seeing me again, and even that she seemed to contain. Her smile was tenuous, trembling. Her frail frame withered more by the years, she looked emaciated with the sunken contours of her three score or more. She shook a little, from age I was sure, as her watery blue eyes rested on mine.

"Viscountess, may I show you to your rooms?"

I almost gaped at her bold use of my title. Forbisher did. So did Helena. Graham stood stoically.

"Thank you, Mrs. Bellweather. I would be happy to accompany you. Come, Jeremy. We must unpack." Frantic to be alone, I turned and excused myself from Graham and the others. "Miss Simpson, you should accompany us."

A sigh of relief swept through me as the traveling group disbanded. Graham waved us off, Helena remaining with him to discuss some matter while MacCarthy followed a stiff Forbisher to his new quarters on the menservants' side of the great house.

With Jeremy and Simpson and Mary trailing behind me, I followed Bellweather's slight form from the grey gloom of the Saxon lord's hall, up the worn stone stairs to the keep, and into the house that I feared.

Chapter Eight

Bellweather uttered no words as she led us from the great hall through the upstairs keep, then into the long hall from which spread the many arms of Darnley Castle. Like an octopus spreading out its tentacles from its head, Darnley Castle was a creature of many eras. Over the centuries, different Darnley lords had added wings to the castle as their families had grown or their fortunes had waxed.

This long hall, once a cloister for exercise on dreary days, was as dark and dank as it must have been when first built in the thirteenth century. Though the carved intricacy of oaken walls and floors pleased the art historian in me, the narrow windows of muddied glass made for a lack of light that denied the hall its rightful glory. Bellweather paused before the massive oak door at the far end and indicated that Jeremy and I, along with Simpson, were to be in the oldest addition to the castle. This meant we were to be alone. Far from Graham, who, of course, was to be in the newest wing of the house, which for almost a century had served as the chief residence. And far from Helena, whose rooms had always been located there ever since I'd known her. Jeremy and I were to be housed in the medieval wing—alone. I turned and breathed more easily.

Beyond the oak door was a solar, where Darnleys

had embellished the colorless stone walls and vaulted ceilings with functional but decorative tiers of wind braces, tie beams, and dark wooden buttresses to the gabled roof. Chandeliers meant for hundreds of wax candles hung from the center of the rafters, while along the walls tapestries depicted the tragedies of the Yorkist and Lancastrian rivalries for the throne of England. Once a sitting room for the women of the medieval period, this solar was now punctuated with massive medieval chairs around even more monolithic oak tables. So much the rage in the current Victorian era, the furniture denoted the somber splendors of yesterday and today.

My eyes traversed the room and noted two doors at right angles to each other. Beyond this solar were three connecting bedrooms, none of which I'd ever occupied. Yet, as with the rest of this meandering mausoleum of England's architectural heritage, I knew the wing's history—and some of its architecture—from my perusal of the castle's bounteous library.

The largest bedroom, behind another ornate carved oak door, was the master room, where the Yorkist Eliza Darnley had truly lain down her arms against her beloved enemy, the Tudor spy, Clifford Chadwick. This bedroom was where Eliza and her husband Clifford had not only made their peace, but had also planned their fortune and, of course, created their sons and daughters, the ancestors of Graham and Helena and my own Jeremy.

Bellweather cleared her throat. "I prepared this room for you, my lady, because it is far from the other wings. I thought you would like a bit of privacy— and, of course, the lovely view of the gardens."

"Thank you, Mrs. Bellweather. I am flattered by your memory of my preferences. I do appreciate your thoughtfulness." I smiled at her expectant face and nodded at my son and his governess. "I think you might show Master Jeremy and Mrs. Simpson to

110

their rooms. I will reacquaint myself with the room."

"As you wish, ma'am. Lucile is at your disposal, but do ring for me if you need anything—anything at all." She excused herself with a small curtsy and, with a tilt of her head, beckoned Jeremy and Simpson to follow her through the other door off the solar.

I strode forward, pushed up the iron latch and, with both hands, opened my door. The housekeeper had chosen well. This part of the house, "Eliza's Wing," as it was called, was a labyrinth of secret staircases and concealed rooms. Staircases where Catholic monks had fled from raiding Scottish presbyters—and, later, Henry Tudor's tax collectors. Rooms where Eliza had plotted for her cousins, the noble Yorkist clan. And the secret entrances and stairs to each of these chambers were all in my bedroom.

Behind the alabaster fireplace was one room, lined with tomes, most of which Charles had said were hand-copied texts, especially Bibles—Catholic versions left there by renegade monks. To gain entrance to the secret room, one had to find the exact center of the fireplace and step on the two center hearth stones, one foot on each, toes exactly parallel to each other and to the carved gargoyles that snarled from the middle of the stone mantel. Beneath the stones a giant lever pushed against another, opening the portal about four inches, wide enough for a man or woman to enter the room sideways. Inside, a corresponding pressure on the floor stones shut the aperture.

Charles had explained it to me one day soon after we had arrived at Darnley.

"I often came here as a child, even as a young man." He chuckled and his black eyes gleamed wickedly. I took his look for husbandly romantic interest in me. "I enjoy the solitude, and since few know precisely how to open the wedge in the far stone wall or how to close it from the inside, the room is completely secure. There are few places where one is completely secure, wouldn't you agree, my dear?"

I stammered something.

He eyed me almost impersonally. "Perhaps security of place is what you need to flower. I will introduce you to its values. Shall we say, tonight?"

At his perfunctory tone, I shivered and nodded.

He never introduced me "to its values." Actually, I breathed a sigh of relief when he never mentioned it again. Yet, I worried too because he never mentioned—never even implied—that we should discover its values. In fact, from the time we arrived here at the castle, Charles seemed to grow more and more distant, emotionally as well as physically.

I walked to the balcony doors, which the library's records say one Chadwick wife added to allow more cheer to enter the dreary interior. I opened both panels to admit a burst of crisp northern air.

From that day when Charles and I had spoken here, I had been confused by his growing inattentiveness. Not that he had ever been overly attentive. No, indeed. Yet in the beginning, I would have said that he had a normal man's interest in me.

He had courted me with courtesy and with all the romantic delights a young girl of my social background expected. That he was an English lord probably made me endow him with more grace and charm and style than any other. Certainly, no American beau seemed to compare to him.

But then, Charles had charmed me with his superb dancing and his witty conversation. He had piqued my interest by sending to my home his daily bouquets of roses and hydrangea and violets. He had beguiled me with his words of praise for "the satin shimmer of my white-gold hair" or the "amethyst sparkle of my eyes." He had wooed me by being debonair with my New York friends and respectful to my doting mother. He had even won over my doubtful father with his sober responses to Daddy's

112

many objections to our marriage.

Our relationship had certainly progressed in a normal manner. During our courtship, Charles had performed the normal courtesies of taking me by the elbow to lead me from dance floor to punch bowl; he had hovered over my every wish while at teas or socials. If he had held me too daringly close while waltzing or cut short the amount of time before he held my hand or stole a kiss, I welcomed his advances. After our marriage, he had even offered me the convenience of waiting until the second night after the ceremony before beginning our conjugal union. He had explained that we should both be rested, at our very best. He, of course, *always* seemed at his best. Whereas, waiting another day and night only made my nerves more raw. I never told him. But I think he knew.

He knew because when he came to me that second night in the pitch-black room, removed his dressing gown, and laid it at the foot of our bed, I froze. He kissed my forehead, caressed my jaw, then let his hand trail down my torso. He knew what he was doing. I did not. My mother had been kind to me but not terribly informative about the facts of marital bliss. Charles's cursory caresses did nothing to persuade me about the value of his actions. He continued his explorations. I felt touched, but strangely . . . untouched. He persisted with harder, swifter probing fingers. I began to feel disturbed and knew I should have felt attracted. I willed myself to become more tender, more loving. I reached for him to kiss his lips. He pulled away and gave me kisses along my throat and then . . . oh, my . . . along my breasts. My responses to that encouraged him. He quickly took the act to its next logical conclusion.

With a pat to my head, Charles rolled away, stood, and donned his dressing gown. He strode away and closed the door to our bedroom. I was left alone in the lavish honeymoon suite of The Grand Hotel in

New York, bewildered.

But with the optimism that had been my hallmark and my heritage, I greeted my new husband the next morning with cheer and what little I knew of womanly flirtation. He smiled tolerantly, then shook out his morning newspaper. He came to my bed again that night and the night after.

Every night, in fact, until we set foot in England.

From then on while in London, his nightly visits diminished. Perhaps once or twice a week, he would grace me with his presence. Always in the dark. Always in the same manner as the first night. I grew to conclude that this was what conjugal relations were like. Short, tepid couplings of two bodies. I never asked for more. He never gave me anything other. Then we arrived at Darnley and his visits dropped to once or twice a month.

I felt relief. And great guilt. He was my husband and I should have welcomed his attentions, whatever their nature. I loved him, I repeatedly told myself. I loved him and he loved me. But now, during the day, in the brightness of sunlight, I began to see in him what I had only felt at night in the dark.

Charles had been bored with me.

Lucile cleared her throat.

Startled at the depths of my reverie, I turned to her. She had followed me out onto the balcony. A pretty thing, no more than sixteen, with black hair and black eyes, she had once hung around the kitchens as a waif. Household gossip had it that she was a by-blow of the old earl, my father-in-law. If she was a Chadwick, she had Chadwick ambition. Even as a very young child, she'd helped the cook so much that one day Cook had rewarded Lucile and made her scullery maid. Now, here she was upstairs!

"I'm delighted to see you again, Lucile. You've gotten a promotion to the upstairs. Good for you."

"Yes, ma'am. Thank you, ma'am. I can call you ma'am, can't I? You won't get mad at me or noth-

114

ing if I—"

"No, Lucile. I understand your problem. Few people here know how to address me. But I believe that titles are not the measure of a person. If you will be available to me now to unpack and to help Simpson with my son—whom you may call Master Jeremy—I will be very pleased with you."

"Thank you, ma'am." She curtsied. "I don't want to displease the new lord. I want to make my way in the world, and doing good here at the castle is very important to me. Why, Lord Darnley, he's been so good to all of us. Not like working for the old earl, his father. Or for the viscount, who was a terror. Why, when he was lyin' in his bed dyin', he used to holler the house down and rant for this or that. I could never keep up with his wants. But I had to. We all did. If we didn't . . . well, the old earl would have us on the carpet before breakfast, he would. Why, I remember—"

I held up my hand. "Thank you, Lucile."

I could bear no talk of Charles. And certainly not talk tainted with gossip from the servants. I had my position to maintain, and while I might no longer want or need titles, I needed my dignity. And I would have Lucile keep hers as well.

"I wish to hear no more about my husband."

"Sorry, ma'am. I know you loved him."

She turned away, and I watched her go to her duties of getting water for my ewer and fluffing the pillows. When the two Surrey brothers came in carrying my trunks, she quickly went to them and began her sorting.

I spun away from the sorting and sifting, then blinked my eyes to clear my visions of the past so I could view, instead, the beauties of Darnley's gardens. A maze of boxwoods and hollies and evergreens, shaped and pruned and coaxed over the centuries by ladies or nuns or hired gardeners, the feast of its wonders was best sampled from this

115

balcony. I had first seen the garden from one of the other wings, the Georgian one to be exact. But none offered the full view of its intricate pattern as did this one. I shook off my doldrums and turned to survey my bedroom.

An octagonal room to the casual observer, the room by all rights should have matched the rectangular exterior of this wing of the castle. Yet, whoever had designed this wing had done so with an eye and an ear to the sights and sounds of medieval England. Torn by border raids from the north, and beset not only by Lancastrian enemies from the west and south but also by attempts to land upon the Yorkist coast east of here, Darnley Castle had never been completely secure. This wing reflected that insecurity.

To my far right stood the stark white fireplace. Almost as tall as I, that fireplace was just as deep. Sinking back to the real exterior of the castle, the fireplace hinted at the deception of the octagonal room. Yet, few noticed the deception because of the room's extraordinary beauties.

The first of those beauties was the bed. Directly opposite the fireplace, the bed was a huge affair, its black-red stained frame and posts holding aloft a canopy of scarlet silk embroidered with silver. The voluminous draperies of the same scarlet, now pulled back with huge red tassels, could envelope the bed and its occupants, sealing in warmth and shutting out the cold world. According to the records, Clifford Chadwick had ordered the bed made and installed here against this wall. A precursor of the type of bed known as the "Elizabethan State Bed," this early Tudor wonder had served the first Chadwicks well. Clifford had spawned six sons here, a prolific precedent for all Chadwick earls who thereafter did Clifford proud.

At the foot of the bed where Clifford Chadwick must have received retainers and written his correspondence stood two footstools upholstered in the same material as the coverlet and hangings. At juxtaposition stood a brace of X-framed chairs, those derivatives of folding medieval chairs meant for itinerant medieval lords. More wood than upholstery, the chairs looked surprisingly comfortable, probably due to the thick cushions that were cloth of silver embellished with scarlet embroidery. Beyond stood a squat chest of drawers and above it hung a mirror of some later period. This, plus the folding privacy screen, marked the concessions to a female occupant's vanity, while the thick Turkey rug before the fire gave some modern comfort to the age-old room.

Just then, Jeremy burst through the connecting door, a flustered Simpson just behind him.

"Mommy, Mommy! You must come see what's in my room!"

I smiled at him and nodded to Simpson in dismissal. "Let me guess. A horse with wings?"

"Do you suppose there really are such things?"

I chuckled and ran my hand through his hair. "Only carved in mantels. Would you like to see what's carved in mine?"

When I showed him the gargoyles, his eyes bulged. "Miss Simpson has no carvings in her fireplace, Mommy. Only you and I. Why?"

"I suspect because this wing is similar to many other castles here in England. This room is for parents, and yours is meant for children. In fact, your room is really meant for many children. The nursery, it is really called. And Miss Simpson's room is meant for the nurse or the governess. A simple arrangement which meant the adults were close to the children. The reason Miss Simpson's room has no carvings of animals on her fireplace is because that room was always meant for servants who lived quite simple lives and were not considered part of the family."

He considered that a moment, but then he caught a glimpse of the balcony doors. "My room doesn't have doors to the outside, either."

"All a part of the plan, my love. Children of old were contained rather strictly, I'm afraid. Their outings were carefully planned. Balconies were for adults."

He made a face.

I put out my hand. "Let me show you something meant for every adventurous child." I led him toward the two central stones of the hearth. "Mark my steps, here and here. Now, stand perfectly still and watch."

Slowly, with the creak and groan of ages, two large stones in the wall to my left slid forward. Beside me, Jeremy gasped.

"Mommy," he whispered, frozen to his spot.

When the stones had reached their meager limit, I looked down at my son. "Would you care to discover the secrets of the Darnleys?"

His black eyes twinkled.

"Come." I led him by the hand toward the aperture and we peered inside. Only six or so inches wide, the opening was enough for a human to pass through sideways. Dark as a sepulcher, the triangular room was lit only by the daylight from my bedroom. Yet Jeremy and I could see a few volumes that lined the longest wall, the trestle rough-hewn table, and the solitary wooden chair before it. Cobwebs and dust covered everything.

"Mommy, who lives here?" whispered Jeremy in awe.

"No one, my love." I turned sideways and slid inside, taking him with me. He and I stood before the trestle table in the chilled silence. "I do know that many people hid in here. You see, in the library are accounts—diaries and letters and other documents—that tell of the lives of people in the castle. I will take you there this afternoon if you like."

"Oh yes, Mommy."

"You will probably not be able to read the accounts—the handwriting is too complex and the English very old—but I know you would like the

118

stories. I will show Miss Simpson and she can tell you some of the tales. I will certainly tell you those I know." I smiled at him. "The one that strikes me most is the story of how the first Chadwick—Clifford was his name—was hidden here by the young heiress of the manse. Her name was Eliza Darnley. A beauty, the records say, who believed this Clifford when he arrived here and told her he was a Catholic priest. Really, Clifford had been sent here to spy on Eliza Darnley by his lord and master, the noble Henry Tudor of the house of Lancaster. You see, Eliza was a longtime supporter of the rival house of York for the throne of England. The Yorkists and Lancastrians had been fighting over the throne of England for more than a century when Clifford set foot in the castle.

"As the story goes, Clifford came to fill the post of priest to the Darnley household and village. He lived here inside the castle, I know not exactly where. But it is told that wherever he was, he filled the mind of the lovely Eliza. She sought him out at first for spiritual advice, but later for friendly comfort. She plotted with her cousins, the heirs of the house of York, to retain the throne for themselves. And all the while, Clifford watched her movements. Then he, growing more enchanted with her daily, gave her what advice and comfort he could. Spy that he was, he took all information she freely told him and sent it to his cohort, Henry Tudor. Soon, as the fortunes of Henry rose and those of the Yorkists declined, it became apparent to the Yorkists that some spy existed in Eliza's household.

"When she discovered the spy might be Clifford, Eliza suffered great torments, it is said. She demanded a confession, and when he would not yield, Eliza pulled a dagger on the man. Torn by his own duplicity, appealing to her love for him, Clifford finally revealed the truth. Thus, he gave her the opportunity to choose between turning him over to

119

her cousins or hiding him in the castle. When her Yorkist cousins finally came, she secreted Clifford here in this room. For hours, her cousins searched and found no trace of the priest.

"Days later, safe from the Yorkists, Clifford emerged. Eliza gave him a new suit of clothes, one horse from her stables, and bag of gold coins. As Clifford departed in the still of the night, he vowed he would return for her. She reportedly laughed and cried at the same time, and then told him to never darken her door.

"However, one year later, Clifford did return. Infuriated, Eliza again pointed a dagger at his throat. But his friend, Henry Tudor, now king of England, interrupted her efforts and gave Eliza an ultimatum: either marry Clifford at noon on the morrow or die for her treason at sunset. She chose, of course, to live. And live she did, quite well with Clifford for many years."

I turned to smile at the enraptured face of my son. "Clifford and Eliza became the first Earl and Countess of Darnley. They are your ancestors of whom you can be proud."

"I would like to hear more stories. Are my ancestors all good men and women?"

I arched my brows. "I think they must have been, my love."

We tell our children tales to make them proud and upright, honest and brave. Life's indignities, people's perfidies, we leave for our children to learn firsthand and then explain as best we can.

I smiled once more at Jeremy. "I'll show Miss Simpson the collection of documents so that she might immediately begin to make the family's history a part of your daily lessons. And when you begin, you must come to me with your tales and I will try to match them with discoveries in the house."

He thrilled to that idea, clapped his hands, and ran backward. "I'm off to get Miss Simpson."

I watched him exit the secret room and waved goodbye to him. I heard him shut the connecting door, and then I turned to the tall, thin bookcase along one short wall. I strode forward and eyed its second shelf. The cobwebs and dust told me that no one had touched it in years. Probably not in the five years since Charles had moved the two volumes of Greek myths that still stood there, grasped the rough handle in the bottom plank, and pulled upward, as I did now.

Now, I heard once more the creak of stone, the groan of wood. I stepped back. The bookcase slid forward and stood at a right angle to the wall. I took a step around it and through the thin aperture, peered down into the blackness of the stairway.

The stairway I had once dared to take spread before me. I smiled in self-satisfaction. Once, when Charles was out riding, I had come here and opened the bookcase door. Taking a thick wax candle, I sailed down the stairs and discovered a treasure trove of medieval artifacts amid a maze of tiny, secret rooms that had hidden God knew how many people with how many secrets. I spent hours here and returned twice more before Charles warned me of rats and mice, perhaps even bats. I shuddered. Still, I hungered for the adventure. I overcame my fear and went a few more times. After I became pregnant, I forced myself to stop my almost daily explorations. I feared for the effects of the damp atmosphere on my unborn baby's life.

Yet, ever after, I remembered the joy of discovery I had experienced along this stairway.

Suddenly, a gust of fetid air assailed me. I covered my mouth. I had forgotten the malignant potency of that cloistered air. The burn of a candle helped for more than merely lighting the way as the smell of it helped to clear my head. I stepped backward and, at that moment, jumped when something brushed my legs.

An animal screeched.

I slid into my bedroom and peered inside the secret room in horror. A rat? A mouse?

Around the stone, a small black head appeared with snow-white muzzle, long graceful whiskers, and two perky white ears. Huge green eyes.

She mewed.

"Samantha!"

Samantha!

I bent down and put my hands out to her. She ran toward me and purred with great pleasure as she rubbed her body against mine. I patted her sleek black fur.

"My dear," I crooned, "I hadn't thought you survived. But, of course, you are young, and I suppose they would not have been so cruel as to throw you out." I gathered her close as she raised her finely sculpted head, batted her lovely emerald eyes at me, and meowed in delight.

I laughed and hugged her. She rubbed against me.

"She welcomes you the best way she can. And claims you as her only mistress." The trilling voice from the doorway was none other than Helena's.

Samantha stilled and hissed.

"Hush." I smiled at Helena. "Someone kept her."

"You have Graham to thank for that. Uncle Albert consigned her to the barn. But Graham insisted she return to the house, lest she grow ugly and fat on the barn mice."

"She has remained in perfect form."

"Graham said she should be here to welcome you back. I agreed with him." Her eyes held mine and told of other meanings.

"You had more hope than was reasonable."

She walked in and took one of the chairs. "But now you are here."

"You both are vindicated."

She threw me a small smile and glanced about the bedroom, eyeing Lucile a long moment. "I came to

122

see if you approve of Bellweather's choice." She rolled her eyes, meaning Lucile as well as the room.

I stood with Samantha cradled in my arms. "Bellweather knows me well in many ways," I said meaningfully, and glanced toward my maid. "I would not wish to be in the Georgian wing of the house. It would bring back too many painful memories. Besides, I plan to take advantage of the opportunities afforded by the extra rooms and stairs." I nodded toward the secret room.

She laughed. "I had no idea such things interested you."

"Secrets are always very interesting. The Darnleys seem to have acquired the knack of keeping theirs hidden longer than others."

"For more reasons than others."

"They are such grievous secrets?"

"I know they are."

"But these secrets, behind this wall, are so long dead, they hurt no one."

"Ah, but you have certainly heard that the evil men do lives after them. What you may find behind that wall or others here are inherited characteristics in the clan. Faults, frailties that send you running from all Darnleys in horror." She leaned forward to whisper so Lucile couldn't hear. "Some of us have very bad traits."

I stared at her. "You fear I'll find faults in the Darnleys which will turn me from my son?"

"Among others."

"That will not happen, I assure you."

"I hope you're right."

I tilted my head. "You fear for me?"

"For years."

"You needn't. I am self-sufficient."

"I would say *resilient* is a more appropriate word, my dear. Resilient to have survived so much so well."

Resilient. The same word Graham had used to describe my character.

123

Helena stood. "I'm off to my unpacking—and a good nap to rid me of this infernal headache. I get them so often." She smiled curtly. "But the doctor says they are incurable. So . . . I suffer through. But now that I am here at Darnley again, I feel so much better. Don't you? I am eager to see the countryside atop a good horse. One never gets a decent horse in London, you know. I do so miss my daily ride. I'm off. See you at dinner."

Chapter Nine

The stone walls of the old manse reverberated with the knells of the grandfather clocks as they trolled the hour of eight. Hurriedly, I kissed Jeremy on his tousled head.

"Good night, my love. Sleep tight to rid yourself of that cold. Tomorrow, if you're better, we'll go on an adventure."

"Through the secret wall or out riding?"

I made a moue. He loved to ride, even as a child of three. Since the destruction of my father's business and, of course, the sale of our horses in New York and Saratoga, neither Jeremy nor I had ridden horseback.

"If you are good and fall asleep quickly and complete your lessons for Miss Simpson, we will do both. But only if your sniffles are better."

The imp shut his eyes tightly. "I'm sleeping already!"

I laughed. "Good night, my dear. Sweet dreams."

I made my way through his bedroom door, through my dressing chamber, and into my room. As I emerged into the solar and the long hall, the last chime rang throughout the house. I picked up my heavy black velvet skirt and ran toward the Georgian wing.

The last major addition to the castle, the Georgian wing dated from the turn of the century, when a series of Georges had held the throne of England. As surely as Eliza's wing reflected the history of the period during which it had been built, so too did this wing represent the incidents that had intertwined the fate of England and the Darnleys.

Passing the corridor that led to the third main wing—Charles's Restoration, as it was called for the second English king of that name—I hastened up the grand staircase. Its majestic square black skeleton rose three floors. Splotches of drifting moonlight illuminated the cold stone steps and mingled with the eerie flicker of the gas lamps stationed in the corners at its landings. Massive mahogany balusters supported the wide ramped handrail, which I grasped as I ran silently up the blood-red runner to the second floor.

I paused at the doorway to catch my breath. Both mahogany doors were closed as they usually were, simply to cut down on the drafts that wended through the castle. I composed a serene expression upon my face, grasped the brass knobs, and entered the salon.

Helena and Graham conversed before a fire, which the servants had laid within the gilt chimneypiece. Helena sat in one of the citron upholstered side chairs. Her stiff gown of burnt cinnamon, against the shadows of the celadon walls, cast a sickly glow about her. Even the glitter of gold in the appointments of ormolu wall sconces and the sharp reflections from the pair of Rococo pier glasses could not compensate for the mismatch of that dark cinnamon. I would almost think she were ill. But, of course, I knew better. Helena had always been extremely robust. And except for her complaint of headaches—which were probably a fabrication to allow me more privacy—I had not found her anything less than what she had been when I had left here.

I crossed the room to them and made my apologies

for being tardy.

Graham accepted them with a wave of his hand. He set down his whiskey glass and stuck his hands in his trouser pockets. Dressed for dinner in the country, he wore the ebony informal dinner coat and trousers with the air of the gentleman at home. Certainly, by his broader smile, he looked more relaxed than he had in London or Southampton. He even sounded more relaxed.

"Come in, Vanessa. No apologies are necessary. We have just gathered. I am glad to hear that Jeremy has retired early. He is not used to the chill of an English autumn. May I serve you a sherry?"

"Yes, thank you." Of what importance was it that I had a glass of sherry? Helena, who held one small glass of it herself, would not disapprove. And Graham was not so duplicitous as to offer me something simply to criticize me afterward for accepting it.

"I am worried about Jeremy's cold, though," I said. "I would have brought him down to dinner with us, but I thought it best he retired early."

Graham had moved toward the red and gold lacquer Chinese cabinet where the liquors were customarily kept. Standing before one of the pair of mirrors, he took a crystal sherry goblet and began to pour.

"Good God, I'm grateful you didn't bring him," declared Helena. "I simply cannot dine with children about. They do not know how to converse. It ruins the appetite."

"Oh, but Jeremy is really quite polite, I assure you, Helena."

"Polite he may be, my dear, but do let Simpson and Lucile fuss over him in Eliza's wing, will you? I simply cannot digest with children flitting about. It brings on one of my headaches and you know, Graham, how I suffer with those."

I accepted my sherry from Graham. Perhaps I had

been mistaken. Perhaps Helena was truly afflicted. "I am concerned about these headaches. Do tell me when did they start?"

"Oh, it is nothing, my dear, nothing."

Graham sputtered, "Nothing?! Vanessa, they are so bad she can't see. She has to take to her bed. I wanted her to go see my doctor in London. She refuses."

I turned to Helena, my one true friend in this family. "But why? Perhaps he can help—"

"I'm sick to death of doctors, my dears. Sick to death. They have no remedies for me and I refuse to take laudanum every night. Pah! A nervous woman's cure! I am not nervous. I do not want to become an addict simply because I have a few headaches. There is nothing wrong with me except that I am just getting older." She chuckled a bit.

Graham and I glanced at each other, each glance telling the other to drop the subject. So I looked beyond him, over his shoulder. A new painting hung there. I had always loved the paintings in the Georgian wing. I liked the landscapes, but I loved the portraits more. I circled Graham and came to stand before one I had never seen before.

"This is wonderful of your father, Graham. When was it completed?" I searched the corners for the artist's signature.

He walked toward me and offered me my glass of sherry. "Father commissioned some fellow recommended to him by an old schoolmate. Arnold Pendergast was his name. What do you think of it?"

I stood back and considered my father-in-law's features. The black hair and eyes to match. The self-indulgent half-lidded look that my husband had inherited. I shivered and sipped some of my drink.

"It is very like him. He was quite handsome. Very self-possessed. A portrait should convey the principal characteristics of its subject."

Graham stood in back of me, and when he spoke,

his breath ruffled my hair. "What characteristics would compose a portrait of me?"

I spun about and faced him. "Your perseverance."

His onyx eyes glittered. "What if I offered you a commission to paint just that characteristic? Would you do it?"

"Oh! I would love to. I have never had a commission to paint a portrait."

"But you are capable."

"Well, yes. I have always dreamed of . . . but, no. I could not."

"What's the matter? Don't you want to paint me? You know me well enough, I think."

"Oh, yes. Well enough to do a better rendering than most. But—"

He cocked his head and took a sip of his whiskey. "Well, out with it."

"We have less than a week until the reading of the will."

"How long *does* it take to paint a man's face? Weeks? Months?"

"At least a month, and the reading of the will is scheduled for next Tuesday."

"Vanessa, no one is turning you out the moment the solicitor finishes reading. Besides, there is that other matter we discussed—Nathan and his wife, remember?"

"The Rothschilds are one issue. This is an entire portrait taking days and days. Anyway, it won't work. I have already booked return passage to New York."

"And when does your ship sail?"

"October fifteenth."

"Three weeks. More than enough time."

"Hardly—"

"We shall work every day."

"I have no oils, no easel."

"Oh, but you do. I had MacCarthy purchase some last week. We brought them up from London with us

129

in the baggage. By now they should be piled high, waiting for you in my study."

I examined his eyes.

He examined his glass.

"You have had this planned."

"Let us say that I saw an opportunity to have my portrait painted quickly and painlessly. Good God, why do I want to sit for one of these things for just anyone?"

Helena harrumphed. "Why do you want to sit for one at all?"

"Custom. Every Earl of Darnley has commissioned one. The castle is full of them. I thought since we had an artist in the family, it would be expedient. Particularly while you are here, Vanessa, and waiting for the reading of the will. I would not want you bored."

"That is very thoughtful of you."

Thoughtful, indeed. In London, he had revealed to me that he wondered if his father had truly named him heir. Or if the gentleman had had a change of heart and named Jeremy. Now, feigning confidence in his inheritance, he wanted a portrait done. Which emotion of Graham's was the true one?

He raised his glass. "It's settled, then."

"Not quite," I added. "I'll take no money for it."

"Then you'll not do it," he replied.

"But I cannot take money from you."

"Then I cannot give you the honor." He widened his eyes. "You need the honor and the addenda to your artistic credentials. True?"

"True. It would do much for me in New York. A start to a new life."

"So, then," Helena interjected, "why not do it, Vanessa? Take Graham's money! It's as good as anyone's."

I met Graham's eyes evenly. "You win. A new portrait for the new Earl of Darnley, and you shall pay me." He began to speak and I held up one palm.

"I have no idea how much. But I shall consider it and tell you when I've decided."

I smiled at him in pleasure and gratitude. We would be spending hours together. Hours . . .

His eyes searched mine. "I'm glad it is settled so easily." He raised his glass to toast me. "To my portraitist."

We all drank.

He looked at me. "I hope you've had a chance to settle in."

"Completely. I think I will find it very comfortable."

Helena placed her glass upon the small tea table. "Vanessa actually likes Eliza's wing. Quite out of character, I'd say."

Graham cocked a brow. "Is that so? Why?"

She smiled. "Because our Vanessa is a creature of society, my dears. She always was."

I tried not to frown. "I'm afraid I don't know what you mean."

"Perhaps," said Graham, "Vanessa would prefer a lighter topic of conversation, Helena."

"No, Graham. It's quite all right. I would like to know what Helena means."

Helena raised two perfectly arched black brows. "I simply meant that the apartments here in the Georgian are more modern. The furnishings are more plush, the art more appealing, the servants closer. That's all."

"I find the feather bed extremely comfortable, Helena. I had a nap on it this afternoon and slept like a baby. And the chairs owe much to the expertise of the carpenters and the upholsterer. As for the art, it is true that I never found much in the brooding of the medievalists. That is no loss. Neither is the proximity of servants. I am delighted you've given me Lucile, Graham. She is a charming girl, bright and eager. But over the past year, I have come to rely totally on myself for all my needs. I feel no lack. Any inconvenience which you might assume is important is, I assure you, more than compensated for by the marvelous view of the gardens.''

What I did not say was that I prized the utter privacy of Eliza's wing. Instead, I sipped my sherry. Thick and sweet, it filled my senses.

Helena shook her head. "Well, I will tell you, I never liked the appointments. I prefer the amenities of the later periods." She swept out a hand toward the salon. "The exotic nature of Chippendale, the lavishness of Rococo. The serenity of Romney. The classicism of Wedgwood. The convenience of gas-light and bellpulls." She sighed. "I don't have many amenities in my tiny house. So whenever I visit here, I take every opportunity to enjoy the ones available.''

"Since father died," Graham said to me, "I have tried to persuade Helena to sell her house and move here, even if it is just into the summer cottage. I am more in London than here and the place needs someone to manage it. But she won't hear of my proposal."

I went to the Italian settee and sat before Helena. "Your house no longer pleases you?"

She threw back her head to laugh, mirthlessly. "Oh, my dear! It *never* pleased me!''

"Really? I thought you bought the house because it was convenient to your charities."

"No, no, no. I bought the house, my dear Vanessa, for the same reason most people buy a house. It was what I could afford."

"Then why not take Graham's suggestion? Move here."

She set those black-as-hell Chadwick eyes on me for only a moment. Then she dropped her lids, rose, and walked toward the window.

I glanced at Graham.

He shook his head.

Helena's voice drifted toward us.

"I'm so tired of charity," she growled through

gritted teeth. "Charity makes one weak, beholden. I have lived all my life on the charity of my Chadwick uncle, so that I am repulsed by the idea of charity from the hand of my cousin. My younger, unmarried male cousin."

She spun about to face us. Her eyes—I could see even from this distance—were lit with a demonic measure of anger. They riveted on Graham.

"I can no longer take your charity. It only serves to point out how dependent I have always been. How much in thrall I have always been to my richer, kinder relatives. I hate the degradation of it. Beholden as I have always been, the very nature of it limited me from the start. Conceived by a minister's runaway daughter and an impoverished youngest son, what future could I have expected? Particularly as a female? Eh?"

She paced the forest-green rug like a cat in a jungle cage. "None. I had no chance to make a better life for myself. Disinherited as my father was for his folly of loving the local parson's daughter, he could not worm his way back into Grandfather's good graces. Not with a sickly wife and a mewling female infant as proof of his desertion from his family duty.

"Hah! When my mother died of consumption and my father of drunkenness, Grandfather and Uncle Albert must have danced for joy! Just rewards for the disloyal son.

"But Grandfather couldn't ignore me, could he? After all, what would his peers think of a man who let a six-year-old live in squalor? More important, what would His Maker think of a man like that? And Grandfather was dying, quickly and insidiously.

"It was he who, on his deathbed, ordered your father"—she pointed at Graham—"to bring me here. For the sake of the family honor.

"Pah! For the sake of the family honor, your father followed his father's instructions. He sent the governess to fetch me from the cottage in York. I

133

remember the look on her face when she saw me for the first time. She was appalled by my dirty appearance, my threadbare clothes. Barely able to touch me, she brought me here and put me in the nursery upstairs with you, Graham, and Izzy and Charles. From then on, your father gave me my due—food, shelter, clothes, an education in the early years equal to you boys.

"Dear Uncle Albert . . . He let me into the nursery with the three boys—the heirs. Dear Uncle Albert let Charles teach me how to ride and shoot and play cards. He let me dress as was befitting my station—as a poor relation. A useless girl. Without proper parentage. Without a dowry. Without a future.

"I always felt it. Always knew how subservient I was. I saw how the staff looked at me, as if I were an upstart and no better than they. One day, Charles caught the upstairs maid sassing me. I was here only a month or more and frightened of everyone and everything. Only Charles made me feel comfortable, welcome. In his best hauteur, Charles took the maid to task, ordered her into his chamber. My God, what was he? All of twelve? She must have been fourteen or fifteen. Charles bade me follow him to his quarters. There across his four-poster, he made her spread herself and bare her back. Then he took his riding whip and, there before me, gave her twenty lashes."

I gasped.

Graham gaped.

Helena, her eyes wide with the visions of yesteryear, went on. "She moaned. Ah, how she cried bitter tears. And her apologies flowed like water afterward. She scurried from the chamber. Charles turned to me and told me always to confide in him if any other servants were so bold again."

Helena inhaled and drew herself up with great pride. "But of course, no one ever dared go so far again. The little maid remained for a few more years and then she left, pregnant herself and in disgrace. So

134

finally, she could sneer at herself." Helena clapped her hands in glee. "Those who look down their noses at others *should* have reason to despise themselves, don't you think?" She turned to us, her smile sardonic. "It is their just reward."

I was speechless.

Forbisher appeared and loudly cleared his throat. "My lord, dinner is served."

Thank God. I rose so quickly, I almost spilled my glass of sherry. In an instant, Graham was there to assist me. He then turned and beckoned Helena with a smile. She came, the only sound in the room that of her awful stiff cinnamon satin gown crackling against the furniture as she walked.

We entered the dining room. The indescribable splendors of Ionian white and gold designed by Robert Adam met my eye. His Corinthian columns with gold-topped filigree and the white pilaster table with matching chairs adorned in pristine white brocade gave a brilliance to the room. I could scarcely see its beauty, so blinded was I by a vision of Charles delivering twenty lashes to a housemaid.

Graham assisted me to my chair at one end of the Chinese Chippendale table. I arranged my gown around the legs of the chair, making more fuss than was my usual wont. I scarcely knew what to say, how to proceed. Helena certainly was still lost amidst her reverie, her face a mask of plaster as stark and immobile as the marble busts upon innumerable pedestals here and there about the room.

I looked to Graham.

He met my gaze briefly, then assisted Helena to her chair at the center of the table and marched to the other end to take his own seat. He placed his napkin in his lap with one hand and signaled to Forbisher with the other. The meal would begin.

I breathed deeply. Forbisher disappeared into the alcove at one end of the magnificent room. When he emerged, he trailed behind him an array of servants with their offerings. A steaming soup with fennel, a cold vegetable sauté of squashes, a main course of partridge with a bitter sauce and sweet young carrots, a rack of lamb, a salmon stuffed with leeks and potatoes, and finally the fruits and cheeses. All were served with stoic faces, impeccable precision, and silence. Absolute silence.

Into the void, Graham stepped serenely. I applauded him and followed his lead.

We spoke of Bellweather's fine choices for the meal, the crisper weather here in the north marches, the fortunes of the German Empire, Bismarck's ironfisted rule and his view of the power of the British Empire. Helena joined in with a few contributions—the salmon were running well this year, the Germans were crafty and needed watching, and Kaiser Wilhelm was more barbarian than we gave him credit for.

"The kaiser may be related to the English throne," Helena concluded as she ate a morsel of Stilton, "but only by marriage, not by blood. The Germans, I think, retain an elemental characteristic of the barbarian hordes. They have very elemental urges. Primal tastes. And power is a primal force. To the strongest go the victories. While the Germans might not yet be supreme, they know that the show of force is one important step in achieving it."

I set my silver down with a clank upon the Sevres. "I have suffered from the hands of those who use power indiscriminately. If what you say is true, someone will stop the Germans from their quest."

Helena just stared at me a moment and then burst out laughing. "Oh, my dear"—she put a hand to her chest, but her laughter permeated the air—"how innocent you still are. After all that has befallen you"—she could not stop laughing and put her napkin to her mouth—"you think someone will rectify a situation?! How ludicrous! Tell me," she said, leaning down the table and piercing me with

136

those black eyes, "have you rectified the situation that your banker, Mr. Morgan, put your father in? No, of course you haven't. Nor shall you. Ever. To the victor belong all power and all rectitude. Charles knew that. Yes, he taught me that quite well."

Graham peered at Helena. She turned her head to him, an imperious smile upon her face. But when she saw Graham's implacable nature, she sighed.

"I see you find my views unacceptable." She gathered her napkin and placed it by her plate. "Very well. I seem to have developed one of my headaches. If you will excuse me . . ." She rose.

Graham made to stand.

She put out one hand.

"No, no, please. I insist that you both remain seated. You, Graham, to a pipe and port. And you, Vanessa, to your coffee."

With a small wave of her hand, she bid us both adieu and swept from the room.

Graham gave instructions to Forbisher for coffee to be served in the drawing room. He then stood and strode down to my end of the table.

"Shall we try to find some suitable topic of conversation by which we might both recover?"

I pushed back my chair and stood. "I think we must."

He offered his arm and I took it, emotions churning inside that I couldn't yet identify.

Forbisher opened the door and when he closed it, Graham and I both let out a sigh of relief at the same moment. We looked at each other.

Graham's brows arched. "I heartily suggest a brandy."

"Oh, absolutely."

He moved away to the Chinese sideboard. The two snifters he filled were fit for giants. I accepted mine from him with huge, questioning eyes.

"Drink it, by God. We both need it after that."

I took a large draught and swallowed slowly. The

burning sensation could not eradicate the harshness—no, the virulence!—of Helena's words.

"It did not seem to matter what her subject was," I said to Graham who stood near me. "She was unspeakably . . . utterly . . ."

"Hateful."

I let my eyes meet his.

He searched mine for a moment, then he walked away.

"Why, Graham? What has happened to her?" I followed him as he moved toward the mantel.

"I have never seen her this vocal." He considered his brandy a moment and took a sip, then turned to face me. "She is different. More sharp. But I must admit, I really have not seen her much in the last few months. And maybe her sharpness is grief. After Father died, she seemed to absent herself from me, more than was necessary, I felt. Yet, come to think of it, she has really become quite scarce since Charles died." He paused, looking straight through me, almost the way Charles used to do, and I shivered.

Yet, I saw something else in his countenance.

"What else bothers you?"

He dismissed the subject with a shake of his head.

I knew. "The story of the maid shocked me as well. I said before when we saw Margaret in Southampton that I shouldn't be surprised at any revelations of Charles's misdeeds. But I am surprised once more. Flogging a servant seems so archaic. Yet we both know many still do it."

Graham snorted. "Perverse is what it is. And Charles was perverse enough to do it." He spun about to face the fire.

Drawn to him, I set my glass beside his. In profile, his marvelous face aglow with the burnished flames, he seemed obsessed as he clenched and unclenched his jaw.

"What troubles you so, Graham?"

"I'm trying to remember. . . ." He seethed and

138

kicked at the brass grate. "Damn, damn. What was her name? Mary? . . . Maria? . . . Mary Beth? . . . Mary Beth, by God! Yes!" His dark eyes grew round with remembrance. "She was a sweet girl. Red hair, red as they come. With tons of freckles. An upturned nose and obliging blue eyes. She had been here since a young child. I think she was orphaned by one of the typhoid plagues which constantly swept the countryside. She worked this wing upstairs, if I remembered correctly. By God, yes! I remember Izzy telling me about her. How Mary Beth had somehow gotten on Charles's wrong side and how he had it in for her. Izzy and I had shuddered for the girl. We knew enough, you see, to understand that no one should ever go into Charles's disfavor. But, my God, I never, *never* suspected he was beating her!"

Suddenly, as if a bolt of lightning had shot through him, he stood straight. He cursed mightily and narrowed his eyes. He faced me, a man possessed. "I remember the talk through the house when she left. Yes, yes! Izzy had heard that one of our maids was caught in Charles's bedroom. Izzy and I thought she had been caught stealing. But no. Later—days later—I heard from the stable boy that a housemaid was about to have a baby and if the earl, my father, found out, there would be hell to pay."

"So Mary Beth left the house."

My voice seemed to bring some sanity back to Graham.

He peered at me. It was moments before he spoke.

"Yes, she left. I'm not sure what happened to her. But I remember—oh, Lord, I remember—Charles boasted even more about his prowess with women. How he had proven to everyone how worthy he was to become the eleventh Earl of Darnley. Because he had sired a son."

I shook my head. "Miraculous conception."

Graham narrowed his eyes at me. "What?"

I inhaled and cleared my head. "I—I just meant . . ."

What could I say? I was embarrassed to be speaking of private matters once more with my brother-in-law. Matters no lady discussed, not even with her husband. Not even with her mother, for heaven's sake!

Graham stood still as stone, waiting.

"I simply meant that Charles's prowess was . . ."

"Legendary? Notorious? Despicable?"

I hung my head. "Yes, all of those."

Graham lifted my chin. "Look at me," he whispered.

I willed my body to resolute rigidity. But my eyes would not obey. They fled his scrutiny.

When he spoke once more, his whisper had diminished to the thread of a tone. "Vanessa, what do you mean, my dear? That Charles was not loving or kind to you? He didn't beat you, did he?"

I shook my head.

"Thank God. I wouldn't believe he'd dare. What then? I say, look at me." His eyes probed unmercifully into mine. "Do you perhaps wonder how he could have sired so many because he never treated you with any—"

"Yes! Yes!" I tore myself away from him. I stalked the room. Graham stood rooted to his spot. "He always seemed in such a rush with me. At first, I thought that was how it was supposed to be—quick, painful. So . . . I don't know . . . incomplete! Of course, no woman ever speaks of such things. How was I to know what to expect? What to do? How to meet him? I accepted his actions."

I stared at Graham.

His face went white. "He did not show you love. He showed you merely the act."

"Oh, please!" I put up both hands and turned from him in shame. "I should never have broached this subject." In panic, I made for the door.

Graham's hands clamped my shoulders. In a second he turned me, and I—in great confusion and mortification—went into his arms. His body trembled. My eyes closed. Safety and solace seemed to be only here with him.

He buried his lips in my hair and murmured into my ear.

"Ah, Christ. Charles was a devil and I can scarce believe he was my brother. He did you such disservice. Made you live unfulfilled."

Ashamed beyond comprehension, I groaned. He caressed my shoulders softly.

"He hurt you just as he ruined that poor girl. He charmed you, but I think he must have blackmailed her into his bed. The talk about her was that they were often found together. Ah, Vanessa . . ." He stroked my hair. "Sweet Vanessa. He was not fit to wipe your shoes."

My arms stole around him as I burrowed myself into his embrace. "It's over with. Buried."

"What you have endured unjustly is beyond reason. You are worth so much more."

Tears misted my vision as I lifted my eyes to his. "It is worth much to me that you value me as you do."

"I always have." His eyes went to my mouth. "I always will."

I knew what he meant to do. I knew and did not stop him. I waited, mesmerized by the charm of his desire. I waited, and in a magic moment I was rewarded for my patience.

He kissed me. Kissed me as I'd only twice before known a kiss could be. Twice before, in his arms. This time, his mouth met mine, his two wet, hot lips matched to my own. His mouth was open, seeking, molding, searching for a response.

I met him and—oh, joy of joys!—I was not sorry. No! I was enraptured with the delight of his little kisses at the corners of my mouth and the bow, then back once more to press my whole mouth against his. His tongue defined my upper lip and tested my desire

141

to have him fill my mouth with it. I surrendered to his lead. He groaned and I urged him closer. With ardent force, he ravished my mouth and, in the process, bent me backward in his arms. My knees went weak.

He swept me up and took two paces to the settee. Now in his lap, I went into his arms so quickly, so willingly, the breath left my body in a whoosh. I put my hands aside his dear face and set my mouth on his once more.

"Ah, Vanessa," he moaned into my mouth. "You taste like heaven, my sweet." His hands plunged into my hair and pins flew to the floor. With greedy, grasping fingers, he crushed my curls and thus, with handfuls, ran his fingers down my throat to my chest and the tips of my breasts. Hard and reaching for his touch, my breasts burned as his fingertips settled on the bud of my nipples.

I'd never known possession like this. Never known I could yearn like this. Yearn for something so elusive that years of yearning—and years of unfulfilled desire—set alarms ringing in my brain.

What kind of madness was this? Where did it lead?

To disappointment.

To heartache.

I jerked away from him.

"No, no." I was pleading, demanding. "Let me go. Oh, please, Graham, let me go."

He went still. His hand went to my cheek and came away wet with fresh tears. His passion-filled eyes grew mellow.

"Darling, don't cry," he whispered as his eyes watched his hands smooth my hair across my shoulder. "We won't do anything more. You're not ready."

I bristled. Ready? *Ready?!*

I wiped my cheeks with both hands and pushed away from him. Avoiding his eyes, I stood on wob-

142

bling legs and rearranged my gown.

"You are mistaken, sir. I will never be *ready*."

"Your body is."

"You, sir, are very bold."

"Yes. In my circumstances, I think so. So must you be, for what we must face here together."

"We face nothing together."

He was upon me in one bold move. His hands seized my shoulders, his arms circled my waist. His virile body clamped to mine like an iron vise. "We face *this* together."

His mouth swooped down and captured mine. Like a pirate claiming his prey, he possessed my mouth, my body. He filled my mind with silken longings for some mysterious emotion as his lips branded mine. Once, twice, three times. Breathless, I was undone and lay limp in his arms.

He put his lips to my forehead and then, with a finger beneath my chin, raised my face. "Look at me, Vanessa. What began between us years ago was based on more than pity. The way your body responds to mine tonight proves it. Don't bother to deny it. Your breasts, your mouth, your eyes, give you away. It is the proof I have lived for, longed for. You are here with me for the next few weeks, and by God, I mean to use every minute of them to discover if what we feel is more than lust."

I pushed at his massive chest to no avail.

He smiled serenely. "Lust is what you fear. And rightly so, my sweet. You were undone by Charles's version of it. But no longer. For the next few weeks, we will see how powerful it is. How it complements other emotions. So you will sit at breakfast and luncheon and dinner with me. You will paint my portrait in the mornings and ride with me in the afternoons. You will converse and smile, and in that time, we will put to rest the speculation of the years."

He set me away from him and steadied me as I left

143

his arms completely.

"Good night, Vanessa. Sleep well, my dear."

With a composure I did not feel, I turned my back on him and left the room. But as I fled the Georgian wing and returned to Eliza's, I ran like a madwoman, fearing what I fled was the truth.

Chapter Ten

The next morning, I went into breakfast serenely. One look at Graham told me he had slept more peacefully than even I could feign.

His smiling countenance welcomed me into the dining room. His solicitous nature recommended the kippers and biscuits. His blazing black gaze burned my body, making my knees melt and my breasts sizzle.

I cut short my trip to the sideboard and sought my seat. Then I tried to eat without conversing. He would not allow it, so alive was he with comments about the morning's news of trade and politics and the social escapades of Prince Bertie.

I excused myself and would have left had he not called me back with a question of when we should meet for his first sitting. Gad, the portrait!

"Ten. Ten o'clock," I told him, instead of remembering my manners and asking.

He agreed.

Promptly at ten, he appeared in his study, just off the library. I had been there since eight, arranging my easel, discovering MacCarthy's choices in paints, brushes, thinners, and glazes and declaring them good ones. I had also been there, chewing my lower lip and trying to decide on lighting and effect—and the wisdom of this venture.

I stared at him, this virile, dashing man who was wearing the most ghastly black suit I'd ever seen. "You don't intend to have your portrait painted in that?"

"Why not?" He spread his arms and glanced down his body.

"It's . . . not suitable."

"Not suitable? But my father had his portrait painted in a black suit. My grandfather did as well. What's the matter with this suit?"

"You are not your father or grandfather." I put down my sketchpad and pencil. "You have golden hair."

"From my mother. But I have the Chadwick's black eyes."

"No reason to wear black. In fact, a reason not to." I crossed my arms and surveyed his form. "Haven't you something blue or violet?"

The hint of a smile graced his lush mouth. "I have a violet cravat the same color as your eyes."

"We are painting *your* portrait, sir, not mine."

"The castle needs one of you."

"No, sir. The castle needs one of you, and you, sir, need something to illuminate the power of your features."

He crossed his arms and cocked his head. "You think I have good features?"

"Yes. Strong Chadwick features."

"Like Charles?"

Was Graham baiting me to compare him to his brother? I hated all reference to my husband. "Charles's strength was a mask." I turned and began to take a seat to wait for him. "Yours is as palpable."

"And illusory as well?"

"No," I breathed, and busied myself arranging my paints across the table. "Pervasive."

Graham caught my arm and led me toward the door.

"Very well, Vanessa. You want color. You shall choose it, then."

He took me to his dressing room—with the hall door open, of course—while he proceeded to remove not only his coat and waistcoat, but also his shirt. For minutes, I was treated to the sight of his back, with sculpted scapulae and his expansive chest with molded pectorals. My fingers twitched with the temptation to twine themselves in the thatch of golden hair smothering his chest. I continuously fidgeted in my chair, my eyes searching for some safe haven.

Just when I could stand the tension no longer, I jumped from my chair and advanced to the rack of hanging garments. MacCarthy's ministrations were evident in the meticulous order and pressed perfection of each article. I put out my hand, then turned to Graham.

"May I?"

"Naturally."

My hands flew over the evening dress shirts. "Too formal." The stark simplicity of business attire. "Too ordinary." But on the far wall, a different sort of clothing beckoned. Beige and navy Norfolk jackets with trousers to match. A soft grey flannel seaside coat. A deep green redingote with velvet collar and buttons. And several large white shirts that flowed from their hangers.

"This is what we want," I announced, and turned to see Graham considering me with shocked amusement.

"I hardly think that *suitable* for a formal portrait of a Chadwick." He removed a satin grey waistcoat and silk dress shirt, so that once more I was treated to the sight of his bare chest. "Let me show you." He took the shirt I held and moved to his armoire, from which he pulled a wine-red vest and a purple neck scarf. When he turned, the man before me was no Graham I'd ever seen before.

147

Yet I smiled. "That's more like it."

He spread his arms once more. "This is what I wear well out to sea! If my ancestors saw me in this, they'd climb down from their frames and scold me."

"But the impression is uniquely you," I insisted.

"As the youngest son, I never expected to merit a portrait. Therefore, I have always been *uniquely* myself and only rarely obeyed my father willingly. The last time I obeyed him, I rued the day ever after." Graham went quite still.

"You know that day as the one I came to see you off to New York. When I had the divorce papers in my hand. My father never told me until afterward that that is what they were. He revealed it to me when I returned to the London townhouse. I was out of my mind after that. I left for Singapore, Hong Kong. Anywhere was good enough. Nowhere was far enough. I hated myself. I hated my father. But most of all, I hated Charles for what he'd so callously done to you."

I had listened with growing heartache. "You did not know they were divorce papers? But what did you think they were?"

"My father told me they were papers consigning your dowry back to you. I believed him. I believed him because I wanted some excuse to see you again. Some excuse aside from the real one."

I turned away from him. "Please, let us return to your study. I have no stomach for these memories."

Once more in his study, I took up my station before him with sketchpad and pencil in hand. Since we had the attire finally correct, the pose possessed my imagination.

I frowned at him. "In those clothes, you cannot sit. You must stand."

Yes, that was it. I rushed forward and pushed aside papers and books from his desktop. I took the brass bookends and moved them to the credenza. Then I reached for his hand to take him from the formal Louis Quinze chair he had chosen.

"Here. Perch on the edge of your desk."

He did as I commanded, a quizzical smile lifting his generous mouth.

"Do you like this better?" Graham crossed one leg over the other and lifted his jaw in a regal pose.

I inhaled and shook my head. "Still very stiff."

Ha! What was I referring to? His pose or my attitude?

I considered the morning light streaming through the tall windows. It warmed the smaller room off the cavernous library. But it also gave great brilliance to Graham's golden presence. I had put one hand on my hip and analyzed my continuing dilemma.

"Now, if you will turn this way."

I had turned his head slightly to the left so that the sun cast shadows across the sharp planes of his cheek and chin. His hair gleamed with gilded highlights. I brushed my fingers through the locks at his forehead and they fell down across his brow, as if the sea wind had blown them there. I placed one arm across his molded thigh so that his hand draped between his legs. I took his other hand and splayed his long, blunt-edged fingers atop his kneecap.

I stood back. "You still look uncomfortable. Not you at all."

"Not bloody likely I'll be able to hold the pose for hours, either."

I nodded, then my eyes skimmed the room. I clapped my hands when I found what I needed.

"Don't move," I ordered, returning with an over-stuffed footstool with which I knelt to place at his feet.

I surveyed my work. "With a lift to your leg upon that footstool, your entire body relaxes."

"He looks like a pirate!" came a voice from across the room.

"Helena!" Graham was laughing. "Come join us.

149

What do you think?"

"I think the whole effect rather startling." She sailed in, her gown of dark navy complementing her complexion only slightly better than the color of the night before. She glanced down at me, still kneeling upon the floor. "What do you mean to do to Graham with this portrait? Imply he is a pirate? A thief?" She was smiling, but there was a serious edge to her tone. "I thought you had come to terms with your station in life, my dear."

Graham's brow furrowed. He broke the pose and stared at Helena. While I sat confused, he shook his head.

"Helena, Vanessa is merely presenting her interpretation of my character."

"Whatever her interpretation, Graham, I wish to see the family name upheld. This rendering of you as a—"

"Sea captain," I interjected.

Her black eyes found mine. "A sea captain does not connote your station as heir to the family estate and title."

Graham pursed his mouth and considered his hands. "Helena, I wish to allow Vanessa her full range as an artist. As for me needing to uphold the family honor, I am painfully aware of that burden. However, a simple portrait will not rectify the ravages of misdeeds performed by others before me."

Helena smiled. "Well, of course, Graham, I agree. I merely thought that after the will is read and you are made heir, you would wish to proceed in a manner that makes an immediate but lasting impression."

I rose from the floor. "The impression of this pose will be of a man who is independent, determined. Don't you see, Helena? Graham can be viewed here as himself. Quite different from the others."

"From Charles, you mean."

I bit my tongue.

She patted my arm. "I understand all too well, my dear. Different from Charles's father, too." She sighed.

Graham cocked a brow. "From many other Chadwicks."

"I am a Chadwick, too," she declared proudly. "We are not perfect, but we are a force to reckon with. Isn't that right, Vanessa? And I would see you, Graham, recognized not only as one of us, but as our leader. So do your portrait as you wish. I will extol it"—she beamed at both of us "—for its subject and its artist. In the meantime, I came to tell you that I am off to the village to visit a distant cousin. One of my mother's sister's girls. Lovely woman. About to give birth to her sixth child. Yet, all of them are poor as church mice, which, of course, is precisely what they are. Church mice." She shuddered, then cast off her doldrums and gave a little wave. "I'll see you at tea."

I went to pick up my sketchpad.

Graham's gaze still centered on the door. "Helena is brutally honest."

"It is what I value most about her."

"Really? I have always wondered about the basis of your friendship. She is so unlike you."

"We have always been good friends. She was a great help to me when I first arrived. She was honest then about what I must do to gain acceptance by society. She taught me English customs, Chadwick ways. She was the one who first brought me here and introduced me to the wonders of the family library. She even exposed me to the family records. Thanks to her efforts, I felt more like a member of the family, as if I might belong here."

"We could have done more."

I saw remorse upon his face. "You must not blame yourself. You were away so much of that year and a half I was here in England. You couldn't do much."

"Oh, but you are mistaken. I could have done more. When I met you, I had an Englishman's reaction to your American origin. So priggish, so very small of me. I realized it within a week or two. And then I came to know you, really know you, and I—I knew I had to get away. I *chose* to be away. Chose to sail to as many ports as possible. But perhaps, if I'd stayed in England, I would have been able to see what was happening here. Perhaps I could have stopped it. Saved you."

"Don't be foolish, Graham. You couldn't. Whatever the problem was between Charles and me, you couldn't have saved the relationship. And knowing what I now know, I would not have wanted you to save it. Had none of the sordidness occurred and we remained together as man and wife, I would have died a slow death here with Charles."

"You love him no longer, do you?"

"I sometimes question if it was love or merely infatuation. Whatever I might term it, even the pain of his rejection has dulled in the morass of tragedy I've experienced since our divorce. I wish the pain of all those tragedies completely gone. By coming here, I hoped to put it to rest completely. If only—if only I understood *why* Charles did it, then I might be able to live a full life once again."

I glanced around me. "This is a fine old house. A home to so many noble Chadwicks and Darnleys. I wish I could find some logical reason for Charles's actions so that I might once more appreciate the good qualities of the family. After all, my son is a Chadwick, despite what Charles may have thought or what your father may have believed."

"What if there is no logical explanation, Vanessa? What if there is no reason except that Charles was who he was, what he was? What if Charles did it merely because he was self-centered and spoiled? What if such self-possession is an inherited trait? Can you then bury your dead? Accept your past and the

Chadwicks' foibles and sins? Can you find peace and love your son completely?"

"Oh, Graham, I have never seen self-centeredness in Jeremy. He is a child of light and love and loss. He is sweet and sensitive without any trace of the hauteur which typified his father. I credit myself that Jeremy is my child as well as Charles's, and I see qualities in him that I have nurtured. And, despite what you or anyone may think, I think nurturing is a key to good character.

"As for finding peace for myself, I work for it daily. And now that I am here—at the very place where my good name was snatched from me—I will confront my past and work for freedom from it every moment of every hour I remain in Darnley Castle."

I turned from him and began to concentrate on my task. My art, so little exercised this last year or so, came back to me slowly. But my desire to return to it came back with a rush. I stepped into my task with a keen awareness of my subject. Discussion died as I delved into the joy of rendering his perfect body, his sublime face, and his potent character onto the lifeless canvas. Here would be a Graham all would remember. For his grace, his kindness, his devastating handsomeness.

Then followed a most unnerving experience. I found myself too often standing before him, lost in the black wonders of his eyes. He allowed my forays, meeting my stares with an openness and patience that made me more eager to convey the beauties of his soul to the canvas. When the hour was over and Forbisher appeared to notify Graham of his business appointment, I mourned his loss.

Graham approached me and smiled, his eyes in tender communion with mine, and whispered for my ears alone, "I will see you at luncheon. And we shall ride at one."

Luncheon was another affair of blithe conversation and ravenous lingering looks. I ate little, my stomach churning with some appetite the food could not satisfy.

Then and there, I quickly decided Jeremy should come riding with us. I leaned over to him during the soup and asked him if he would like to accompany his Uncle Graham and me. From far down the table, Graham had arched both brows at me and expressed surprise because of Jeremy's continuing sniffles. Nonetheless, I insisted the air might do him well.

Graham went ahead to the stable and had Mike, the stable boy, outfit a sweet dappled pony with white mane and tail.

"Welshie's a gentle feller," young Mike assured an eager Jeremy as he clapped his hands and mounted with an agility that pleased me. Anxious to get on with his discovery of the countryside, my son had spurred the little pony and led the three of us down the bridle path.

As we traveled through Darnley's meadows and forests, Jeremy exclaimed his love of the trees and flowers, while Graham supplied the exact names for his inquisitive young mind.

But though Graham's words were for Jeremy's benefit, his eyes constantly melded with mine. I knew what he did. I felt what he meant. I could not sit the saddle, even sidesaddle as I was, and I squirmed to be free.

When the raindrops began to fall, I raised my face to the sky as if in thanks. Deliverance was at hand.

But delivered from what? And from whom? Graham or myself?

I shook off a frisson of excitement and acknowledged anger. Anger at my actions—and, truth be told, my inactions.

We trotted back to the stables, dismounted, and ran for the house. In the great hall, I made curt excuses for Jeremy and myself, then retreated to my apartment.

I paced the floor. The afternoon loomed before me.

154

How would I take my mind from Graham?

I'd bring Jeremy into the library! That was it! I'd read him a few stories from the family histories.

I went into his room and announced my intention to Simpson, who looked grateful for the free time.

Jeremy bounced up and down. We made our way to the cavernous oak-lined library. At once, Jeremy's keen eyes lit on the huge red leather family Bible, lying on the center reading table.

"Tell me stories," he begged me, and I settled him into the tufted corner of an overstuffed wing chair near a mullioned window.

I took the family bible on my lap and thought of the story I liked almost as much as Eliza's and Clifford's.

"Over eight hundred years ago, England was an island ruled by a king who grew weaker by the year. Across the ocean, in what is now France, lived a young man who wanted to be king over England. He raised an army and crossed the Channel, landing and taking a stand at a place called Hastings. The French man won and called himself William the Conqueror.

"Immediately, to put order in his new domain, he sent out men from his army, whom he called his retainers, to take over the lands from the old king's vassals, the Angles and the Saxons. One of those retainers was a friend of William. His name was Geoffrey, of a small town called Arnleigh in Normandy. And he had become a friend of William when the two of them were boys, and Geoffrey had taught William how to hunt game with falcons. Geoffrey, you see, was the youngest son of a Norman count, and as the youngest, he was neglected by his father and his mother. He took up training falcons to fill his time and his heartache for being the youngest and, therefore, so unworthy."

Jeremy frowned. "That's not nice. Why didn't his daddy like him? He didn't hurt his daddy, did he?"

"No, my dear. But that was the way of the world

then. Oldest sons got lots of attention and love."

"Too much," came a velvet voice from across the room.

I looked up and there he stood in the doorway of his study.

He'd changed his beige riding habit for a more casual pair of thigh-fitting fawn trousers, white silk shirt, and charcoal jacket. The combination set off every dynamic feature the man possessed—body, complexion, eyes. Dear God, the eyes could devour me whole and I'd still sit here defenseless.

He walked forward and came to stand in back of Jeremy, his hands going to my boy's shoulders and gently squeezing him, his eyes caressing my mouth.

"Tell us more, Vanessa," he rasped.

I licked my lips. Geoffrey, Geoffrey . . .

"Geoffrey had trained many falcons and was reputed to be the best teacher of falconry in Normandy. He was also a strong warrior, supposedly more than six feet tall with coal-black hair and eyes— the hallmark of the Arnleighs and the Chadwicks ever since."

"But I'm a Chadwick and I have blond hair," fretted Jeremy. "Why?"

Graham came round to sit next to Jeremy. "Because your mother has blond hair and your grandmother—my mother and your father's mother— had hair almost as platinum as your mother's. Those things add up and suddenly, no matter how much black hair you have in a family—poof!—a blond!"

I was examining my hands, trying desperately not to wring them. This was the very subject that I had feared. Jeremy's paternity still sent chills through me. It was the thing my husband had thrown in my face as proof of my so-called "alienation of affection" with that horrible man George Hayden. It was the thing I had always feared discussion of, particularly after Jeremy was born and he had hair that was blond—not Chadwick black—hair as blond as

156

Hayden's. I knew when I returned here with Jeremy I took the chance that someone might remember this and take it as proof that Jeremy was no Chadwick.

Jeremy was scowling. "But lots of people have blond hair. How do you know I'm a Chadwick?"

Graham smiled. "Oh, I know, Jeremy. I knew the first moment I looked at you."

"You did?" Jeremy asked, sitting forward.

Graham nodded.

I sat, terrified.

"How?" asked Jeremy.

How? asked my heart.

Graham reached out and, with both thumbs and forefingers, grasped Jeremy's earlobes. "You have wens on each lobe. Little bumps. Not too many people have them on even one ear. Only true Chadwicks have them on both."

My sweet lord. Wens. On earlobes. Even I—a mother who knew every inch of my baby's anatomy— even I had never considered that!

Graham was smiling at Jeremy.

Jeremy was asking for the rest of the story.

I looked at Graham and I knew he could see my astonishment and joy. With his consoling eyes and a tilt of his head, he told me he was amazed I never knew.

"Shall I finish the story, my dear?" Graham was asking me.

"Please. I would like to hear you tell it," I told him.

His eyes went stark with tenderness as he whispered, "I can tell you many things."

My heart was beating so loudly I was sure the servants could hear its tattoo in their hall. "Please do. Geoffrey—Geoffrey's tale, that is, please."

"For now." He said it like a vow.

Then he turned to Jeremy, imparting a tale of a youngest son who won a place in a king's heart, a domain for himself, and then conquered the fear and enmity of the young Saxon girl he grew to love.

"And Rowina loved her husband so much," concluded Graham, "that when he died, she composed a book of verse to his ardor and his valor. I gave the book to a friend of mine—a professor of literature—at Cambridge last month to study, copy, and publish. He will see it is preserved as well. You see, it is one of the few surviving original books of verse from the Norman period." Graham put a hand to Jeremy's knee. "So now, young man, I think it is time for your nap, isn't that right, Vanessa?"

"Yes, it certainly is."

"Run along up to Miss Simpson, Jeremy."

"Yes, sir!" Jeremy scampered away, but quickly came back and reached his little arms up to his uncle. Graham bent down and then Jeremy planted a big, wet kiss on his cheek. "Thank you, sir. I feel better—about my ears, I mean."

I clutched my hands to my chest! Did he know? Had he overheard some conversation that made him question his paternity? Oh, no!

"I always wondered—since Mommy and I live so far away—if anyone would ever think I was really a Chadwick. I would like to be, 'specially since I know about Clifford and Geoffrey."

Graham grinned at the boy in his arms. "Yes, I can understand that, Jeremy. I would like to be like them both myself."

Jeremy left us with a little wave.

I couldn't take my eyes off Graham.

He came forward, took my hands, and brought them to his lips. He branded each palm with a kiss. He folded my fingers, placed my hands against my chest, and explored my eyes. "I love him, Vanessa. You have nurtured any terrible Chadwick trait right out of him."

"I am so pleased you care for him. He has been the world to me."

"Is there room for another in your world?"

I wanted to speak, to say a thousand things. Yet of

158

all the affirmations I could have given, I could find no courage.

I found more fear.

I stepped back and cast my eyes around the shelves. "I must think. I—I think I should leave you and—and perhaps read a book. Yes, I—" I glanced at his disappointed features. God, how I hated to hurt this man!

"Forgive me, Graham. I wish to read in my room."

"Very well." He let my hands drop and stepped back. "But please know that you may use the library at any time, Vanessa. Simply because I conduct my business from my study is no reason to absent yourself. I would welcome the company."

"Thank you. I will take your invitation another day, perhaps. Now I wish to read upstairs."

Now I wish to be alone!

I took an old edition of *Canterbury Tales*, then made my way to Eliza's wing and the sanctity of my apartment. With Jeremy napping, I was totally free for the first time since the afternoon in London when I'd landed in Abercrombie Mews.

No one had threatened me since then. I sighed now and acknowledged that Graham had been correct. Whoever that man was, whatever he had wanted of me, he had not followed me here to Darnley Castle. I was safe. Safe from physical harm. But was I safe from emotional turmoil?

No! I would not think of that!

Now, today, with that freedom in hand, Chaucer and his tales held precious little attraction for me. I shut the book with a whack!

I stood and paced my room once more. But as I glanced at the far stone wall, I knew what really attracted me—what really might divert me from my musings—were the tales that lay behind that wall. Down those stairs. In those secret rooms.

I took two candles.

Samantha mewed and stretched herself upon the

crimson coverlet.

"Want to go exploring, my pet?"

I took a kindling taper from the fireplace. The slender wick of one candle flickered to life.

"Come along, Samantha. We might find a mouse or two."

She cried and lunged off the bed.

I placed my feet squarely in the corners of the old hearth stones and the far wall creaked open.

I slid inside the musty cell and lifted the candle. Shadows rolled this way and that. I walked toward the bookcase, placed my hand against the lever, and lifted. Once more, I heard the telling creak of stone on stone. The bookcase and its wall slid forward and I slid round it, my foot on the top of the stairs.

Worn so by years of stealthy fugitives, the steps of stone sagged from the wear on their polished middle. I took each one gingerly, careful lest I trip over some article that had fallen there. But my path was sure and easy, as sure and easy as if someone had swept the stairs in full knowledge of my adventure this afternoon. The candle gave good light, showing me the ordinary elements of a staircase long hidden from light of day. Things like spiders and their intricate webs, as well as larger insects caught there in various stages of decomposition. Things like mold and mushrooms and fungus as dark and thick as oil.

I was barely five or six steps down when I caught sight of some scribbling on a wall. Words long faded made no sense to me.

I held the candle higher. Samantha, winding herself between my legs, kept her opinion to herself. I gathered my skirts and took the next step. As I remembered, the stairs now turned one hundred and eighty degrees, probably to run beneath my room and the solar. Here, if I remembered correctly, began a number of interesting configurations that told tales of Darnleys long forgotten.

Like the drawing in this small niche, where some

160

MORE PASSION AND ADVENTURE AWAIT... YOUR TRIP TO A BIG ADVENTUROUS WORLD BEGINS WHEN YOU ACCEPT YOUR FIRST 4 NOVELS ABSOLUTELY *FREE* (AN $18.00 VALUE)

Accept your Free gift and start to experience more of the passion and adventure you like in a historical romance novel. Each Zebra novel is filled with proud men, spirited women and tempestuous love that you'll remember long after you turn the last page.

Zebra Historical Romances are the finest novels of their kind. They are written by authors who really know how to weave tales of romance and adventure in the historical settings you love. You'll feel like you've actually gone back in time with the thrilling stories that each Zebra novel offers.

GET YOUR FREE GIFT WITH THE START OF YOUR HOME SUBSCRIPTION

Our readers tell us that these books sell out very fast in book stores and often they miss the newest titles. So Zebra has made arrangements for you to receive the four newest novels published each month.

You'll be guaranteed that you'll never miss a title, and home delivery is so convenient. And to show you just how easy it is to get Zebra Historical Romances, we'll send you your first 4 books absolutely FREE! Our gift to you just for trying our home subscription service.

BIG SAVINGS AND FREE HOME DELIVERY

Each month, you'll receive the four newest titles as soon as they are published. You'll probably receive them even before the bookstores do. What's more, you may preview these exciting novels free for 10 days. If you like them as much as we think you will, just pay the low preferred subscriber's price of just $3.75 each. *You'll save $3.00 each month off the publisher's price.* AND, your savings are even greater because there are never any shipping, handling or other hidden charges—FREE Home Delivery. Of course you can return any shipment within 10 days for full credit, no questions asked. There is no minimum number of books you must buy.

4 FREE BOOKS

TO GET YOUR 4 FREE BOOKS WORTH $18.00 — MAIL IN THE FREE BOOK CERTIFICATE T O D A Y

Fill in the Free Book Certificate below, and we'll send your FREE BOOKS to you as soon as we receive it.

If the certificate is missing below, write to: Zebra Home Subscription Service, Inc., P.O. Box 5214, 120 Brighton Road, Clifton, New Jersey 07015-5214.

FREE BOOK CERTIFICATE
4 FREE BOOKS
ZEBRA HOME SUBSCRIPTION SERVICE, INC.

YES! Please start my subscription to Zebra Historical Romances and send me my first 4 books absolutely FREE. I understand that each month I may preview four new Zebra Historical Romances free for 10 days. If I'm not satisfied with them, I may return the four books within 10 days and owe nothing. Otherwise, I will pay the low preferred subscriber's price of just $3.75 each; a total of $15.00, *a savings off the publisher's price of $3.00.* I may return any shipment and I may cancel this subscription at any time. There is no obligation to buy any shipment and there are no shipping, handling or other hidden charges. Regardless of what I decide, the four free books are mine to keep.

NAME _____

ADDRESS _____ APT _____

CITY _____ STATE ___ ZIP ___

( )
TELEPHONE _____

SIGNATURE _____
(if under 18, parent or guardian must sign)

Terms, offer and prices subject to change without notice. Subscription subject to acceptance by Zebra Books. Zebra Books reserves the right to reject any order or cancel any subscription.

GET
FOUR
FREE
BOOKS
(AN $18.00 VALUE)

ZEBRA HOME SUBSCRIPTION
SERVICE, INC.
P.O. Box 5214
120 BRIGHTON ROAD
CLIFTON, NEW JERSEY 07015-5214

loyal Catholic had carved a cross into the stone and etched beneath it *Semper*. Always. Or farther down, where a wooden door high enough and round enough for a slim woman or youth to walk through seemed a good hiding place. I paused to open the door and peered inside. Empty except for a few earthenware jugs that stood just inside.

I shut the door and went on.

Four more steps down led me to an alcove that had long remained in my mind's eye. An alcove where I had found the means for many an afternoon of joy.

Here, I pushed against an ancient door and it opened easily. I held the candle above my head to illuminate the vaulted room, smiling at the sight.

Here was a room meant for historians of England's political struggles. For here, assembled in one room, stood a king's ransom in medieval archery. Bows and arrows of every shape and size, every delicacy, every purpose. I moved forward in fascination. I touched one giant instrument of death, the famed English longbow, at least six feet long. I knew just by looking at it that Graham would be taller than this bow. Then I quickly dismissed the idea and turned for a smaller version, one that stood against the wall, left there by some hunter perhaps. I picked it up and tested its feel in my hands. I stretched the bow. It bent with ease. After all these years, it was still resilient. A credit to the craftsman who had created it. I yearned to feel its power and searched the ground for arrows. A quiver filled with arrows that seemed just the right size had fallen on the floor. I grabbed it up and made for the stairs.

I knew the way out. This arsenal was but a few steps above the exit to the stairs. I took the candle, and careful lest I go too fast and blow it out, I made for the door. Once more, I unlatched an ancient door and suddenly was outside in a secluded courtyard.

Surrounded on three sides by several small additions to the old castle, this courtyard was a perfect place for the medieval lords of Darnley not only to train their archers but also to loose them on the enemy. The courtyard's only avenue of exit lay close by a copse of trees, wherein a band of archers could easily disperse to the perimeters of the moat and the castle's outposts.

Eager to try the bow and refresh my knowledge of archery, I rejoiced that the rain had suddenly stopped and I could walk outside. I picked up my skirts and made for the copse. I looked back at Samantha, who sat and curled her tail around her body, content to remain near the castle. I walked on. Beneath a canopy of ancient oaks, I chose a knot in an old tree as my mark and lined up the arrow straight with my eye. Remembering my father's instructions, I set my sight and let the arrow fly.

I hit the outer ring of the knot. I took another arrow from the quiver, lined it up, and tried once more. This hit was better still but not up to my best performance. Finally, by the fourth arrow, I knew I'd recalled the best of my ability. I pulled back, straight back, aimed, and released my fingers. Bull's-eye! I had not lost my touch.

I turned and there he stood.

"I never knew you could use a bow and arrow." He nodded toward my collection of arrows in the tree.

"There is much about me you don't know."

I turned and strode forward to the tree, and began to remove the arrowheads.

"Where did you learn?"

"My father once took me on a trip out west when he was involved in the expansion of the railroads. I learned how to use a bow and arrow from a Lakota Indian who was an interpreter for the railroad company. He was a good teacher."

"You are a good pupil." He came to stand behind me and I felt his body heat my own. I struggled with one particularly stubborn arrow and he reached around me, encircling me with his arms, and said, "Let me."

I flushed with boiling need. It burst upon me as anger. "I can do this!"

"I know. You are capable of anything," he said softly.

I spun around in his arms and frantically searched his eyes. What were we speaking of?

His mouth curled into the semblance of a smile, but his eyes grew ominously enticing. "You astound me with your capabilities. I long to prove to you how multitudinous they are." His eyes drifted closed and opened once more. "Until tonight," he whispered, then was gone.

"My lord, the coachman said Miss Chadwick told him to return for her at ten o'clock. Since Miss Chadwick will not be with you, may I now serve dinner, my lord?"

"Certainly, Forbisher," Graham nodded to the butler.

I fumed in my chair. Dinner alone with Graham. Not even Jeremy to save me from—oh, dare I acknowledge it?—from ruin.

"Well, it appears that Helena is enjoying her visit. It is unfortunate Jeremy was so hungry he begged to have his dinner and could not join us. Hmmm?"

I didn't look at Graham, but I could tell he was not at all unhappy at the prospect of dinner for two, alone. I was a mass of confusion and could not trust myself to respond.

I didn't have to.

He came forward and offered me his arm. "Let us go in, shall we, Vanessa?"

I tried to stop the trembling of my limbs.

"I must tell you," he offered smoothly while he looped my hand around his forearm, "even though I hate you in black, I do like this gown. It is the best of all I've seen you in."

I gazed up at him. "But it is just like the others."

"I know, and as soon as the will is read, I hope to God you don a few blues and greens and purples. I appreciate the style of this one, however." His eyes fell to the lace netting through which the swell of my breasts rose to a high pointed collar.

I swallowed hard. "It is an old ball gown of my mother's, which I altered as a mourning gown."

"Yes, I assumed as much." He led me beyond my appointed place at the long dining table. "No, no, come down here and sit with me. Since there are only two of us, we must be closer. Wouldn't you agree?"

No, I would not.

But politely, I sat down. I fiddled with my napkin as the servants marched in and began to serve the soup. Once more my appetite deserted me. I sat through the courses and marveled at Graham's unceasing ability to find dinner conversation. Had I heard of this and how did I like that? Had I ever been there? Tried that? What would I do if I did?

Great God, how did I know?!

By the time they cleared the cheeses away, I was a mass of bubbling fury. Again, I was angry at myself. For succumbing to Graham's charm. His spell. His plan.

That was what had made my life a misery with Charles. I would not repeat the mistake!

I rose so suddenly my chair almost fell backward. I caught it just before it crashed to the floor.

"I—I must retire, Graham. Forgive me. It has been a long day."

"You won't join me for coffee and brandy?"

"No. No, thank you." I put one hand to my head and could not meet his eyes. Instead, I made for my room.

The solitude offered no comfort. I prowled like a hungry cat. The clocks struck ten. I wondered if Helena had arrived home, but here in this wing, I had no way of knowing. I undressed and donned my nightgown and robe. I lay down in the featherbed, punched the pillows, but could not rest. I climbed down from the mattress, searched for my slippers, which Samantha had once more used as a bed, then padded to the far wall. I picked up my book of Chaucer and turned up one gas lamp. There was nothing for it. Perhaps I did need a brandy.

I fastened my robe about me and left my bedroom. Out in the hall, I noted how the servants had turned down the gas. The ancient manse seemed alive with shimmering shadows. I made my way to the library and, opening the door and sliding in, headed straight for the cabinet where the old earl had kept his prized collection of continental liquors. Lit by the glow of an autumn moon, the room needed no further illumination. So I avoided turning up the lamps. Instead, finding a glass, I poured myself a drink and took it to the window. Outside, the wind buffeted the closest trees, creating silhouettes against a few fleeting clouds.

I sipped. I felt more languid. I sipped again and held the glass up to the light, wondering if I needed liquor to quell my nerves. I closed my eyes.

The brandy worked its way into my bloodstream, its warmth spreading to my limbs.

"Is brandy really what you want, Vanessa?"

I gasped and the glass almost slipped from my fingers.

I turned and there he stood. He had removed his coat and cravat. His snow-white shirt gaped open to reveal his muscular chest. In the moonlight he looked half angel, half devil.

"I am sorry, Graham. I merely wanted something to help me sleep. I had no idea you were here."

He strode to stand before me. "No, of course not. If you had known I-was here, you would have stayed away."

I walked around him. The movement was so

abrupt, the room so dark, my footing so unsure, I lost my balance when my slipper tangled in the carpet.

Graham had me in his arms in a moment. I smelled brandy on his warm breath and I writhed to be free.

He scowled at me. "Stop that." He clutched me to his chest.

"Let me down."

"No, by God. I'm taking you to bed."

"No! I won't—"

"Allow it?" He glared at me, but kept walking toward the long hall and Eliza's wing. Then he laughed sourly as he took the stairs two at a time. "Ha! By God, that's rich. You won't allow it." He practically bounded down the hall and shouldered open my bedroom door. He placed me on my bed and backed away so that I could not see his face. "I don't want to be *allowed*, my sweet. I want more, much more. With you, I want to be *welcomed*."

Chapter Eleven

Tangled in my robe, I awoke the next morning with stiff and aching limbs. No wonder! I had paced the floor most of the night, full of anguish. I had fallen asleep only after I had made a few important decisions.

I recalled them now with pain that made my heart ache as vitally as my body.

First and most important, I would not let my heart rule my head ever again. Devastatingly attracted to Graham as I was, I knew it was lust, just as he'd described it, just as he'd exhibited it. And just as he'd concluded, I could not venture into its realm. Lust was the very trait my late husband had displayed. Lust was the very trait Graham now called forth from me. Not love, never love. And certainly not with Graham, of all men!

But love—that sensitive regard for another, that gentle nurturing of a sweet soul—was what I longed to find with a mate. Yet, while I could rhapsodize about love, I had finally admitted to myself in the wee hours of last night's darkest despair that I was not sure I knew what love was. I had loved, for lack of a better word, and lost. I had done so in a most cruel way and could not—dare not—do it again.

If I ever found a man whom I admired, I might

consider marriage. But he would have to be a saint to take me. For my background would do nothing for him socially or otherwise. In fact, my mere presence could make him an object of ridicule, a laughing-stock. I would not have it. Nor would I have Jeremy subjected to it. Therefore, the very possibility of finding such a creature to love and cherish me and my son was ludicrous.

My second decision was to avoid seeing Graham privately. While he seemed to pop up everywhere, I told myself that if it continued to happen, I would simply pick up my skirts and leave. My resolution was merely a restatement of my grandmother's saying: "If the path is covered with ice, choose a safer way."

I was sure if I avoided him, his demeanor would even. His erratic swing from sweet to surly would end. Meanwhile, my erratic emotional swing from frightened to enthralled would stop as well. It had to! I could not let lust or romanticism lead me toward disaster—not with Graham, not with any man ever again.

I propped myself up on one elbow and pushed back the scarlet bed hangings. A warm beacon of sunshine spread across my bed. Knowing from the angle of it that the hour must be nine or so, I swung my feet over the edge of the bed to dress for breakfast. Certainly by this time, Graham would be in his study at his paperwork or receiving business callers. I would be able to slip into the dining room and eat in solitude.

I felt about with the pads of my feet for my slip-pers. These past few days Samantha had taken to lying on them—when she wasn't lying on my bed, of course. So I had a devil of a time locating them. This morning, I had to get down on all fours to find them where she'd left them flush against the headboard wall. I reached in and, with great difficulty, slid them out.

"Samantha! Samantha, where are you?" I stood up and slid my feet into their warmth. "Here kitty, here kitty, kitty." I put my hands on my hips and peered around the room. "Well, you are right not to come out. You have been a bad kitty and I do wish you'd stop absconding with my slippers!"

Giving up on her, I concluded she must have bounded out earlier. Perhaps Lucile or Mrs. Bellweather had come to check on me for breakfast, and Samantha had taken the opportunity to prowl the castle for a mouse or two.

I grasped the bellpull to call for Lucile, and within minutes I was dressed for the morning—and for my purposes. Because of my usual ten o'clock appointment with Graham—and my need to sequester my body and soul from him—I chose an old gown, albeit of spring muslin in hydrangea violet. Its style was dated, a high-necked princess polonaise that buttoned down the front and whose full flared skirt required no bustle. Over three years old, even its charming color had faded. No one would find me attractive in this. Then, anticipating the cool drafts of the castle, I asked Lucile to fetch me a crocheted shawl of pale ivory cashmere.

"I doubt you'll need this beyond mid-morning, ma'am," Lucile offered. "The day is so warm, it feels like June instead of late September."

"Wonderful! I have great plans to enjoy it, too!"

"So does Master Jeremy."

When I turned, she supplied the answer to my unspoken question. "He was up at dawn, it seems. Miss Simpson took the opportunity to start his lessons early. He finished so quickly, he asked to go riding. On that pony Lord Darnley gave him yesterday."

I frowned. I couldn't remember if Simpson rode or not.

"Oh, don't worry, ma'am," Lucile said, once more anticipating my thoughts. "The stable boy went with him. Young Mike is a good boy. Forbisher's nephew and all of fourteen. He'll take care of Master Jeremy just fine."

I went down to breakfast and, much to my surprise, found Graham over his coffee, his newspapers shoved aside, his attention fully on Helena.

She clearly was arguing with him. The only words I heard were *dinner* and *preservation,* but when she saw me, she snapped her mouth shut. "Good morning, my pet. How did you sleep?"

Graham harrumphed. "I hope better than I."

I let his implications slide. "I slept well. Like a rock."

"Really?" he frowned. "I'd say the rocks hit you"—he pointed to his lower lids—"right here."

"Yes, my dear," Helena joined him in his scrutiny. "You do appear rather piqued. Could you be getting Jeremy's cold, I wonder?"

"Yes, I might." I moved away to the sideboard and selected bacon and a poached egg. As I took my seat, Forbisher appeared and poured my tea. I thanked him and he nodded. The less he said to me, the better he seemed to like it. I felt downhearted. Some people, I supposed, you could not win over—not with a smile, let alone an explanation.

I let my shawl drop to the back of my chair and took a few hearty sips of my tea. Its strength warmed me, even if it did nothing for my growing case of nerves.

"You should dress more warmly for the north," Graham grumbled, his eyes slithering down my throat to my breasts. "That dress, charming as it is, might do for today, but not beyond. Perhaps, Helena, you could take Vanessa into your dressmaker in Darnley and purchase a few woolens for yourself and her."

170

"Absolutely not!" I put down my fork with a thud. "I'll not accept your charity."

Helena put her hand on my arm. "My dear girl—"

"No, Helena. You didn't like charity. Neither do I."

"But I took it."

"You had no choice. You were a child. A blood relative."

"For God's sake!" Graham almost yelled. "Pay me back, then. From your commission on the portrait. I will not have you ill in my household and that's final!" On that, he thrust down his napkin and stalked from the room.

Helena put her napkin to her mouth, and I was not sure if she hid a smile or surprise.

"Well, Vanessa, shall we go when you have finished Graham's sitting at eleven?"

"I won't do it."

"Yes, you will."

I glared at her.

She smiled knowingly. "You don't remember how difficult Chadwicks can be when they want their way, do you?"

Oh, I remembered. I remembered how Charles would pout if I wished to leave some gathering earlier than he had planned. I remembered how his father would hound the staff if his coffee were too strong or his whiskey and soda too weak. I had not seen as salient a streak in Graham, but I feared nurturing it.

"Very well. I will go."

"Wonderful. I have not had the chance to visit my dressmaker in so long. No money, you know." She stirred her coffee absently. "How I'd love to have just a little to enjoy a few pleasures. A good horse from a decent stable in town. A carriage of my own. I hate so hiring cabs all the time. One never knows who has inhabited them before you. I don't long for much more. Perhaps a new hat from my old milliner, Germaine on Bond Street. I get so tired of refashioning my own netting or dashing about for the best price on decorative feathers. I would adore being able to hire another upstairs maid, too. I need more help but have so little money. Meanwhile, Irene has been a dear, but she is getting on, almost sixty now, and her rheumatism gets worse daily."

Throughout her monologue, I sat silent. My anger gone, assuaged by hearing the woes of another, I found myself concentrating on Helena's predicament. She was so unlike me. She had no talent she could ultimately turn to earnings. No proclivity to take a position in a shop. No loved ones—close loved ones—to work for or worry over as I did Jeremy. She had only a closed little life—her small but respectable house, her elderly but crippled housekeeper, her limited and limiting charities, and . . . nothing else.

"How have you stood it all these years?"

She stared at me a moment. "I could say it is habit. Born of routine. From the cradle, one does what one is told. Particularly here in England. Particularly if one is female and orphaned. One takes one's pleasures where they are apparent, and then too soon one discovers time has sealed one's future. The die is cast and escape to other worlds has been cut off by one's own habits. Youth goes and, with it, boldness. Hope shrivels."

"If it is any comfort at all, I think I have seen this malady afflict other women here in England."

"I agree. Women have taken such a back seat in this society. Why, only recently, Parliament passed a law which allowed a married woman to control her own money. Outlandish, if you ask me. We are no more than chattel here. You know it, firsthand."

"And I escaped."

"And at what price, I ask you? I know any number of women who find themselves swept off their feet by

172

the charms of English dandies, and what do they get with their marriage certificates? A drafty castle. A brood of children with the obligatory heir and a spare! And the right to order about a bunch of unruly servants! Not my cup of tea, I'll tell you!"

"No? I can't speak for the drafty castle or the unruly servants, but I do know you would have enjoyed children, Helena."

She went still, her mouth drooped. "Yes," she whispered, "how I would have loved a child. A little boy. With black hair and—"

I smiled into her tormented eyes. "Black eyes. A Chadwick child, for certain." I put my hand over hers and squeezed it in friendship.

She shivered. "Yes, a Chadwick. We seem to be a dying breed, my dear. Your Jeremy is the last. And yet, we Chadwicks were once so prolific Queen Anne proclaimed in court how envious of our many sons she was. Here we are reduced to Graham and Jeremy. I always was astounded that Charles didn't conceive with you sooner."

"Charles kept himself very busy." The words escaped my mouth before I analyzed their outrageous veracity. Yet Helena—bold and honest as she was—continued the conversation without a moment's pause or castigation.

"Oh, I am quite sure you did your duty by Charles, my dear." She patted my hand repeatedly. "Yes, yes. And as we know, he did his. Although not always in your bed. That Hamilton-Fyfe woman made him the talk of London and Rome for many seasons. God, how crass can one woman be!"

"We saw her in Southampton at the hotel. Did Graham tell you?"

Helena lifted her brows. "No. He did not. Why is she here?"

"Visiting her parents, I assume."

"And how do they both fare, the count and his

wife? How does she look? Sickly? Thin?"

I tilted my head. Was that another example of Helena's defense of the family honor? Wishful thinking, perhaps?

"No, not sickly. But hateful. Toward me. She saw me during dinner and she—"

"Yes? She what?"

"She and I did not speak, but I could tell she still holds me responsible for her failure with Charles. She loved him."

"Pah! She did nothing of the kind! She enjoyed his body as he enjoyed hers. She gave; he took and returned to her a knowledge of her own appetites. It is simple. She embellished what they had together with a veil of romantic drivel. Do not fool yourself, Vanessa." She shook a finger at me. "That woman had an abnormal desire to capture Charles. Foolishness! No one could capture Charles. Not you. Not her. Not any playmate Charles ever had. He was incapable of loyalty. Spoiled from the cradle by a spoiled father, Charles was incapable of loyalty to woman or man. Incapable."

Stuck to the chair by the power of her revelations, I felt tears form in my eyes. "How I wish I'd known."

"Don't you think we all wish the same?" she whispered.

"How well do you know Margaret?"

Helena shrugged. "Well enough to say she was too innocent for her audacity." She sipped her coffee. "Why?"

"She may have tried to threaten me."

"Explain yourself, my dear."

"While we were in the hotel in Southampton, I received a threatening note. It told me to go home. I could not imagine who could have done so bold a thing. Neither could Graham."

"My God, you showed it to Graham? What did he say?"

174

"To ignore it. He felt it of no consequence. He was alarmed when we saw her, but he generally did not think her capable. Then, of course, we got to London and that terrible man accosted me in the Mews. Afterward, I felt it must be he who sent the note."

"And do you still think it is he?"

"It must be so. I've had no other incidents. But I must count as an additional threat the other note."

Helena put her hand to her throat. "What other note?"

"The one which was delivered in the morning mail a few days after my attack."

"Good God, Vanessa! Why have you not told me of this?"

"I wished to forget it. With so much else to think of, I did forget it—for a while."

"Did you tell the inspector?"

"No. Graham persuaded me that it is a family matter. An old grudge. I think he is right."

I didn't fully believe it was as innocent as I made it sound, and I could tell by the look on her face that Helena didn't, either.

"Family matter, indeed. Old grudges have a way of making for mayhem, my dear."

"That man from the Mews is not here. Margaret is not here. Neither is Atherton."

"Atherton? What in God's green earth has Atherton to do with this?"

"I found her going through my things the first night we were here. I thought she might be in search of jewels or trinkets to pawn. In my fear, I wondered if she might seek the messages and destroy them."

"And why would she do that?"

"I have no idea. But I did find it odd, unsettling, too, when I learned from the employment agency she came from that she was once in service to the Hamilton-Fyfes."

"My lord," Helena breathed. "I had no idea. You

175

went to the employment agency? My, my. You are resourceful. So that's where you were when you became lost. Clever girl to look up the agency. What did you do? Talk to the other servants?" I nodded and she grinned. "How utterly fascinating."

"Yes. I was also surprised to learn that you yourself had given her a reference. How do you know her, Helena?"

"Why, from Lady Stafford, of course. Carolyn is one of my oldest and probably one of my few remaining friends in Yorkshire. She adored Atherton, who was in her employ for years. Caro claimed Atherton was quiet, efficient, and utterly capable. I am amazed at Atherton's breach of ethics. I shall tell Graham, of course. You did, didn't you?"

"No. To be quite honest, I had forgotten about it until now. What with so many things happening, especially the event in the Mews, I have forgotten much."

"Well, I should say so! And quite rightly, too. Don't think another thing of it. Go and earn your commission, will you, my dear? I shall meet you in the great hall at ten minutes past the hour, and we shall enjoy a nice ride into town in our very own phaeton. I know a lovely little tearoom where we can have a delightful luncheon. And we shall have a jolly time."

"Good. I will see you later."

She rose to leave. I bid her goodbye but watched the doorway for long minutes after she'd disappeared.

What was it about the conversation that nagged at me?

I tried to recall every word, every nuance. But whatever the source of my discomfort, I could not find it.

I shook my head and picked up my fork to finish my breakfast. To confront Graham alone, I needed all the fortitude I could gather.

Shouts in the hallway made me turn my head. When the double doors burst open, I could make no sense from the din created by Forbisher trying to talk above the cries of Lucile.

"Mrs. Chadwick," the somber man presented himself before me, "if you will come with me, please . . ."

"Tell her, tell her . . ." Lucile cried.

Forbisher trained haughty blue eyes on the girl.

"You are too excited, Lucile. Calm yourself. I cannot relate any information if you are comporting yourself in this manner."

"Whatever manner it is, Forbisher, tell me what I need to know."

"Your son, ma'am—"

I rose from my chair.

"—has had a riding accident."

Lucile cut him off. "On the southern meadow beyond the path through the woods . . ."

"Lucile!" Forbisher hated the girl usurping his power.

Feeling an aversion to the rivalry here, I stepped between them. "Forbisher, what is his condition? Where is Jeremy? Was your nephew with him?"

"Yes, ma'am. Your son is fine, just a little shaken. He's in the servants' parlor, ma'am, having cocoa. My nephew is a good boy, ma'am, and would not allow your son to be hurt, ma'am."

I rounded on Forbisher and scanned his now-concerned face. "I would expect so, Forbisher. For Jeremy would never hurt Mike nor anyone else here. Have you told Lord Darnley?"

The chastised butler shook his head. "No, ma'am. Lord Darnley left the house a few minutes ago rather in a huff. I have no idea where he is."

"Very well. Show me the way to the servants' parlor, Forbisher. And quickly, if you will. Lucile, find Simpson and send her to me."

Lucile curtsied and hurried off. Forbisher, his posture a little less erect, led me out into the hall, down the staircase, and through the Georgian foyer to the third wing of the house, the Restoration.

Not having been here too often, I didn't remember how dingy it was. With all the fraying upholstery and dust-covered draperies, the Restoration wing had been aptly named because restoration was what it needed for itself, certainly. Yet, I took only cursory notice, my mind preoccupied with laying my hands once more on my son. Indeed, I followed Forbisher so closely, he had to pick up his pace to accommodate me. He almost flew down the servants' stairs, along a dark corridor, and into a room warm and cozy from a huge fire going in the wall fireplace.

At the long, planked glossy table sat Jeremy, laughing and joking with the older stable boy, Mike. Both clutched large cups of cocoa. I could tell from Jeremy's demeanor that whatever the nature of his accident, he was feeling well now. I breathed more easily and approached them calmly.

Mike stood immediately, looking for all the world like a long, skinny jackrabbit. He swallowed once, twice, then licked his lips. His blue eyes, so like his uncle's in color, were unlike his uncle's in the wealth of emotion they held.

He could hardly keep from crying. Tears swam in his eyes.

"Good morning, ma'am," he mumbled, casting his eyes to the floor.

I went to Jeremy, who stood up immediately and tried to wriggle away from my seeking hands. Meanwhile, Mike went on.

"It's all my fault, ma'am, it is. I let Jeremy canter. I didn't think we were going that fast, Mrs. Chadwick, not on that meadow. It's flat there, it is, ma'am. I let 'im canter, but old Welshie, the pony, he's too old for going beyond a walk, 'e is. I didn't think a canter was fast enough for Master Jeremy to fall like 'e did."

I put a hand to his sleeve.

"Don't cry, Mike, please. I believe you did the best you knew how."

"Yes, ma'am, I did. I did."

"I know that area of Darnley lands well. The terrain is flat, easy to traverse on a horse." I turned to Jeremy. "Stop wiggling, Jeremy, and let me see you."

I ran my hands over his little body as he mashed his lips together, embarrassed at this motherly attention in front of his bigger friend, Mike.

"I'm fine, I am! I am!"

"Stop stamping your feet at me, young man!"

"I didn't hurt myself. I just fell off Welshie."

"Have you forgotten how to ride so soon? You were on Welshie yesterday and did quite well."

Jeremy hung his head.

"He fainted, ma'am," Mike supplied on a whisper. "He was out for only a second or two, but when 'e fell, 'e must've got a blow on the noggin'."

I stared at Jeremy. "Did you hit your head?"

Jeremy looked at me through long lashes and grimaced. "I was only playing games. I *was*. Mike didn't know."

I glanced over at Mike, who was frowning.

"You fell on your head, Master Jeremy. That was no game. 'E hit 'is head, ma'am. I wouldn't lie to you, I wouldn't."

"Thank you, Mike. Let's see your head, Jeremy."

I ran my fingertips over his scalp and found no lumps or bumps. I set him away from me, my hands on his forearms, and I looked him in the eyes. They were bright and clear. I felt his head. No fever. Certainly, if he had broken any bones, we'd have known it by now. The resilience of youth had saved him a hard lesson. Yet, he had another to learn.

"The fall was severe enough, Jeremy, to make Mike very concerned about your health. If you

179

pretended to faint and were only playing games, then I think you owe Mike an apology. Mike was in charge of you and he thought he was going to get in trouble because you got hurt. You can't do that to your friends! A game is not a game when someone gets hurt. And he thought you were hurt. Go on . . ." I shoved Jeremy forward. "Apologize."

Eyes downcast, Jeremy did his duty by the stable boy. Then he turned to me with trembling lips. "It is my fault. I was going faster than Mike wanted me to. I'm sorry, Mommy."

He ran into my arms and I hugged him close. I smiled over his shoulder at the stableboy.

"Mike, you've done a good day's work here already. I appreciate your care of Jeremy. And you, young man"—I pulled Jeremy away from me and smoothed his shock of hair backward off his face— "you have learned not to play games. Servants are people who deserve our respect, Jeremy. They are often responsible for us. And in many, many ways, they often care for us. As Mike cares for you."

Jeremy was still ashamed and would not move.

Mike checked my eyes, then took my cue and laid a hand on Jeremy's shoulder.

"Master Jeremy, I'm glad you're better. Wouldn't want anything to 'appen to you, I wouldn't. May 'e come with me, ma'am, to rub down Welshie?"

Jeremy, knowing this was a sign of forgiveness from Mike, questioned me with hope in his eyes. "May I please help Mike with Welshie? I'm good as new, honest I am."

A rustling skirt signaled the approach of someone. I looked up at Simpson.

"Ma'am, I'm not sure he should."

I stood up.

"We'll let him go, Miss Simpson. Mike, you bring Jeremy to Miss Simpson at eleven, will you? Thank you. Run along now. Goodbye, boys." I turned to a hand-wringing Simpson.

"Don't fret, Miss Simpson. He has to have some fun. After all, he is a little boy and can't stay cooped up in this castle every day."

"But, ma'am, he should be punished."

"He has already been punished the natural way. For his boldness, he fell. And for his mistaken impression of how one treats servants, he has apologized. If he learns those two things this morning, that is twice as much knowledge as I would demand from all the schoolrooms of the world in one day, let alone one morning!"

She nodded and bit her lip. Unhappy she was, but as I gazed beyond her, I saw a full contingent of servants who stood stock-still in various stages of surprise—some openmouthed, some smiling, some returning my gaze with wide-eyed admiration.

Chapter Twelve

Once more I stood in the forest before the same tree I'd found yesterday. Eager to get on with my practice, I tugged at the arrowheads I'd sunk into my handmade hay-filled target hung on the knob of the old tree trunk. Thankful no one could hear me, I said a few unmentionable things about the quality of my skill. Dazzling sunlight filtered through the massive oak leaves as I struggled and won my way when the arrows came free.

Walking five yards away from the target this time, I took up my archer's stance once more. I had begun quite close, and gradually over the afternoon, as my eye and arm adjusted to the resilience of the bow, I moved farther and farther from my target.

I sighted my target, released my fingers, and watched my arrow fly.

Bull's-eye!

My skill brought a smile of joy to my lips, the first in so long. But I thrilled more to the solitude I had found this afternoon. Jeremy, his riding escapade long over and his lessons completed, was at his nap. And Graham had been called on business matters to York—mercifully before our ride. Helena, claiming she was done in by our morning trip to York and by my rejection of all but two new gowns, had opted for an afternoon of quiet correspondence. I knew, of course, that she was really exhausted by the morning's argument over my liberal treatment of Jeremy.

"You not only let him dine with you as an equal but, my dear, you let him take to riding with the stable boy! If this ever gets out that you are breaking code on such things, why, Graham will be the laughingstock of the countryside. You can't do it, I tell you. You may be American and egalitarian but, my dear, this *is* England and we *are* the leaders of social form."

I had disagreed with her until I grew weary of the fight. Finally, I had quieted her when I looked at my entwined fingers and said, "Helena, I know you have the best interests of the family at heart, but I must remind you, I am who I am and I will not change the way I rear my son because of some codes with which I don't agree."

"But you must! You are one of us!"

"No, my dear, I was never one of you. I was welcomed for my money and sent away because Charles wished to be totally rid of me for some inexplicable reason. I did not then nor will I now uphold a social system which teaches people to be so cruel to one another, all in the name of order."

I knew by the way she turned a shoulder to me that she had been offended. I felt badly she took my independence as an affront, but that was the way it would remain. We spent the rest of our visit in cool, polite conversation about nothing of any importance.

Now I marched forward, took another arrow from my target, and shrugged off the memory of our morning. I wondered if she would broach the subject again.

If she remained vexed with me, her attitude could match Graham's. Since this morning at breakfast, I had seen him only for our sitting. And the latter had been more harrowing than I could have imagined.

Going straight to Graham's study from the servants' kitchen, I was relieved at first over Jeremy's well-being and felt very chipper. Thus, I had forgotten Graham's mood at breakfast and how he had stormed out. So when I arrived at his study door, I halted at the sight of him.

Graham, his hair windblown and his clothing askew, was dismissing Forbisher, who was finishing the story of Jeremy and Mike.

"The upshot is, Master Jeremy is well, my lord."

"Did you call for the village doctor?"

"No, milord. Mrs. Chadwick—"

"Yes, I take the responsibility for that, Graham. Jeremy is unhurt. His biggest bruising came from his ego when he had to apologize to Mike." As I explained, I could feel Forbisher beside me, nodding and smiling.

Graham turned pensive. "Very well, Forbisher. Thank you. You may go."

By Graham's quick intake of breath, I could tell he was still peeved with me from this morning.

"If you wish to skip the sitting, Graham, I will understand."

"No, I do not wish to skip the sitting. I wish to sit now. Let's get on with it!"

"But your clothing is not—"

"I don't care. Paint my face, Vanessa."

I stared at him. "But your expression is not relaxed like yesterday."

"That is because I am not relaxed like yesterday!" He yanked off his waistcoat to reveal a once-starched white shirt. "There, is that better?"

It was terrible. His eyes were hard spots of coal. His jaw was granite. His muscles forged iron. I felt as if I were painting a statue. Throughout the hour, I had to keep reminding myself of my task as an artist. But he had closed himself off from me, barricading the kind gentleman I longed to see and paint. I was in anguish when the hour ended. I knew we had accomplished nothing this morning. Nothing to benefit the portrait and nothing to break the war of wills between us.

But out here in the sunshine and the wind, I had escaped him for the afternoon. Glorious and golden, this afternoon might be autumn's last burst of brilliance before the cold winds of the north swooped into these climes with snow and frosty air.

I took up my quiver and bow and decided to go exploring. Today was an ideal day for it. And I knew exactly where I wanted to go—a place I had discovered on my solitary walks years ago. A place I had longed to sketch and paint. A place more auspicious and inspiring than Darnley Castle. A place older by far than the Chadwick or even the Darnley lineage.

I left the copse and headed east toward the sea cliffs. The wind from the North Sea whipped my hair from its coil and sent the mass curling into space. I did not care. I welcomed the freedom. Reaching the edge of the cliff, I looked down to the shore. Waves in ten foot walls sailed forward and crashed to the rocky inlet. I took a step and peered downward to look for the cottage Graham had mentioned when he told me of Izzy and Charles. Sure enough, it still stood. Greying and dilapidated, it appeared like an aging sentinel to any craft that might brave the inlet's rocky shore.

I turned and sought the path up the hill. Winding through berry bushes and scrub, the path was rocky and quite steep. I placed my feet securely before taking each new step. If I fell here—as local legend told many had—few would know, let alone be able to save me from a swift drop over the cliff to the rocks below. But I was not afraid. My father, who had taken me on excursions to the Dakota territories and Kansas, had also seen fit to take me cave exploring. When one knew how to survive in the darkness, one could accomplish wonders in the sunlight. Naturally, I reached the top easily.

Proud of myself, I marched upward, and facing the sea, excitement mounting in my breast, I closed my eyes. Fully ready for the treat I'd offered myself, I opened my eyes and pivoted.

There she was. As thrilling, as majestic as she had been when she'd been built more than one thousand years ago. The last surviving complete Viking fort in the British Isles. Tall and spare, made of irregular sharp stones set one atop the other in a symmetrical patchwork, the walls reached for Valhalla. Never, not even in the daunting aspirations of Gothic Christian cathedrals, had I seen such striving, such yearning to be one with the heavens.

"In many churches," came a familiar rich voice from behind me, "I feel unimportant."

I knew it was Graham. I closed my eyes, no need to turn to hear him better.

"But here, I always see in the structure of these stones a nobility which renews my belief in mankind. Do you think they knew they would display that in their architecture?" He drew quite near.

"Like a portrait, architecture displays the humans who inspire it. They knew." I turned my head as Graham came to stand beside me.

Dressed in a grey business frock coat and contrasting pants of black, he seemed as if he had just returned from his meeting in York. If it were possible, his whole demeanor showed greater signs of stress than this morning.

He stuck his hands in his pockets. "I had no idea you liked to come here. I would have suggested it if I had known."

"Why? It seems I needn't tell you where I would like to come on my retreats! God, Graham, I do not know where to find solitude."

His whole body sagged. "You are displeased with me, I'm sad to see. I cannot spar with you today. I have had too many worries this morning—Jeremy and my fleet first among them. I shall leave you to your solitude."

He turned instantly and I felt the lack of his

person. I had hurt him deeply. I could feel the pain he felt and my heart split in two. He had invited me here to England, met me at the dock, treated me like an honored guest—No! a worthy relative. And I had been rude.

I hurried after him. As he began the descent I called to him, and when he paused, I managed to catch his sleeve.

"Oh, Graham. I apologize. I do not want you out of sorts with me. You know the reason I seek to be alone. I like your company too much. There, I said it. If you would like to accompany me to the top of the tower, I would like it. But you must promise me one thing."

"Name it."

"While we are there, you must speak only of pertinent things—the sun, the sky, the scenery. No business, no family troubles. Let us enjoy the moments together, Graham."

He smiled an iota, a sad expression. "I would like that, too, my dear. Just the joy of the moment."

He smiled more fully now and reached out his hand. I took it, and together we trudged back up the path and into the fort. Inside the front arch, a huge hole in the roof let streams of sunshine light our way.

"A noble place, I always thought," Graham said. "I can see them sitting here conferring—"

"Or here"—we stood beside a central pit—"cooking their game."

I stepped over a fallen wall to what had been the inside of the main hall, where the ravages of time had dimmed but not obliterated an etching of mythical animals in the stone.

Graham turned and grasped my hand. "Let's climb to the tower."

Up the steep, winding stairs, we walked until daylight once more broke through the solid stone walls. We walked upon the battlements and peered over the edge to the cliffs and shore below.

I pulled back. "Oh, the height makes my head spin."

"Don't look down. View only the horizon." He stood beside me and there, with the sun upon his golden hair and bronzed countenance, with his exquisitely perfect profile offered me, I let my eyes enjoy the view.

He snapped his head around. His eyes met mine. I tried to turn away but couldn't.

"What business troubles do you have?"

"You break you own rule, my dear. No business, remember?"

"Tell me. I would know your sorrows."

"Two of my fleet ran aground in a violent storm off Madras last month. Fifteen hands were lost. All good men."

I bit my lip. "Are the ships seaworthy at all?"

"The most recent message came with a British troop ship two days ago. My crew is attempting repairs, but the major damage was to the hulls. God knows if they'll be able to hold ballast."

"Have you funds to replace them?"

"We shall see."

"You mean, you'll know after the will is read."

"Precisely."

He would have walked away.

"Don't go." I reached out and drew him back. He would not look me in the eye.

"Please tell me about the will. What do you know of its contents?"

He shrugged. "Not much. Darian Osgood, Father's solicitor, came to me soon after Father died and told me who was named in the will. Father made a codicil which stipulated that everyone and anyone named in it must be present, or the will could not be read. Darian told me to make sure you came. We have postponed the reading of the will until you could arrive." His dark, bleak eyes met mine. "I praise my father for his plan. I knew of no way to ever see you again."

"You could have come to New York."

"You would have turned me away."

"Yes, you're right."

"I could not bear it, Vanessa. I would rather do without the sight of you for eternity than have you turn me away or worse, once again, have to leave you against my will."

Sweet words, sweet, sweet man. How could I deny how I cared for him? Needed him. Wanted him. I mouthed his name.

Before my mind knew my body's actions, my hand was on his arm, his cheek, his nape. His body melted against mine and his lips took mine, once, twice, a thousand times. In a thousand different ways—gently, fiercely, silently, quickly.

I surrendered to the raging whirlwind that swept through my mind and body. Circling his body with my arms, I let my fingers define his strong back. This was a man. And for now, he was mine.

"Vanessa, darling . . ."

His mouth traveled my eyes, my cheek, my throat. He groaned in animal need, and as he trailed hard kisses down my chest, I leaned back and let him work his will. I let him . . .

I let him unbutton my bodice, push down my chemise, lift one aching, begging breast from beneath, and suckle endlessly there.

Ahhh, God. I had never known such spendor, such wild anticipation.

My head fell back, and as he gripped me by the waist and steadied me, I let him bare the other breast and claim that orphaned one with hot, moist lavings of his tongue. I let him lift me in his arms and take me to some place where he sat and curled me on his lap. I let him murmur against my mouth of his delight in my large, round red nipples, my downy skin, my succulent lips.

I let him bend me back against a sun-warmed stone, raise my skirts, and run his hand up my thigh to the juncture of my legs. I let him place his whole palm against the burning heat of my core and gently circle and press, circle and press.

I moaned and opened my legs wider. He shifted so I lay fully back against the stone. His hand left my center and I cried to have him back.

"Shhh, sweet love, I'll not leave you. I mean to give you more."

He peeled down my undergarments, and when the branding power of his bare hand met the savage heat of my most private skin, I writhed in splendid surrender. His fingers probed, separated, toyed, and stroked my flesh. He found some tender nubbin that had me reeling and reaching for him and something, something . . .

"I know what you want," he whispered against my ear, then put his lips to mine in a luxurious kiss.

"You. You!" I murmured, grasping his nape to bring him close and tease his mouth with mine.

"Only me."

He pressed himself against me. He was hard and hot. He worked at his clothing. And I knew what came next.

I sobbed. "Don't let this end, *please.*"

He paused, only a second or two, but enough for me to register his surprise. He lay his body fully against mine and, with one urgently tender thumb, teased my breasts until they cried for the searing ministrations of his mouth. At the same time, he ground himself against me. I arched off the stone.

"Ahhh, Graham, this is torment."

His burning eyes met mine, his molded mouth smiled. "No, sweet, this is the door to paradise. Welcome me, sweetheart. I would show you."

I shook my hair back and rubbed my breasts against his massive chest, my loins against his marvelous hips, and in that moment, I offered up every ounce of my being to his care. He shifted and the iron might of his body invaded mine. Inch by tormenting inch, he slid inside me.

"Beautiful woman," he murmured. "Here is heaven."

I whimpered at his fulfilling girth and urged him deeper. I kissed his forehead where beads of perspiration formed. I kissed his cheek, and then as he began to leave me, I clutched at his arms.

He caught my mouth with a ravenous kiss, then thrust back inside me. I groaned. He repeated the languorous, driving motions while I swallowed and sighed, undulated and sought his mouth for kiss after trembling kiss.

But then the pressure of my need seemed to spin through my body like a relentless storm. I gasped and called his name. He thrust faster, surer, harder. My very soul seemed to rise somewhere above me. He came with me, and we soared into some breathtaking realm where passion formed every essence of heaven.

I lay panting in his arms. He rested his body against mine and his face against my throat. Finally, minutes or perhaps hours later, I stirred. He raised his head and his black eyes probed mine. His fingertips outlined my lips.

"Your mouth is swollen with our kisses. Do you hurt?"

"No, not anywhere. I feel—I feel wonderful."

"Exactly my thought." He smiled broadly and dipped his head to take a last lavish sample of both nipples. I could not cease watching him as he tenderly raised my chemise and adjusted the lace straps on my shoulders. Then he clamped my shoulders and placed a kiss at the juncture of each arm, at the base of my throat, and on my jaw.

When he pulled his body from mine, I moaned at his departure. He threw me a smile, smoothed my wrinkled skirts, and worked at his own clothing until he stood before me, his body tall and Norselike in the blinding sun.

"Come, darling, it's time we went back."

I took his outstretched hand and stood, but suddenly shy, I could not look at him. He put an index finger to my chin and raised my face.

"I am not sorry. Neither should you be."

Sorry!? How could I tell him that my most vibrant emotion at the moment was not sorrow but surprise at my utter insatiability?

Chapter Thirteen

We descended the mountainside hand in hand, until we reached the edges of the garden. Then Graham took my arm as if we had been merely walking. As the castle loomed closer and closer, I felt the world—the real world—descend on me, suffocate me.

What had I done? Why had I transgressed my own rules when I knew pain would only come of it?

I took my arm from Graham's.

He reached for me. "Vanessa?"

Lucile burst from the conservatory doors that opened onto the garden.

"Oh, ma'am, ma'am, please come! It's Master Jeremy, ma'am, milord. We can't find him! Miss Simpson has been searching for you!"

I handed over the bow and quiver to Lucile, drew myself up, and tried not to panic. "Jeremy, gone?" I picked up my skirts. "Where is Miss Simpson?"

"In the drawing room with Forbisher and MacCarthy, ma'am. The two men have been searching high and low for you, milord."

All three of us hastened inside. When Forbisher and MacCarthy saw us, Miss Simpson turned to face Graham and me.

"Oh, ma'am"—she was sniveling back tears—"I can't find him. I've looked high and low. He's supposed to be napping."

"Where were you, Miss Simpson, that he got away?" Graham asked her.

She fidgeted with her handkerchief. "I was taking a spot of tea, my lord, in the servants' kitchen. I usually do that while Master J—"

"Yes. yes. Forbisher, did you check the stables?"

"Yes, sir. Mike hasn't seen the boy."

Graham turned to me. "Where would he go, Vanessa?"

My mind did cartwheels. If we were home—if we were in my parents' home—he would be in the stable, badgering our groom to let him feed sugar to the horses. But here—here—where would he go for adventure?

I turned to Simpson.

"Was Jeremy dressed when he lay down for his nap?"

"No, ma'am. I had him take his knee pants and shirt off just like I always do, ma'am. I had him don his nightclothes."

"And are his pants and shirt now gone?"

"Well, ma'am, I didn't notice."

"He won't go far without his clothes," I told the others, then pivoted for Eliza's wing.

We went, all five of us, through the castle, down the length of the cloister, and up into the wing where my apartments were. We reached the solar and I turned for Jeremy's door.

It was closed.

"I left the door open," said Simpson.

I paused and put my index finger to my mouth.

Gently, I pulled the latch and pushed open the heavy wooden door. The room was dark, the drapes drawn against the brilliant sunshine. But there under the covers, unmistakable in the dimness, was a tiny body, the face turned from the door, the breathing not quite steady.

I tiptoed in and stood over Jeremy's bed.

"It's no use," I whispered. "We know you went out. Want to tell us where?"

At my first words, his little body had frozen. But as he turned, he vibrated with fear. His face, when he dared to look me in the eye, was crushed in trepidation.

"I didn't do anything—"

"I'm glad to hear it. Stand up."

He did, and I had all I could do not to laugh. He wore his knee pants and a very wrinkled white shirt. He hung his head.

"Tell us where you went? And how you got in and out without any of the staff seeing you?" But, of course, as soon as the words were out my mouth, I had deduced where he had gone.

He lifted an arm and pointed toward my room.

"Did you take a candle?"

He nodded, not daring to look at me.

"What did you find?"

His head came up, and his hand defined something huge and round. "A spider, this big!"

I bit my lips.

"Anything else?"

"Mushrooms! And slimy black stuff!"

"I thought you were going to wait for me to take you?"

"I know. But I thought it would be all right because you'd know where I was."

"Well, we didn't. Look at me. That's because you didn't tell us, but more importantly, you didn't ask us. I'm afraid you are going to be punished for this, young man."

He shuffled his feet, took a glance at the assembled adults, and hung his head once more. "Yes, ma'am."

"You are confined to your room for the rest of the day! Dinner will be here as well. Miss Simpson will be with you the entire time."

I turned and Graham was smiling at me, even if the rest of the staff seemed vexed with a boy's misadventures. We left Jeremy with Simpson.

As Forbisher and MacCarthy departed with tsks and mutters to each other, Graham came to stand before me in the solar.

"I'm off to complete my paperwork. I will see you at dinner." He kissed my temple. "It's so good to have you here, my darling. You put this old house right."

I watched him go and wondered miserably how something that had seemed so right minutes ago could now make me feel so guilty.

"I do wish Graham and Darian would hurry. Dinner will be ruined." Helena scowled as the ormolu grandfather clock struck the half hour. She turned to offer a compensatory smile to her guest. "I do apologize, Blanche. Graham has many problems these days."

"Do not distress yourself on my account, Helena," declared the stately brunette in the ice-blue satin with the wealth of Valenciennes lace at bosom and wrists. "Mother and Daddy and I had a leisurely tea this afternoon."

She smoothed the gown that needed no more ministrations to enhance her noticeable beauty. Her pale skin, her clear brown eyes, her youth, her social grace, her status, all combined to make her the epitome of English womanhood. In contrast, I felt shabby in my two-year-old emerald silk. I inhaled and admitted to myself that poverty might be honorable, but it is not always acceptable. Or pleasant.

I put down my sherry. "Please tell me about your new Preservation Society."

Serenely, our guest arched her thin, perfect brow. "Are you interested in such efforts?"

I couldn't help but notice the surprise in her voice. What did she think? That so-called scarlet women had no other interests but sordid ones? I overlooked her tone.

"Yes, I was a staunch supporter of the Knickerbocker Historical Society. You may have heard of its efforts."

"Yes, indeed I have." Captivated now, she leaned forward in her chair. "We here in Yorkshire have some knowledge of the Knickerbockers. You saved quite a few artifacts from destruction a few years ago."

"Yes, and a patroon's cottage which dated from the seventeenth century along the Hudson."

"We would like to do the same here. We fear that what time does not destroy, man often does."

"Our biggest problem in New York was convincing enough people to donate enough money in time to save the best buildings."

"We have the same problem. Only worse, I shall say. Yes, much worse. We have few wealthy families left in York these days. Few noblemen have the means." For a moment she looked at me with those bright doe's eyes, then glanced away.

I could read her mind. She knew I understood firsthand the plight of English noblemen. Saddled with decaying castles, unproductive estates, and extravagant life styles, England's peerage was falling into financial ruin. There were few means to save it. Most, as my husband had, sought brides with rich dowries. Many, as my husband had, sought rich American brides. A few chose their brides for other reasons in addition—for their beauty or their vivacity. Some chose a woman they loved. From what I knew of them, one or two were happy with their choices. But they, too, learned, as Charles and I had, that money does not make marriage the solution.

I shook myself back to the topic at hand.

"The irony is, the less money you have to save things now means more is needed later."

"I am well aware of that," Blanche sighed. "We were unable recently to save a miller's cottage on the outskirts of York. We lost it to an industrialist who wanted the site for his factory."

"We encountered a similar problem in New York. We saved our building, though."

"What would you say was the most important factor in that?" Blanche asked eagerly.

"Persuasion of the local politicians by one gentleman whose wife served our society. She told her husband to tell the mayor he would either assist in saving the edifice or not receive a contribution for his next campaign."

Blanche laughed gaily. "Oh, that's wonderful! Do you suppose you could come to our meeting Monday? Helena offered to hostess it here. Graham did say it was all right, didn't he, Helena? Yes . . . well, I would love for you to tell us more stories. Particularly like that one. Say you will come. Please."

Monday. The reading of the will was Tuesday—and I was to be here a while to complete Graham's portrait. I glanced at Helena, who arched one brow at me.

"Well, my dear? Will you come?"

"I don't think I could add much."

By the look on her face, I could tell that Blanche understood the totality of my problem. "I think you would add immeasurably. You would give us hope and courage to get our men involved, as you and your friends did in the Knickerbockers. Besides, it would be most appropriate for more than one reason that you attend. You see, our next effort is to save the Viking fort on the cliffs here on Darnley land."

"Really?" I shifted in my chair. The very mention of the place renewed scintillating memories of this afternoon. "How wonderful."

"That old place?" Helena laughed. "I thought we'd given that up as too costly."

Unable to sit, I rose and crossed the room to the fireplace. I had spent the past few hours reliving every moment at the fort. Every caress. Every kiss. Every unspoken emotion.

Blanche continued. "No matter that it will cost a fortune. It will be worth every penny. Why, it must be at least a thousand years old. Daddy says he knows a don at Cambridge who dates it from 792! Can you imagine? I think the fort and its history is so romantic. What do you suppose those Vikings looked like? I see them as tall and blond and very big."

I swallowed. Just like Graham. I turned back to Helena and Blanche.

Blanche was gushing forth. "So much more appealing than what I hear the Saxons looked like—"

"Short and squat, I assume." Helena sniffed in obvious distaste for the entire subject. Clearly from her tone, the Preservation Society ranked as one of Helena's *duties*.

Blanche, poor thing, truly prized the society and now looked cowed. Helena could be cruel at times.

I sought some diversion for us all and nodded toward the piano. "You play, don't you, Blanche?"

"Certainly."

"Would you please?"

"Oh, oh, I—I really must decline. I haven't practiced in weeks, really. I—"

"No matter, I will."

Good God, anything to occupy my mind and body. Anything to avoid discord. Anything to avoid talk of the fort!

I sat on the piano stool, arranged my skirts, then flexed my fingers. I had not played in over a year, but I did not let that deter me. "Chopin, I think," I announced more to myself than anyone else. And then I began one of his polonaises.

I abandoned myself to the demands of the work, the rhythm of the music, the joy of its rendering. God, the freedom of it, the feel of it, flowed from my fingers through my body, and I was captured, enraptured. . . . Just like painting or sketching or making love . . .

Without knowing it, I had concluded the piece and sat with my hands in my lap as the sound of clapping filled my ears.

"Marvelous! Wonderful!" One booming male voice rose above the other accolades.

Suddenly, my hand was being raised and kissed, and I looked up into the round, beaming face of my old friend, Darian Osgood.

I went straight to his arms. "Darian! My goodness, how I have missed you!" I tried to pull away to view his ruddy face but he squeezed me one more time. I laughed. "You'll squeeze the breath out of me!" I chuckled.

He finally pulled away, and his jolly blue eyes ran over my features like a fast-running brook. "Darling Vanessa! You've grown lovelier than I remember. And as I remember, you were a pretty girl." He chucked me under the chin as he used to do. "Now, you rival all the famous beauties of Europe!"

"Darian! You are making me blush!"

He put one arm around my waist as Graham stepped forward.

"Let me do the honors, Darian." Graham's black eyes settled on mine for only a second, but they were kind and sweet and full of promises. Nonetheless, he turned to perform his duties.

"You remember my cousin Helena, Darian. And of course, Lady Blanche Margrave, the Baron of Dunwiddy's daughter."

Darian stepped forward, greeting each woman with a cheerful smile and a kiss on the hand. Graham himself took Blanche's hand and shook it, not having seen her before dinner because of his meeting with Darian.

"Yes, yes," Darian went on minutes later as he settled himself on the Italian settee. "I saw your father, Lady Blanche, just last month in Edinburgh."

"Yes, Mr. Osgood, that sounds to be about the time that my parents were returning home from a month in the north at their lodge."

Graham handed Darian a glass of whiskey, then walked toward the fireplace with his own glass. He turned, one arm slung along the mantel, and his eyes fell over me in approval of my gown. I moved to the opposite side of the room.

Helena asked Darian about his recent expedition to Scotland for the salmon fishing.

Meanwhile, a blushing Blanche addressed Graham. "Before you came in, Vanessa and I were discussing the importance of preserving the Viking fort up on the cliffs, Graham. I know Helena's negative view of that. What do you think?"

I ground my teeth together at the mention of the fort.

"I think it needs some diligent work, Blanche. A cleanup of the floors and the stairs must be your first priority. They're strewn with debris and rocks. Then your major problem will be cutting a path up that cliff so that most can climb without apoplexy!"

Blanche laughed in her most engaging way. It dawned on me that she was flirting with Graham. I took a seat, stilled by the sudden acknowledgment that Graham Chadwick was more than worthy husband material. And with a title, an estate, a business, to say nothing of marvelous charm and looks, many a girl would set her hopes on him.

"What do you think, Vanessa?"

Graham was addressing me.

"Can it be done?" he prodded.

Not quite sure if that was still the line of discussion, I asked, "Cut a path that's safe and easy?" When Graham smiled with those black eyes, I went on. "Yes . . . well, the present path would never do. You would have to make a new one through the forest on the other side of the mountain. There it is

201

less steep. But there, also, is the better view. Being higher, its pinnacle looks down on the courtyard of the fort."

Graham nodded. "But, of course, no one goes through the woods because it is so dense and so much longer."

"But the point of preservation," Helena joined in, "is to save something so people may see it and appreciate it. I think cutting a new path through the woods would serve your purpose more, Blanche."

Forbisher appeared to announce dinner.

Helena rose. "Graham, take Blanche in, why don't you? Darian, you have the honor of taking both Vanessa and myself!"

"I am such a lucky man tonight!"

Darian struggled to get his girth up off the settee as Helena and I smiled down at him.

And for the next two ungodly hours, I kept that smile, wearing it like a leaden mask. While the servants brought food I did not taste. While Helena and Darian chuckled over stories I could not appreciate. While Blanche sat to Graham's right and blushed and giggled and flirted.

And I grew testy.

Blanche and Darian called for their carriages at the same time, and when they were finally led from the drawing room, I sighed audibly.

Helena ran one hand through her hair. "My God, I am going to bed. I have forgotten what effort guests require. Good night, my dears." She smiled at us, picked up her skirts, and sailed away.

I murmured my good night to Graham, rose from my chair, and would have left had he not caught my arm.

"Wait. Don't leave me."

I stared at his cravat. "I must go to bed. I am very tired."

"You won't share a brandy with me? You'll break our custom if you don't."

"I—I can't, Graham. Let me go."

"I need to talk to you, Vanessa. I need to tell you what this afternoon meant to me. How—"

"No. Please, no, Graham. I am so tired. So—"

"Afraid." He stepped closer to me and would have enfolded me in his arms, but I pushed away. "Let me take away your fear. Suppose we simply talk, eh? I'll pour you a brandy and we will sit here, like any other couple, and—"

"No. We are not any other couple. I can't do this. *We* can't do this, Graham."

Paces away from me, he captured me with his mellow voice. "Look at me, darling. That's right. God, I love your eyes."

I groaned and reached for the door.

"Vanessa, wait! I want you to know—"

I paused to open the door and, in that moment, heard him say, "I want to emphasize how well this evening went. It was quite clear to me that Darian remembers you as you truly are and welcomes you as if Charles's accusations had never occurred. And most illustrative of how society thinks these days, Blanche Margrave accepted you, and I think her attitude presages others who will, too."

I spun about, my back to the hallway. "You were not here in the beginning. Blanche did not accept me with open arms, Graham. She balked because she knows. She remembers. Only after I showed her I was not some mindless ninny—some scandalous freak— did she give me the benefit of the doubt. *If* her attitude is any indication of the rest of society's, then were I to venture out into its depths, I would *still* have to prove myself worthy. I do not need the aggravation of it all."

"What of us?" he whispered. "Won't you do it for us?"

I watched him walk forward and I backed away.

He reached for me, but I was quicker and put more distance between us.

My anguished voice created an echo in the stairway.

"There is no 'us.' Today was time out of mind. Forget it and me."

I pivoted and ran! Good God, how I ran!

I stumbled and caught myself, hoisting my skirts higher, higher! Faster, faster, I had to get away!

I reached my room and locked the door. I fell against it, panting for air.

Then the tears came. Copious and hot, they trailed over my cheeks and I wrapped my arms about myself in misery. I threw myself onto my bed and pounded my pillow, thrashed at the mattress. I wept bitterly. I wanted him, I wanted him.

How many times I repeated that refrain I do not know. I only know I was agony itself when strong arms embraced me. When a warm body covered mine. When a moist mouth kissed my hair and whispered words soothed my delirium.

"Shhh, my love, don't cry." Graham turned my head and claimed my lips in a sweet, urgent kiss. "You'll make yourself sick, darling. Don't." He smoothed the hair from my eyes. I hid my face in his neck as he wrapped me closer.

"Oh, Gray, Gray. I promised myself I would stay away from you. . . . I wanted to be resolute. I wanted to be strong and all I am is wanton!"

"You want me?"

I nodded my head and sobbed.

He rocked me in his arms. "Ahh, my love. I want you, too. What else in the world matters?" His hands went to my throat. "I adore you. Your mind, your heart, your body."

He bent me backward, and as if my body acted without my will, I arched up to meet him. I knew what his lips sought. Through the fine silk of my gown and the linen of my chemise, he took the tip of my breast between his teeth, his lips bathing what his teeth gently nipped. Tremors traveled my spine and I moaned.

"I would savor all of your body, darling. I wish to see all of you, sample every charm of you." He kissed me with a ravishing ardor that stole my breath. "Help me."

I could not ignore his plea nor my own rampaging desire. Though his hands would have undressed me, I pushed him away and stood. His eyes glowed like black coals as he watched me slide out of my shoes and then slowly remove my gown, my corset, my petticoat, and my stockings, until I stood only in my chemise and pantalettes.

He stood and discarded his own garments. My eyes enjoyed the sight of broad shoulders with bulging biceps, an expansive chest with a mat of curling blond hair, corded rib cage, lean waist, sculpted hips, sinewed thighs, and upright, naked need.

"Remove your chemise and pantalettes, darling."

I did as I was told. Then I watched him as, in the glowing gaslight, he surveyed every inch of me. "You are a goddess. You deserve far more than this mere mortal can give you."

His words made my eyes flutter even as they made my body pulse to have him inside.

He closed the space dividing us and drew me to the searing fires of his luscious skin.

I felt every cord, every sinew, as my hands claimed his perfection. "If I am a goddess, you are my equal."

He groaned and went to his knees. His hands grasped my ankles and then he began the most marvelous journey, taking me to that same enchanted place I had visited only once in my lifetime this afternoon in his embrace. He bent and kissed my toes, slid his hands up my calves, and squeezed as he kissed each knee. He stroked my thighs and gripped the tops and then—oh, save me—he kissed the juncture of my legs. I buckled but he supported me with two strong hands to my derriere. He murmured of my beauty there and rose to kiss my navel, massage my waist, and lave both nipples with generous swathes of his smooth tongue.

He gathered me up and spread me upon the mattress. With gentle hands he placed me just so, as if he were composing a portrait for his private delight. I watched him through a love-drenched haze. Arms above my head, hair fanned upon the sheets, hips beneath his bold straddle, I burned for him. His fingertips outlined my eyebrows, my cheeks, my trembling mouth, my budding nipples, my stomach, my very center. I bit my lips to keep from screaming down the house.

"Vanessa, my love, I've dreamt so long of how I would learn all of you. The reality surpasses all dreams."

I reached out my arms, aching to receive him. I groaned and he kissed me quiet. I twined my arms around him, wanting to welcome him—all of him—again.

"I can't have enough of you," I told him, and was aghast at my bold revelation.

"Nor I you. But here we shall begin."

His fingers gently parted me; his staff slid securely inside me, and then, then, then, I knew sighing satisfaction beyond my wildest fantasy.

Satisfaction? Ah, God, I knew satisfaction innumerable times that night. So many, in so many varied ways, I could not count. But oh, how I remembered each delicious nuance.

I awoke the next morning after the briefest of sleeps and, in my mind's eye, replayed how Graham had shown me pleasure—no, delight!—time after time. How he had led me into a sensual bliss I had never believed possible.

In one languid moonlit moment, Graham's head upon my left breast, I had told him so.

"I never knew it could be so comforting. So

exhilarating. So exquisitely . . ."

He pulled away to capture my eyes with his own. "Sensual. Yes, if you had not told me as much the other day, I would definitely have concluded it this afternoon when you would not have the kisses end before our final communion." He dipped his head to kiss my nose.

"But I suspected years ago that Charles was not as loving as a husband should be. And I often wondered why you were so receptive to my kisses that one afternoon here at Darnley when we found ourselves in each other's arms. For months afterward, even after I saw you off at the docks, I tormented myself to discover the reason—aside from the obvious one that we cared for each other.

"But now I know that my brother never showed you the truest realms of love between a man and woman. He took no time with you, sweet woman. Thank God, he didn't! That divine task has fallen to me. And I am most eager to show you every aspect of that realm time and time again, my darling. Every aspect."

He had pulled me against his turgid body once more, and from then until the umber hours before dawn, he led me into passion that I not only welcomed but also matched, body and soul.

Still, the rising sun meant discovery, and so he left my arms. As he dressed, he told me he would leave the way he'd come—via the secret stairs.

"I'll return to you that way as well, my love. Tonight and every night." He kissed me with sweet sorrow and disappeared through the crack in the fireplace wall.

I had slept—how long?—perhaps two or three more hours. Now I left my bed to don a robe—without my slippers, courtesy of Samantha, wherever she was—and opened the balcony doors. Another glorious day of sunshine greeted me. I closed my eyes and felt the sun sink into my skin. I ran my fingertips

207

across my mouth. Still tingling from Graham's kisses, my lips curled in the first great joy I'd known in years.

Yes, I admitted in the light of day, I loved this man. Truly loved him. As I had never loved Charles. Never could have loved Charles. My father had been right when he said I would find a worthier man than my husband. Astonishing that it should be my husband's youngest brother!

Eager to see him, to talk with him, to laugh with him, eager to paint his handsome face for all generations to marvel at, I reentered my room and noticed that the fireplace wall had not fully slid shut after Graham left. I walked over and would have stood upon the two hearth stones if something odd hadn't caught my eye.

There caught in the doorway was a splotch of black.

Black fur, white markings.

Still. Silent.

Samantha?

I stepped closer and realized I was right.

It was Samantha, sprawled in death's thrall, her throat slit.

Chapter Fourteen

I tried to scream. No sound came.

Where was Graham? Where?

I ran for the dining room, circling Simpson in the solar. And ran on. On!

"Wait, Mrs. Chadwick! What's wrong?" Her voice died away.

I made the Georgian wing, climbing the stairs on a run. Servants pressed themselves against the walls, a few daring to ask if they could help.

I thrust open the double doors and there sat Graham.

"Gray! Gray! Oh, please, come!"

His chair crashed to the floor as he came to me. Helena rose, wide-eyed, with a frowning Darian at her side.

"What in God name—?" Helena asked, her black eyes wild at the looks of me.

"I need you . . . Oh, Gray, someone . . ." I clutched his arms while tears burned my eyes.

"Someone what, darling?"

"Killed . . . yes, yes, killed Samantha!"

Darian gasped. "The devil, you say!"

I searched Graham's startled eyes.

"It's true, it's true. Come see for yourself, Graham, please."

He stroked my hair down my back and led me to a chair. "Come sit down over here. Darian, get me some spirits from the drawing room, will you, please?"

I heard Helena's skirts rustle as she came closer.

"What nonsense is this about the cat?"

"It's true, I tell you! Her throat is cut. And not there in the secret room, either. They did it someplace else! I can tell from the looks of the body!"

"Here, Vanessa." Graham put smelling salts beneath my nose. He went down on one knee before me and smoothed my hair away from my face behind my ear. I tilted my head into the caress, tears pouring from my eyes at his tenderness. "Don't cry anymore, my dear. That's right. Now, why would anyone kill Samantha? It's prepos—"

"It's obvious she is suffering from a bad case of nerves." Helena returned to her place at the table, then went on conversationally. "Did you know, Darian, our Vanessa has had a terrible time ever since she arrived here in England? What with threatening messages and an attack in London by someone the police inspector called that Jack the Ripper! Why, I tell you, Darian, Vanessa's been in quite a tizzy. No wonder she's overreacting to things."

I rose from my chair. "I am not overreacting, Helena." I wiped the tears from my face and faced Darian and Graham. "Those letters did come to me, one of them when Margaret Hamilton-Fyfe was practically in the next room of the hotel. Atherton did go through my belongings. That horrible man in Abercrombie Mews did attack me! I am not imagining those things! They did happen! And so has this: Samantha is dead. And someone *did* kill her. And placed her there on the threshold of the secret room to frighten me! Go, Graham. Go see Samantha for yourself!"

Graham was staring at me. "Atherton went through your belongings in London?"

"Yes, yes."

"Helena, you told me the woman was sterling!"

"She is. I have no idea why she might be going

through Vanessa's personal items. Perhaps Vanessa asked for a certain item and sent Atherton to get it, hmmm? These things do happen and we forget—"

"I did not forget! I was appalled! But I went out that afternoon to check on her references. She has a few interesting ones. Did you know, Graham, that aside from the Reginald Staffords, Atherton once worked for the Hamilton-Fyfes?"

"What?" Graham shot a look at Helena and back to me. "You went out that afternoon to check on Atherton's references? How did you discover—?"

"Servants know each other's background. They gossip. It was a matter of asking a few questions."

Helena snorted. "You doubt Graham's ability to hire good staff?"

At first confused by Helena's rabid tone, I now grew irritated. "No, Helena. At that point, I was suspicious of anyone around me whom I did not know, because so many threats had come my way."

Graham frowned at Helena. "You did not tell me Atherton was once in the employ of the Hamilton-Fyfes."

"Of what importance was it?"

"So you *did* know she had been employed there?"

"Of course."

"And you still recommended her to me?"

"Good staff is hard to come by, Graham. And you had emphasized how you wanted everything in your new London house in place before Vanessa came. I assisted you in every way I could. That's all. I did my family duty by you, Graham."

"Yes, Helena. You did your family duty." Graham turned and in his face, I saw concern. "Please understand, Vanessa, if I'd known about Atherton's employment history, I would not have hired her." He ran a shaking hand through his hair and could barely look me in the eye. "I will go to your room and investigate this incident."

Darian stepped forward. "If I may come with

you, Graham?"

"Of course, Darian."

I watched them go, then turned my eyes in Helena's direction. She was examining me.

"Recklessness is not the way to capture a man's heart, I'll tell you. There are other ways . . ."

Incredulous, I narrowed my eyes at her. "What *are* you implying, Helena?"

"Implying? I am implying nothing, my dear. I am *telling* you that I know about you and Graham. If I couldn't feel it or see it with my own eyes, I heard with my own ears last night—the two of you whispering here in the hallway. And I gather from the way both of you know about the current condition of the Viking fort and the fact that both of you—in rather disheveled form, I might add—were seen yesterday descending from its heights, you have sampled the delights of its scenery. Hmmm. Imagine trysting in the broad daylight in a dirty old fort! Ahh, Vanessa, you may have been able to fool me before with Charles, but I see you now as you truly are. And you truly are a charlatan. A seductress, just as Charles declared. I never believed it then, but I do now. Graham has had his head turned by you. You do not know, of course, but before you returned, he was as good as engaged to Blanche. Now, just what do you hope to gain by this sordid affair with him, eh?"

Crushed by this revelation about Blanche and Graham on top of all the other problems apparent in this discussion, I remained in place. By her posture and her countenance, I knew Helena had more to say.

She stirred her tea, contemplating its depths.

"Of course, Vanessa, I know what you want: You want the earldom for your boy. And you will do anything, *anything* to get it, even couple with Graham. I am afraid I had you wrong from the start. You are a conniving little American."

She took a sip of her tea and stirred in more sugar. "Except today, there is a vast difference from yesteryear, isn't there, Vanessa? Today, you are a pauper and you *need* this earldom to survive. Well, I tell you, Graham is smart. He isn't fooled by your fakery. He'll have you," she laughed heartily. "He'll take every liberty you offer. All men do, you know. But afterward, they don't marry you. They create some excuse—too young, too plain, too poor. Pah! And Graham won't marry you, either! Imagine! Marry his brother's widow! Ha! The very idea is absurd! No, no, Graham is in need of Blanche. Blanche who has two virtues you no longer possess: She's a virgin, and she has a sizable dowry!"

I reeled with her rejection. Chilled by yet one more Chadwick's incorrect assessment of my character, I opened my mouth to rebut. But what good would it do to defend myself? What good had it ever done? As in years gone by, circumstantial evidence damned me. Helena had evidence. She drew certain conclusions from it. Some of them were true. That she was wrong about most things did not destroy the evidence she had to make right conclusions about other things.

"Convicted unjustly once more, I will not argue with you. I am tired of fighting this family. I never should have returned."

"How true, my dear." She smiled at me, placid in her imperialism. "Graham would have thought of a way to get Darian to read the will without you, regardless of what Uncle Albert demanded."

"Rest assured, I shall never return again."

She sighed. "I am sure you'll be safer in New York, my dear. There, no one has any reason to threaten you. Or . . . do they?"

That salvo hit me squarely in the chest. I could not breathe, but I'd gladly writhe in hell for eons before I'd let her see it.

"I always honored the Chadwick family name, Helena. I valued it and contributed to its power, not only with my money but also with my heartfelt interest. I learned that from my own noble family.

213

But never did I learn to uphold my family if they were wrong. And the Chadwicks have wronged me, Helena.

"I thought you saw that and understood it, because you yourself knew how the Chadwick family—part of the English caste system as it is—could destroy its own members. The Chadwicks must repent of many sins, and hideous disregard for its members' individuality is one. The list began centuries ago, I'm sure. But those I know of begin in this century. First, Charles, in all his perversions, was destroyed by the very name of Chadwick and its so-called glory and power. Izzy, too, I gather. Then there is you. And me.

"But not Graham. Not yet. I pray, not ever. And not Jeremy. I will take him home to America. Far from here. Where a man is judged by what he accomplishes for himself, not by his pedigree and not by some social code that erodes a man or woman's honor before they're out of the cradle. Above all else, I will save my son from the foibles of his family heritage, and I will stand resolute against any attempt to impart the truly scurrilous Chadwicks' nobility and honor."

And then I left her.

"Exactly how severe is this disaster off Madras, Darian?"

Across from me in Graham's study, Darian sat in a wing chair, fingering his watch fob. He shook his head and pressed his lips together.

"I'll tell you, Vanessa . . . " He glanced toward the door where Graham could reappear any second. "He's lost five more hands at the latest report. The most recent word is from the Foreign Office, which got a telegram from one of their men in Calcutta. Graham's crew, like the rest of the natives in Madras, all have typhoid. If they die, *if* he can repair those ships, *who* will he get to complete the run and sail them home?" Darian took a handkerchief from his trouser pocket and wiped his brow. "I tell you, Graham may never recover from this."

"He needs quite a bit of capital to pull out of this, doesn't he?"

"Astronomical amounts, I'd say."

"Will inheriting the earldom save him?"

I knew I'd taken a chance in asking so bold a question. But I gambled that Darian, knowing me and liking me as he did, would overlook my arrogance and give me some hint.

Darian's eyes skittered toward the door. "Barely. If he sells some of the land . . . *If* he can even find a buyer among the gentry, he might make some money. If he sells some of the paintings, the Romneys and Holbeins, he'd do well. He is reluctant to sell the family's priceless acquisitions, of course— and that's a testament to his courage and honor. But an English gentleman must do much to save his family heritage nowadays."

"Yes. Even marry a woman he does not love." I spoke of Charles.

"But Blanche loves Graham, and many times a woman's love makes the marriage."

I swallowed back the black abyss of despair, rose, and walked toward the portrait. Graham, in vague outline, his handsome features in repose, peered back at me. "So, you think they will marry soon?"

"He told you? He asked me not to. Said it would upset you. I see it has. It must be difficult to see people happy in their choice of marriage partner when you thought you had chosen wisely.

"Ah, Vanessa," he sighed. "My God, but you've been done wrong here, my girl. I know you loved that husband of yours. He was a hellion, and while many a girl pined for him, Charles knew his station and his mind. When he sent word that he was marrying an American girl, I tell you, I thought he was totally out of his mind.

Darian paused and frowned. "Charles'd always acted . . . well . . . oddly. But when I met you, I knew Charles had done the finest thing in his life. I could see how you loved Charles. I thought it would make a better man of him. It didn't. He was too used to his pleasures. And after you left, he turned more surly. And when he died, he was a shell of a man. On his deathbed, he told his father how he had wronged you. Charles died a horribly painful death, you know."

"No one has told me, although I would assume he did."

"Yes, the tortures of the damned, excuse me my bluntness, my dear. But, true to form, Charles did not recant his sins. Most of them against you and Jeremy. And he died in abject pain. Syphilis does that, I hear. Makes you suffer unmitigated torment."

I closed my eyes. Syphilis. The disease he earned from his debauchery. I had feared it—for myself and for Jeremy—and had searched for signs of its presence in us both. I had taken two mercury cures to ensure its absence, but when neither Jeremy nor I exhibited any signs of lesions or internal disorders, I thanked God. Meaning that Charles's incubation of the disease had not transferred to us.

Darian went on with his reverie in hallowed tones. "I hate to see you suffer more. Forget I said anything about Blanche and Graham, will you? Nothing is final yet. And normally, I do not give family secrets away."

I faced him. "I know you don't, Darian. I want the best for Graham. He has been kind to me. Inviting me here to hear the will—"

"Well, my dear, he had to! We could not have a reading if you did not come. The way Albert had me write that will of his, the document cannot be read— no title granted, no estate entailed, no monies distributed, not even a brooch bequeathed!—until everyone named in it is assembled here in Darnley Castle."

So it was true. I had to be here. I was named in the will, or Jeremy was. Or both. The old earl had been crafty once more, manipulating people to his ends. I inhaled.

"And there is no way at all Graham could have gotten you to read the will without me?"

"I am paid by the Darnley estate trust, Vanessa. And I am bound by my honor as the estate's solicitor. No, neither Graham nor God himself could change the old earl's stipulation. Why do you ask?"

"Vanessa wonders if I told her the truth, that's why, Darian."

We both turned to see Graham in the doorway, his eyes boring into mine.

"I owe Vanessa an explanation, it seems."

"I think so."

He entered the room, a sheaf of papers in his hands. "Well, then I will elaborate for you, Vanessa. If you had not come, my father stated that no one would ever inherit a penny. The Darnley estate would pass to a charity; the castle would be vacated, sold, and the profit would go to the charity. No one would become Earl of Darnley. The Chadwicks would be turned out into the cold. My father told me so with his dying breath. Darian confirmed it hours later. I have not lied to you, Vanessa."

He turned toward a very uncomfortable Darian.

"Here, Darian. I signed those documents I told you to create yesterday. All three of them. You will see these are my signatures."

Darian rose and took the papers from Graham. "Thank you, Graham. I will look these over before Tuesday."

"No. I want the arrangements final before Tuesday, Darian. And make sure the date stands. Regardless of what the will says, I want yesterday's date to stand on these papers."

"Certainly, Graham. As you wish. I think I will go now. I will see you both Tuesday morning at ten."

I gathered every morsel of courage I ever possessed and spoke my mind. "Darian, please wait. Graham, I am quite distressed by events here in England since I arrived. The death of Samantha this morning is merely the most vile of them all. I wonder if we might have the reading of the will sooner. Monday, perhaps?"

Graham's gaze blistered me with its fire. "Why?"

"Truthfully? I am afraid. For Jeremy more than myself."

"I told you I would keep you both safe."

"I fear you can't, Graham."

Darian cleared his throat. "And I fear what you ask is nigh to impossible, my dear. Twenty-three people must assemble for the reading. Do you know how difficult it is to get twenty-three people to come together at one time in one place? Damned difficult, I'll tell you. Even though you are here—the most difficult person of all of them to get—I can't do it. Not on such short notice. No, I'm afraid you'll have to wait, Vanessa."

"And if I can't?" I was whispering, my eyes on Graham's.

Darian tsked. "Then you know the consequences, my dear. You know the consequences."

We stood for long moments at an impasse. Darian cleared his throat once more.

"I must go, Graham. Send for me if you need me more today. Or tomorrow. But of course, tomorrow is Sunday, and my wife doesn't like me to miss church. Likes to have me in the pew with her, you know."

He shook hands with Graham and kissed me on the cheek.

"Take care, my dear. These things that have happened to you lead me to believe that someone merely wants to see you squirm. If they meant any real harm, they would have done something . . . well forgive me . . . something more terrible sooner than this. Graham runs a good house here. You are safe with him. I will see you Tuesday at ten. By eleven, we

218

shall all be finally free."

He left Graham and me in a void.

I walked to the window and gazed out over the garden. I slowly turned and faced him. His eyes were upon me but I could not read their depths.

"I feel very odd. Samantha's death leaves me strangely calm."

"It follows your normal pattern of reaction to terrible things."

I narrowed my eyes at him. "I suppose you're right. At first, the mind fails to comprehend the horror of things. But after a while, the elements fall into place and reason takes over."

"You accept the occurrence and deal with it." He rounded his desk and sat down. He faced me, his hands steepled before his mouth, his eyes assaying me. "You still want to leave, though. I am amazed. After all we have meant to each—"

"No!" I had one hand up. "No. How much do you think I can stand?" I meant Samantha's death, Helena's misjudgment of me, the man in the Mews, the notes, and now—now!—the knowledge of Graham's impending marriage to Blanche.

"Anything. Everything. Jeremy is worth the price."

"Ahhh, God, yes!"

"I gave orders that your wing is to be guarded round the clock by servants. I tell you, Vanessa, when I left you this morning, the door to the secret staircase was closed. So whoever killed Samantha knows Darnley Castle well. We found evidence that she was killed at the lower door to the secret staircase."

"If what you say is true—and I don't disbelieve you—then the culprit could be any of the staff."

"Except MacCarthy and Simpson, who have never been here before and don't know of the secret staircase. In any case, your wing will be secure. Even the outside entrance to the secret staircase will be patrolled. No one will pass there to hurt you or Jeremy."

"Thank you."

"You're welcome. Naturally, that means I cannot come to you tonight. But then, I would assume you would forbid me the joy of that now, anyway. I detect something in your eyes that makes you wary of me. What is it?"

"Blanche."

He peered at me. It took him a second to make a conclusion. "No marriage agreement exists."

"Yet."

He dropped his hands and clutched the armrests so tightly that his knuckles turned white. "I doubt ever."

"She's lovely, well-bred, and rich."

His eyes blazed. He stood, walked to the window, raked his hair, and cursed profusely.

"And I thought, Vanessa—nay, I dared to hope—that you could love me. Completely love me. What a fool I am! You will never trust a man enough to love again. I see that now. You think I am playing all odds so that—if on the outside chance Jeremy inherits the title and estates—I could marry you and still control the money and the power of the family." He faced me, his visage a ruin of regret. "I was wrong about you, Vanessa. Wrong. I bear you no ill will. You are the product of your past. As we all are. God help us all, as we all are!"

I do not know how I managed to survive the rest of the day, except that I applied myself to numerous chores. I sat in on Simpson's lessons with Jeremy, then read him a story. When rain came and then broke, I sent Lucile to tell Mike to saddle a horse for me and Welshie for Jeremy. My son and I went riding in the crisp air as dark clouds scudded overhead. Graham did not come with us, naturally. But two footmen did. As protection. Though I explained to Jeremy that they came for the outing; and he—God bless him—accepted it.

That afternoon, I took the two footmen with me to

the forest and the three of us tried our best at marksmanship. They were not so skilled as I in archery and I managed to teach them a bit of finesse. They were grateful for the knowledge. I was grateful for the protection and the few spots of laughter.

But I was still frightened. And sad. Desperately sad at my loss of Helena's friendship and Graham's regard. Helena's friendship, I soon decided, was not worth my remorse. She had grown colder these last few years, and whatever the causes, I could not be among them. If she chose to side with family honor instead of seeing things clearly, then she, too, was a child of her past. I could do nothing to change that.

I would soon return to my life in New York. Hopefully, a little more financially secure and a lot more worldly than when I'd left. And I would gladly leave all this pain and anger behind. With some financial backing to salve the wound, thanks to my father-in-law, I would live a better life. An honorable one. Free of the degradation I suffered here.

My only pain now was my unfulfilled love for Graham.

Oh, how right he was! I would never love again. Not after this last revelation of a man's duplicity! This morning I had thought love a possibility. I had embraced it and would have told him of my feelings had not Samantha met her untimely death. Had not Helena told me of Blanche. Had not Darian told me of Graham's desperate need for money.

Luckily, I saw neither Graham nor Helena the rest of the day. I arrived in time for dinner, to be told by MacCarthy that Graham was out and Helena was dining in her room. I ate alone.

I retired early but did not sleep. I heard the footsteps of the house guard outside my door. Saw them from my balcony window. Shivered at the thought that someone might break through. I even went in on tiptoe to assure myself of Jeremy's safety. He slept peacefully. Simpson's door was ajar, and from the sound of her snoring, I could tell she slept as deeply as he.

I awoke the next morning to slashing rain upon the windowpane. Creaky with tension, my bones moved slowly. I went down to breakfast. Despite the fact that it was seven, Graham's and Helena's places had been cleared. Again, I ate alone.

Amazingly, MacCarthy, not Forbisher, appeared as I sat over my second cup of tea. "Lord Darnley instructed me to tell you that he regrets he will not be able to pose for his portrait this morning. He has pressing business to attend to in the village."

"Thank you, MacCarthy. I did not expect to work on Sunday, anyway."

Sunday or any day, I did not expect to work on the portrait ever again!

A commotion out in the hall captured both MacCarthy's and my attention. We looked at each other.

The downstairs maid Mary—young and pretty and out of breath—burst through the dining room door.

"MacCarthy! Oh, MacCarthy, come with me! Oh, Mrs. Chadwick—oh, Lord, I don't mean to frighten you, but—but come to the master's study! The master—the master's—"

I was out of my chair in a shot. Graham? Someone had hurt Graham? Oh, God, no! No! Why? Who? Who would hurt Graham? In his own house? In his study!

I thrust open the doors, MacCarthy close on my heels, the maid right behind.

No one was there. Graham was not there! Thank God, thank God.

The gloomy day cast grey shadows everywhere. The place where sun normally streamed, the place where Graham would usually stand while I rendered his likeness—oh, my God!

Someone had slashed his portrait to ribbons!

Chapter Fifteen

I grasped the handgrip as the coach veered around a perilous turn in the rutted road. Jostled beyond reason, I peered out into the storm that had swept the shire since yesterday. The winds and beating rain chilled me to the bone. I gathered Jeremy closer to me. He squirmed. The toy soldier he held in his hand had failed to amuse him miles ago.

He sneezed and I offered him my handkerchief. As he took it, I prayed for a speedy resolve of my situation. Soon I would be free. Free of this place, my past, and, yes, free of my nemesis. Free of this need to feint and parry with a shadow—a person who had the gall to threaten me while he or she accumulated the nerve to confront me. I hoped I could endure these last score or so of hours, feinting and parrying myself, so that whoever wanted me gone would think me far away. Far away from Darnley Castle, far away from whatever inheritance the old earl had left me or Jeremy, and far, far away from Graham.

Yes, that's what my foe wanted. Graham. I had not realized it until I stood staring at his slashed portrait.

Whoever opposed me was possessed by jealousy. Yes, jealousy was the motive in this masquerade! Whether that jealousy was based on Graham's regard for me and our subsequent relationship, or based on a resentment that by the old earl's will I might be reinstated in society, I had no substantive clues.

Whoever was doing this was clever. Secretive. And now, with the death of Samantha and the destruction of Graham's portrait, my nemesis was turning diabolical. To send old clippings and threatening notes was one thing, but to attack me in the streets and kill my pet was brutal. To ruin my work, slashing the portrait of Graham, I could only take as a warning to him and a threat to me.

My utter frustration in deducing who my foe might be made me shake now with fury. I had been over this time and again. Who had been with me constantly since my arrival? Only Graham. Who had something to gain by my departure? At first, I would have said that it was Graham. But now, knowing what I did about the conditions under which the old earl's will had to be read, I could not point solely to Graham.

Beyond those two questions, I asked myself others. Who could follow me from Southampton to London and onto York? No one I knew of. Who could do it and not be detected by me or Graham? Again, I knew no one, and I believed that if Graham knew, he would have investigated it days ago.

Who, then, knew the castle well enough to place my Samantha in the doorway to the secret staircase? It could be any of the servants, from Bellweather to the scullery maid to the groom, and I had no way of detecting specifically which one of them might carry a grudge against me.

Who would slash my portrait? Again, anyone in the house.

I clutched my son closer. I had no answers except one: I would not be foiled. I knew what I would do to save the situation for myself, Jeremy, and, yes, for Graham. I had made up my mind yesterday morning as I had stood staring at the ruined portrait.

For long minutes, I had shook with fury. Then, I ordered MacCarthy to bring Forbisher to me. When both men appeared, I told the butler to clean the mess and clear the study of all oils and supplies. I vowed that when Graham returned, there would be nothing that remained of me or mine. Nothing.

I ordered my trunks taken upstairs to my apartment. MacCarthy stepped forward and cleared his throat. He now joined his new comrade, Forbisher, in an attempt to have me stay, doing everything short of getting down on his knees to beg me not to go.

"I must, MacCarthy."

"Lord Darnley will be furious."

"So be it."

"But where might I say he can find you?"

"You can't."

"But, ma'am . . ." He flushed a thousand shades of embarrassment, unable as a mere servant to broach family business.

"I know, I know. The will." The infernal will! "Forbisher, please have the coach and four brought round. I'll need the space for my trunks."

The butler's fear of Graham made his body shake. "But, ma'am, I can't order the coach—"

"You know you can, Forbisher. Either do it, or Lord Darnley learns I walked from this castle, baggage in hand."

As if the morning's events had not been wild enough for human tolerance, Lucile rushed into the study. Utter fear paralyzed her eyes.

"Ma'am, Mike wants to see you."

"Mike?" I frowned. "Why?"

"I don't know, ma'am, but he is insistent."

"Very well. Bring him in."

I stood there, Forbisher and MacCarthy behind me. Mike came in, his cap in his hand. Twirling it round and round, he hung his head. When he saw his uncle and MacCarthy, too, he blanched.

I tilted my head in question. "Shall I ask them to leave, Mike?"

"No, ma'am. I—I want you to know I mulled this

over and over. I thought I'd better come tell you, though, I did. I knew you'd understand. Like no one else would, ma'am."

"What, Mike? What will I understand?"

I purposely inhaled and exhaled slowly to calm my raging fear.

"Well, ma'am, everyone knows how someone is after you and how you need a guard so that—so that you don't get 'urt." He was worrying his lip. "Well, ma'am, yesterday when you went for that ride with Master Jeremy—"

"Yes, what about it, Mike?"

"I 'ad to put a different saddle on Welshie."

"I don't understand your point, Mike. Please explain."

"Well, ma'am, I did saddle 'im with 'is usual saddle, but when I went to tighten the girth straps," he swallowed a couple of times, "the strap broke."

I raised my brows. "Perhaps it was damaged when Jeremy fell from his horse the previous day."

"That's what I first thought, ma'am. But then, I thought 'arder on it and went back to look again at the strap."

I held my breath. "Yes? And what did you find, Mike?"

"Someone cut that strap, ma'am. I knows they did. The place where they cut it is smooth as only a knife cut can be. Only they didn't cut it all the way through, no, ma'am. They cut it jus' enough to make it weak, so that if Welshie did more'n a walk, something might happen."

"So when Jeremy trotted on Welshie, the effects might have been made worse by the weakness in the girth strap?"

Mike nodded.

"Why didn't you tell me this yesterday, Mike?"

He was twirling his cap again, eyes to the floor. "Well, ma'am, I was afraid you'd think I 'ad not been doing my best for you. Maybe that I was to blame.

226

Maybe I cut the strap. Maybe—"

I put up one hand. "Enough, Mike. I understand. You are not to blame. And no, I do not think you are involved in the threats to me. I am grateful for your honesty. You may leave."

I turned to Forbisher and MacCarthy. The two men were frozen with horror.

"Now, Forbisher, get me that carriage."

No words left, Forbisher turned and departed, a defeated man. MacCarthy could only stare at me.

Within the hour, the coach came around to the front entrance. Before I climbed inside the black conveyance, I ordered the driver to take me to the inn in Darnley village. I knew he would spread the word where I'd gone. He'd be compelled to reveal my destination, not only to Forbisher and MacCarthy, but most certainly to their lord and master Graham. Graham would soon follow me, as surely as the sun and the moon. But I would not be there.

No, I would not be in Darnley. Within minutes of reaching Darnley village, I had ordered another coach. Even though it was Sunday and a devil of a day to scare up a hired hack in the country, the innkeeper did it for the former Viscountess of Chadwick. I knew him; he remembered me. He smiled at my request and told me he would ask his brother-in-law, who had a friend who was for hire. His brother-in-law complied, and soon Jeremy and I landed north in the little village of Dortmund. It was there, in the miller's house that also passed for an inn, that Jeremy and I were shown to a clean but sparsely furnished room with crude beds of straw. Jeremy slept dreamlessly. I had stayed awake to pace the floor and contemplate my singular nightmare.

I could not stay in Darnley Castle; I would not leave England and deprive Graham of his ability to save his shipping company.

Yet, I knew not who despised me.

I praised my stars the reading of the will was set for

Tuesday. I had too little money to survive in any inn—even one as elementary as in Dortmund—for longer than two nights. The lack of money and the promise of it after the reading of the will kept me in Yorkshire.

Oh, let anyone criticize me as mercenary, I knew I remained so that the old earl's will might be read and promulgated.

Whatever it held, someone feared its reading. And instinct told me that that same someone—my nemesis—feared its reading for more than what it might say about me or Jeremy. The knowledge gave me more courage. I had come this far. Through this much anguish. This much danger.

I would survive this, too. I hoped my diversion from Darnley village to Dortmund would keep my adversary at arm's length. Certainly, what I planned for the morrow would keep me one step ahead of the man or woman who wished me ill.

Who it could be ran round and round in my brain. The clues were too many, too diverse, the puzzle too complex for me to piece together. The very exercise exhausted me even if it kept me walking back and forth all night across the rough hewn floor.

This morning I had asked the miller to hire another carriage for me. He scoured the village. By afternoon he found me a young man, scrawny and shabby and eager for my fare. His conveyance was a sorry thing, surely over a half century old, creaky and threadbare. Nonetheless, it took us over this awful country road northwest to Pickering. Northwest, instead of southwest to York, where one could catch the London train. Northwest, where few would look for us or few expect us to wait for Tuesday to arrive.

I convinced myself that staying in Pickering meant Jeremy and I might foil whoever dogged my footsteps. I hoped to God I could lose them, confuse them, for one more day—whoever they were. My life depended on it. And so did Jeremy's.

Jeremy twisted in discomfort. I smoothed his hair and crooned to him. He nestled closer.

I sighed. For the thousandth time, I tried to calm myself. I had made the best decision for myself and for many others. I would arrive in Darnley Castle at the stroke of ten tomorrow. The will would be read. My duty would be done. My future would be better. My past would be resolved, if not my reputation put to rights. But I had not come to England asking for miracles. No, I had come hoping for money. And, that almost assured, I felt justified. If my heart ached for the loss of the one man I had truly adored, I would learn to live with the agony.

I had to!

Graham had been right about me: I was strong, stronger than I gave myself credit for. I could survive. I *would* survive!

Driving rain pelted the carriage. Lightning struck land off to my right, and the coach lurched as the horses whinnied and bucked. The vehicle righted itself and I banged my umbrella handle on the top. I could hear the driver cursing, his lash whipping the horses.

"Ho, there!" I called to him through the roof and banged once mòre.

"Getting outta the rain, mum!"

Not likely, I thought to myself. Not by beating those poor horses. But I heard the lashing continue. I felt the horses' pace quicken. But I also heard shouts from behind the carriage. I twisted and looked through the hazy back window.

Hooded figures, two of them, pressed down on the struggling carriage! Two figures, tall in their saddles, their arms in the air, guns in their hands!

I pushed Jeremy down to the floor.

"Stay there. Don't get up until I tell you!"

The coachman yelled at the horses and lashed at them once, twice, three times! I grabbed my umbrella and wished it were a pistol. Good God . . . I had nothing!

I heard shots. Bullets pinged and ricocheted off the carriage. More shouts met my ears. The highwaymen were yelling at the driver. He responded with more lashes to the stumbling animals. I groaned. More bullets rent the air. I fell atop Jeremy to cover him. The sound of hooves came abreast of the carriage. The coach lurched, balked. I felt my weight shift, and Jeremy and I were thrown to the right. I hit my head and Jeremy cried. The coach faltered once more in the muddy road. Lightning illuminated the inside of the carriage, and every detail of the shoddy interior shone like the brilliance of hell. I looked up at the window. One of the robbers had come even with the carriage and his eyes—black eyes!—peered at me. In that instant the coach shuddered. I lost my grip on the door handle, and with the force of demons, I felt myself hurled through the air.

I screamed.

And then the black of oblivion claimed me.

My mind wandered through a maze of miseries, searching . . . searching . . .

I opened my eyes. I felt I was warm . . .

I opened them again. I felt I was safe . . .

I opened them a third time. Darnley Castle! I knew I was trapped!

I groaned.

Someone mopped my brow.

It hurt.

"Go away," I told my tormentor.

"Never," came the dark reply.

I went once more into that void of time and place.

When I emerged, the gas lamps burned low. I moved my head upon the pillow.

I let my eyes define the room. My bedroom at Darnley. Now an invalid's room, if one took in the medicine bottles and bandages and scissors on the nightstand. My hand went to my head, where a bandage wound around my crown.

So it was true. I had escaped the highwaymen, only to return to Darnley. What irony! From danger to danger!

But my greatest danger slumped in a chair across the room, sound asleep.

Graham.

My love.

My greatest loss.

I looked at him with pity and regret. His blond head, hair tousled, sagged on his chest. His clothing, wrinkled and askew, revealed a ravaged man. His hand held a pistol.

A pistol . . .

I struggled up on one elbow and examined the weapon more closely. I sank back and let out a sigh of relief. The pistol was short-barreled, not at all like the long-nosed dueling pistols my two attackers had brandished.

I closed my eyes. Had I really thought there for a moment that Graham might have been one of those cloaked and hooded men?

Why?

I searched my memories of those awful moments before the carriage toppled and the world went black. Black. Black . . . eyes. The hooded man who came abreast of the carriage had black eyes. Just like the Chadwicks. Just like the Chadwicks!

But who . . . who . . . who could it be?

I knew of no other Chadwicks close by. Only Helena and Graham. And it could not have been Helena. The highwayman *was* in truth a man. Burly and loud. They had hurt me, but what of Jeremy?

Jeremy!

I struggled up on an elbow again. I tested my muscles. Pain shot through me and I groaned.

Graham, his black eyes flying wide with horror,

gaped at me. "Good God! You're—"

"Jeremy?" I croaked. "Where—?"

"Safe! In his room. With Simpson." He lunged toward the bed, shot out a hand, and felt my brow.

I shook it off.

"I will not stay here." I swung my feet over the edge of the bed, and the room spun madly. I fell backward, but Graham lowered me gently to the pillows.

"You will not leave here." He smoothed my brow. "I asked you once before never to leave me. Now, I will ensure it."

"You cannot! Whoever pursues me is very clever."

"Your two attackers are dead. Crushed when the coach veered into a ditch and rolled over on top of them."

"Who were they?"

"Two men from Darnley village."

"Who?"

Graham shrugged. "Two brothers. Jim and Johnny Fellowes. The barkeep's sons. Drunkards, both of them. Ne'er-do-wells. Always have been."

"Why would they attack me?"

Graham shrugged. "That's what Darian and I were trying to discern for hours tonight. Those two boys have always been hellions. Used to be good friends of Charles's, so the village gossip goes."

I frowned and licked my lips. "And would they have been in Southampton and London?"

"Not likely. Men like that couldn't even get in the front door of the hotel, let alone deliver a message upstairs!"

"Then, they hired someone to deliver it."

Graham shook his head. "They're very poor. Never having worked an honest day of their lives, they have nothing."

He seemed to stop in mid-thought, as if he hoped I'd let him finish there.

"Yes? But?"

"But they each had three gold sovereigns in their

232

pockets tonight. Gold sovereigns struck during Charles the Second's reign." Finally, Graham's eyes met mine. "Both are from my father's coin collection. I recognized them instantly. Darian and I went to the books where my father kept and catalogued them. All the Charles the Seconds were missing."

"Whoever hired them took the sovereigns to give as payment."

Graham inhaled. He did not need to respond.

"We are no closer to discovering this person than we ever were."

Graham's eyes went to the floor. "I've failed you. So many times. So many times. Whereas you persist. I know now you stayed in Dortmund last night, and I suppose you were on your way to Pickering to throw this person off the track and be able to attend the reading tomorrow. I know you did it for yourself, but I also know you did it for me. How can I thank you? How can I tell you how I admire you? How can I match your bravery with some small measure of protection? Christ, I've tried. I know not where or how he will strike next. But, as God is my witness, I promise you . . ."

"Promise me nothing," I whispered through dry lips. "Only stay away from me. I believe what they fear is you and I together. And I don't know why, except that whoever threatens me wants either something you have or . . . wants you. I cannot stay here. Someone will kill me or Jeremy. I cannot let them."

"I will do my damnedest not to let them. But you must stay here. You have had a terrible blow to the head. You must rest."

"Rest? I am once more in Darnley Castle—where someone wishes me ill! I cannot rest. And you must leave. Now! I'll not have anyone know you spent the night here in my room."

"Rubbish! You are ill!"

"Never that ill!"

233

His entire body sagged in defeat. "I know you have no reason to trust me. I have not shielded you from whomever assails you. I cannot promise you restoration of your reputation. I cannot even convince you of my affection for you. I have failed you. And I thought . . ." he laughed mirthlessly. "I was convinced I would succeed. What colossal egotism. Forgive me, my dear."

He rose. "I have a household guard posted. I asked Mrs. Bellweather to leave you a tray. Some broth and bread and tea, there by your bed. I would have you well before you go. I leave you to recover."

He left, and I knew he took with him all remnants of my innocence. Tears coursed down my cheeks. For long minutes, I could not stem the flow.

Finally, I rose from my bed, a more mature woman.

I ate and drank and felt refreshed. Then I took the pistol Graham had left there and fit my hand to the grip. Yes, I had used similar weapons when my father had taken me out west years ago. I climbed back into bed, plumped the pillows so that I could sit against the headboard, and tucked the pistol under the covers beneath my right hand.

My eyes went to the connecting door to Jeremy's room. I dared anyone to bother us this night.

I nodded off and came awake with a start. I gripped the pistol more tightly. We would survive. We would . . .

The cold click of the barrel against my temple had my eyes flying open.

"Don't bother to scream," declared a self-satisfied voice. "You would not leave, so now you will die."

Chapter Sixteen

I looked up into the face of Helena. My heart crumbled at the sight of her total malice.

She stood there stoically, her lips spread across her teeth in a smile that was none.

"Get out of bed," she whispered. "We're going for a walk. That's right, a walk. Get dressed."

I could only stare at her. My friend. My nemesis. I could hardly believe it.

"You? You've done all this? Sent the clippings, the notes? Hired that man?"

"Yes, me. I sent the clippings. Via a hired boy, of course. When I learned Margaret and her husband were to be in town at the same time, I almost crowed with delight. I knew you'd hate seeing her. Sorry to say, I never hired the man in the Mews, but whoever he was, he fell in with my needs, didn't he? You never knew, never knew. Clever me, clever me."

She shoved the barrel of the gun into my temple.

"Get out of that bed. Move, or I kill you now."

I slid the covers back. Yes, the weapon she had in her hand was the one I'd hidden under the covers. Nothing would save me now but my wits. I swung my feet to the floor.

"Where are we going? How should I dress?" If I knew, I might have some idea of how to escape.

"Your traveling costume. Yes," she snickered to

herself, "how appropriate. You *are* traveling, of course. The destination is quite new, however."

I moved toward my dressing room and noticed how the far door had fallen ajar. Had Helena entered my room through Jeremy's? Even at that, how had she passed the guard in the solar? With kind words of concern for us all, I suppose.

When I moved inside the tiny dressing room, she followed me. My eyes traveled to Jeremy's room and I noticed him on the bed. He slept soundly. I sagged in relief that Helena had not bothered him. Quickly, I took down a serviceable wool skirt and shirtwaist, along with a bolero jacket. Then I grasped my cloak of wool. Who knew what I might need?

"Bring your clothes back to the bedroom," she rasped, and nodded the gun in the direction of my room. "Don't go behind the screen. Dress here where I can see you."

The only person I had ever dressed in front of was my mother. While I knew that under ordinary circumstances I would have felt embarrassment, I trained my sights now on the business at hand. Calmer than I ever could have imagined, I crossed to the chest of drawers where I kept my smallclothes. I glimpsed her in the mirror, standing there behind me with hatred in her eyes.

I withdrew a chemise, a corset, a petticoat, and pantalettes. Then I faced her. My eyes met hers squarely.

"I trusted you," I whispered in fake remorse. "And you did all those things, even killing Samantha and slashing the portrait . . . and arranging for those two highwaymen . . ."

"I know," she giggled. "Clever me. I had you riled, didn't I, my pet?"

"You were my friend."

"Friend," she spat, her nostrils flaring. "Pah! Never! Now, remove your nightgown. No dallying."

I did as I was told. Naked now, my flesh prickled. I

drew my chemise over my head with little jerking motions. My obedience calmed her and she began to speak.

"I played your friend and you believed it. There was a time when I truly would have been your friend. Yes, yes, I would have had some use for you, but you were too innocent, would not join us, and could not comply."

I paused with my hands on the laces of my corset. "Join whom? Comply with what? How might I have obliged you? By going home now? Before the will is read?"

She snorted. Her black eyes shone like the fires of hell. "You never complied!" she hissed. "And going home now won't do the trick any longer, my pet. No, no, it won't. Put that corset on. That's right. Now the petticoat. Yes. And the shirtwaist and the skirt. Good, good. When you go over the cliff, I want you completely dressed. It will be an accident, you see. The blows to your head in the carriage disoriented you, and when you wandered outside, you fell . . .

"Or—or perhaps Graham will find cause to convince himself it was a suicide. Yes, yes, that *would* be delightful. I like that."

She wandered off into her own thoughts a second and the gun drooped.

I stepped closer. She raised the gun to my belly.

"Hook that skirt!"

I did as I was told.

"I am going home, Helena. After the reading tomorrow morning, I am leaving. I am no rival for you for Graham's affections."

She threw her head back and silently laughed like the demented of Bedlam. "That's ripe, that is! You think I love Graham." Her laughter died to a snort of derision. "Don't be ridiculous. I don't love Graham!" She glared at me, triumphant. "I never have! Not the way *you* love him, my pet. Graham is so—so *ordinary*."

I stood immobile, stymied.

She chuckled, and the venomous sound made my toes curl in fear. "You truly don't know. You haven't even the vaguest idea, the tiniest perception, have you?"

I shook my head.

"No, you are too sweet, too kind, too *well-bred*." She said the last as if poison filled her mouth. "I never wanted your Graham. Pah! Give me a man—a man who seizes the world!" She clenched her fist and twisted, as if wringing someone's neck. "Yes! Yes! Not Graham. Charles! Charles! Charles was my choice!"

My mouth dropped open. I watched her rant on, her eyes wide with wild remembrance.

"Charles was my darling man. Ever since we were children, he kissed me and petted me. Made me feel wanted and loved, as no one ever had. As no one else ever did. I was the poor relation—the poor *female* relation! But Charles knew how to make me feel welcome. The day I came here, he came to my bedroom. I was so young and alone and afraid. But Charles came to my bedroom and smoothed my hair from my face and gave me sweet treats. He lay down in bed with me and took me to his chest. Yes, he was a man—even at the age of twelve—and he knew what I needed. Then, later, after that terrible maid sassed me, he showed me how thrilling a whipping could be. He tied me up, too, you know, just to demonstrate . . ." She was smiling serenely.

I was swallowing back bile.

"It was the first of many glorious adventures into the realm of the senses. Here in the nursery, and down in the farrier's shack or the cottage by the sea."

"Izzy!" I breathed.

She sneered. "Izzy! What a foolish boy he was! Izzy thought he could stay and watch Charles and me and not join us. What a little idiot! Charles caught him often following us and making fun. But Izzy didn't make much fun after Charles lamed his horse and left them both to die in the rain, did he? No, no. You see, Izzy had to die for his audacity. He was going to tell his father about us. Can you imagine the nerve? Ha! But Charles put Izzy quiet, finally and completely. Izzy never had the opportunity to tell a soul."

I took a step back against the chest to support myself. Charles had killed his brother. Oh, no, no.

Helena turned reflective. "Izzy wouldn't join us so he died. You wouldn't, either, and that's why you had to go the first time. You were always there, always with Charles or looking after him. My God, the man was surrounded by you. You, with your accommodating ways. You, with your ready understanding. I grew so tired of your eternal presence. I had to get rid of you, and when I told Charles how we might accomplish it, he agreed.

"You see why I loved Charles. He was always so bold. Yes, I understood him. I loved him as no other woman ever did, ever could. And he loved me. We were made for each other, attuned to each other. And no other woman could ever take my place. I told him so constantly. No one was my equal. Not that actress in Drury. Not that silly, vain Margaret Hamilton-Fyfe. Pah! Margaret—who didn't know passion from dishwater. And certainly not *you*. You! The catch of the season. The rich virgin from New York. God, how I laughed at you as you smiled and tried oh-so-valiantly to save your marriage. It was doomed from the start! You never saw it, of course."

She sighed. "Charles never loved you, you know. He romanced you because his father, noble Uncle Albert, cast him out to find a rich wife. Dear Uncle Albert brought Charles into the drawing room one night after dinner, sat him down in a hard-backed chair, and lectured him. The old geezer told Charles to get himself off to New York and not to bother to come home until he'd wed a rich one. Wonderful man, Uncle Albert. Sweet, dear, poisonous man.

Gave instructions, and God help you if you didn't follow them to the letter!"

She inched closer and the pistol muzzle went to my ribs. "I inherited that trait . . . or perhaps I learned it from Charles." She grinned lasciviously. "He taught me everything. How to ride, how to shoot, how to cut girth straps . . . how to make love. He was wonderful in bed. He knew every trick, every position."

I closed my eyes.

"See no evil, my pet?" She laughed. "You never knew what was happening, did you? We were so clever, Charles and I. So clever.

"When Charles grew tired of you—and he knew it once he set eyes on me again here in London—I devised the plan to have you shamed and sent home. Yes, yes. I arranged for that seduction of you by George Hayden. He owed Charles gambling debts and it was an easy way to skip the bill. Hayden loved the intrigue and enjoyed the notoriety of seducing the famous, the virtuous Vanessa. You never knew, did you?" She chuckled softly. "No, you didn't. But we arranged that to get rid of you and take your dowry to boot! Ha-ha! Even crafty Uncle Albert never knew how Charles and I had bested you."

She sniffed and rsied both brows at me as her eyes ran over my figure. "Charles loved me and kept me above all others. We arranged to be together always. Even when Uncle Albert wanted to marry me off, we outsmarted him. Why, before Uncle Albert could get the suitor to the drawing room, I got Charles to bribe a doctor in Scarborough to say I was incapable of having children. But, of course, I *was* capable of having children—and I would have had the heir to the earldom today if he hadn't died. He'd be three now . . ."

Aghast and in sorrow, I put a hand to my throat. "You had a child and he died? How?"

Her eyes snapped back to me. "He was stillborn. A pretty boy, too. He looked just like Charles and me,

240

except for the deformities . . ."

"Your headaches—?"

"Yes, it is the syphilis. Syphilis! I told Charles he didn't need other women. I told him! I told him I was all he needed. But he wouldn't listen, damn him! Him and his appetites. It killed his child. Our only child." Her face screwed up into a gargoyle's grimace. "I see it didn't touch your boy, though."

Beyond her, I saw a movement from behind the screen. Hands appeared, then a golden head of hair. Graham! Graham emerged from behind the screen, and I licked my lips as he advanced on Helena.

She stuck her face close to mine. "So you see, my pet, you won't escape me now. I have waited too long. You may have taken my lover, but I'll be damned if you or your spawn will have this house or any part of what should have been mine! Put your coat on, pet. You go to your reward!"

Graham lunged forward to grab for her. But Helena stepped out of his reach and pivoted. I watched in horror as she fired point-blank.

Graham recoiled, his hand clutching his arm. Shock registered on his features. But then his face contorted into a fiendish rage. Like a volcano that explodes without warning, I saw him erupt in a frenzy of movement. With his left hand, he reached out to Helena, and clutching her arm with the pistol, he pulled her flush to him. She struggled mightily, cursing and kicking, firing the pistol again and again and again until no more bullets left the empty barrel. She dropped the useless thing to the floor.

I wrenched forward to the bedstand, where I grabbed the scissors. But Helena's hand closed over mine. I was too late. Still held by a sagging Graham, she swirled around toward him and, in one flashing second, jabbed upward, catching him in the shoulder, then slashing at his torso a thousand times. In a moment's space, his body went red with blood, his knees buckled, his eyes bulged. I sobbed, but Helena

241

laughed as I ran around her.

I cradled him as he sank to the floor.

Helena ran past me, her arms flailing. "Ha! I saw you! I saw you in the mirror!" She was singsonging like a child. "Leave him—leave him to die! Why, certainly! What a good idea! He'll appear to have died at your hands! Then you, in remorse, will take your own life! Oh, this is too good! Oh, if Charles could only see how well I've done! Leave him, I say!"

I shook my head.

Her eyes practically popped from her head. "No?" she seethed. "I'll teach you not to refuse me!"

She ran into Jeremy's room.

I struggled up from the floor and broke into a run.

Helena had grabbed up a sleeping, disoriented Jeremy into her strong arms. Facing me, the scissors to Jeremy's throat, she grinned.

Torn between a dying, bleeding Graham and the danger to Jeremy, I quaked with fury.

"Put him down, Helena!"

She was backing toward the outside wall. She had nowhere to go; she was trapped. Her threat was a ruse.

"No, Vanessa. Follow me!"

With a squirming, bewildered Jeremy held high against her chest, she slid sideways and disappeared!

How? How? I trembled at the black magic of her disappearance. I ran forward and felt along the wall. In the darkness, my hands told me what my worst fears proclaimed.

Jeremy's room had secret exits, too!

I spun for Simpson's room, shouting for her to wake up and get MacCarthy. She stood in her own doorway, blinking at the wild scene she'd obviously witnessed. At my words, she came fully awake with a start and bounded for the hall.

I returned to Graham. He bled profusely. His face gone to a sickly ashen color, he could not live long.

I bent to kiss his closed eyes. "Forgive me," I whispered.

Then I ran for Jeremy's room.

I paused at the slit in the wall and pondered the need for a candle. Not knowing what labyrinth awaited me, I crossed the room and pocketed a candle from the mantel. I did not light it, though. Helena had gone without a light, which meant she knew the way well. If I lit a candle, she would easily find me. I would have to rely on my brains.

I slid around the aperture and paused to let my eyes become accustomed to the dark.

I felt the stones of the wall and realized that this was surely the other side that ran along the secret stairway from my room. I tested the contours of the stones in the floor. Yes, I could go by instinct.

Nonetheless, I took each step judiciously. My bare feet communicated the years of decay the passage had endured. Cobwebs and crawling insects made my toes spread. Repulsed, I swallowed back the cold fear that wended up my body. I would not let Helena hurt my boy.

My back to the stone wall, I took each step one by one and soon discerned the passage was a mirror image of its companion. Did that mean it had cubbyholes and hidden rooms like the armory beneath my bedroom? I felt along the wall with each step I took. Saddened, I found nothing. What was worse, I could hear nothing.

Where was Helena?

The thought made me travel faster. Faster! God only knew of what she was capable.

I traveled down the stairs to what I thought had to be the ground level, where an exit door must open to the outside. But I found nothing. Nothing! How could this stairway have no exit to the out-of-doors? I must have missed some opening, some portal.

But where? Where?

If I dallied, what would Helena do to Jeremy?

What evil could she concoct next? I knew her to be so very capable, so diabolical, that I shook. I clenched my teeth and turned back up the staircase. I'd find it. I would!

I inched back up the stairs, extending my hands out for my fingertips to touch each wall. Nothing. Nothing. But suddenly my hands felt the outline of a hinge, then the opening of a door. So where did this door lead?

Helena must have gone through here. I pulled it wide, felt around the edges, lowered my head and shoulders, then made my way through the tiny room. If Helena had come through here, she would have had a devil of a time dragging Jeremy with her.

Yet, from the feel of the place, I knew I was in the storage room where I had seen the jars last week. I scrambled on, tugging at my long skirt that caught on the jagged stone floor. If my sense of direction were correct, the door to my side of the stairway was here somewhere. I felt the ancient wall, and in the darkness, my fingers gave me clues. I soon felt the outline of a similar door. I felt the hinges, the latch, the handle. I pulled backward and the wooden door opened.

Here, I was on my side of the stairwell. Here, I was in my element. I licked my lips in anticipation because here—here!—I had access to protection. I stood and took the few steps down, making my way toward the armory. I thrust open the door, then stood there a moment, adjusting my eyesight to the speckles of light that illuminated the room. The moon's brilliance shining through the narrow windows allowed me to find my bow and quiver. The very same I had used only days ago, when Graham and I had visited the Viking fort. I took it from its place on the rack and wondered whose bow this had been. Eliza's? Clifford's? My hand clasped the powerful length of elm. I would have service from this medieval weapon.

Now silently praying that I would find Helena in time, in a place where I might use it, I grabbed the quiver, still filled with arrows from days before, and slung it over my shoulder. Knowing my way well now, I ran. I ran out the door and down the few stairs. Even in the dark, I knew this terrain, these woods. I knew this copse, that path . . . that path straight up to the cliff of the fort.

Toward the east, the somber shades of night parted for a few small rays of sun. Trees stood as silent sentinels to the brooding dawn. I shivered, my feet sluiced with dew. With the stealth my father and I had witnessed in the native American Lakota tribe, I left the path for the dense forest. The other side of the mountain might be steeper but I knew that way as well as the other. I also knew its merits—a view of the Viking courtyard.

The way was steep, still slick with moisture of night. I slipped and fell over rocks and twigs, and sank into ooze. My feet were cut and probably bloody. I could not care. It mattered not a bit compared to Helena's sick-mindedness and her enmity for me and Jeremy.

Panting, I reached a clearing at the top of the mountain. Here, the mountain reached higher toward the heavens, tall as the tower where Graham and I had consummated our love. Here, from this position, I could look down into the courtyard. Here, in the center of the ancient ruin, stood Helena with my son.

I reached for my quiver. Nestling into the hollow of a boulder, I licked my lips, flexed my muscles, and drew an arrow from my quiver. Testing the resilience of my bow, I threaded my arrow. In dawn's calm, no winds blew to divert my arrow from its mark. I took my sight.

Helena was in full view, but wary and canny as she was, she still held Jeremy. Oh, he was no longer held high in her arms—once fully awake, he must have given her quite a struggle—but she held him firmly to her torso, the scissors to his throat.

I swallowed hard and took another sight.

"Helena!"

My voice, a normal pitch, reached out to her in the cavern of the courtyard. I knew she could not tell where I was. No one could detect where the echo originated—no one who'd ever been here. From the way her head jerked to one side and then another, I knew she'd never been here. I felt satisfaction at my advantage.

"Let him go, Helena!"

She laughed. "Come to me! It's you I want!"

"No, you don't! You want Charles and your son. Both are dead. Dead! As payments for your own sins!" I dropped my voice to a whisper, which I knew she could still hear. "Helena! It's you who is the fool. Charles didn't love you."

"Yes, he did!"

"How could he when he went from woman to woman? He laughed at you, you know."

"You're lying."

I was, but my son's life depended on her belief I could never lie.

"He laughed at you often. How you rejected suitors for the silliest reasons. He thought you were a millstone around his neck. Those were his very words to me. Often."

She began to circle, dragging Jeremy with her. "He wouldn't say that!" She scanned the mountainside. "He wouldn't!"

She frantically searched for me, but I was well cloaked by the frailness of dawn's light and by sheltering foliage.

"He always said he loved me! Me! Me!" She lifted her head and I saw the ravages of tears.

Jeremy curled forward, and in the next instant, he rammed his little body backward!

She lunged for him, her scissors outstretched, but

he slithered away from her.

I fixed my sight. My fingers unlocked. My arrow flew. Its trajectory straight and true, it made a perfect path and met its target.

Helena halted, mid-stride, a marionette in midmotion. Shocked, she straightened and stared at the arrow protruding from her chest. She sank to her knees. Her body jerked backward, her face turned skyward. She keened.

Shouts rang through the forest. People were coming from the castle.

Helena fell facedown to the dust. I stood and saw Jeremy scamper down the cliff path, all the while shouting for me.

He hadn't run far when I saw him met by the two Surrey brothers, footmen who had been sent out from the castle. They ran their hands over him and looked up toward the fort. I could see Jeremy pointing upward as he related his tale of capture and escape. John Surrey ran up the cliff and paused at the sight of a crying, writhing Helena, her fists beating the earth, the arrow making her weaker with each movement.

I turned back the way I'd come up. With footfalls more careful than those I'd taken to climb up here, I descended and worked my way through brush and trees, to find my son in Todd Surrey's arms.

Jeremy saw me and balked at the hideous sight I obviously presented. But then he ran to me.

"Mommy! Oh, Mommy!"

I clasped him to my heart.

"Mommy, I was brave."

"I know you were, my dear."

"I knew the passageway. I knew it was dark and dirty, but I didn't cry. I was a big boy. Mommy, she was so mean to me. Why did Aunt Helena do that to me?"

With great trepidation lest he ever discover the depths of depravity to which humankind could sink, I hugged him.

"She is very ill, my love. It affected her mind."

John Surrey, who had gone up to tend to Helena, had returned to stand before me.

"Ma'am, Miss Chadwick is wounded badly."

"Is she dying?"

"No, ma'am. But hysterical and saying things that—" he eyed Jeremy meaningfully, "that come from pain. The arrow is firmly imbedded in her shoulder. MacCarthy sent Rogers for the village doctor. As soon as he finishes with Lord Darnley, I think we should have him come up here to see to Miss Chadwick."

"Yes, yes." I closed my eyes at the thought of Graham dying without anyone who cared for him. I put Jeremy to the ground and took his hand. "Make her as comfortable as she will allow. Come, Jeremy. We must run. Your Uncle Graham is very hurt."

"Did Aunt Helena hurt him?"

When I nodded, he sprang ahead of me down the path.

We ran like the furies, passing teams of servants who seemed to be everywhere in the forest. When Forbisher had sent out a search party, he'd sent out the entire staff. Jeremy and I reached the old tower and came to a halt in front of the other footman, Wilson, who stood by the entrance to the secret staircase, his pistol at the ready.

"Where is your master?" I rasped.

"Where he fell, ma'am. In your chamber."

I took the stairs two at a time, Jeremy close on my heels. I pushed the opening in the wall wider and slid through. The sight of Graham, pale and wooden on my bed, robbed me of what little breath I had left.

People moved about. Simpson hovered over Graham, stroking a cool cloth across his brow. Bellweather appeared behind her, her eyes liquid with tears, her hands filled with a basin of wine-red water.

I sank to my knees beside his bed. I took his hand,

limp and cold. I gazed at his dear face, lax now in his unconsciousness.

"The doctor's not here yet?"

Bellweather moved toward the bed. "It's twenty minutes down to the village and twenty minutes back. If the man's abed and not out to a house call on an emergency, he should be here soon. Forbisher told Rogers he'd give him ten gold sovereigns if he got the doctor here within the half hour. But if Rogers and the doctor don't get here soon, ma'am, I don't think . . ." She broke down completely and covered her mouth with her apron. She turned away in her misery.

I surveyed the two women's ministrations. Graham's shirt was cut open to reveal the nasty work of the scissors. The deepest puncture in his shoulder had stained the white bed linen almost black. The wound he'd suffered in his right arm was from a bullet and that wound seemed to have stopped bleeding now. He had other chest wounds, cuts, it seemed, more than gunshots, that Simpson and Bellweather tended gently. I thanked God that Helena, for all her boasting about Charles's training, was a lousy shot.

I stroked Graham's hand, then kissed it. His hands, which had held me and caressed me . . . His body, which I had loved in lust and in all holy adoration . . . He was broken, bleeding, and all in defense of me!

I could not stop the tide of pain that swept over me. I put my face down on the bed and cried in abject agony for what we all had lost today.

The doctor came. I gazed at him. He was new to the village since I'd left, and I did not know his name nor did I ask. Young and full of energy, he moved quickly, shouting orders for fresh hot water and more clean linens. He stopped to stare at me.

"Mrs. Chadwick?"

"Yes, I am."

He smiled consolingly and glanced at my disheveled condition.

"Come away, Mrs. Chadwick." He took my hands from Graham's. "You must let me near your husband."

I objected, but he did not understand that my objections were twofold. I gave up the futile quest. I had neither breath nor reason to argue with him. He needed to do his work.

I stepped away as someone thrust a brandy into my shaking hands. But when I took it, my quaking sloshed its contents over my already-filthy skirt. I turned and watched the doctor mutter over each new wound he discovered. In the midst of this, Graham's pain-filled eyes opened and he searched the room. When he found me, he opened his mouth to speak but grunted in pain as the doctor probed the hole in his shoulder. I smiled at Graham, my message only that he endure. His eyes ran down my figure and he gaped at my appearance, but then writhed when the doctor once more probed a wound.

For all of his slow preliminary examinations, the doctor then moved like lightning. He cleansed and sutured, probed and finally extracted two bullets from Graham's upper arm, close to the puncture the scissors had made.

"There are no more bullets?" I asked, astonished.

He turned weary eyes toward me. "No. How many should there be?"

"Four in all, I think."

The doctor gaped. "Four?!"

"Will he live?"

The man smiled sadly. "He has lost much blood, but he looks healthy and able to recover quickly. Yes, he will live. What has occurred here today? Sit down. Sit down to tell me while I look at your feet. You are in only slightly better shape than Lord Darnley."

"No. You must go up the cliff to the fort, sir. My cousin is there, wounded. She needs your attention."

250

He narrowed his eyes at me.

"Wounded, too? How so?"

"With an arrow. I shot her in the shoulder. Here"—I pointed to a spot below the clavicle. "Rogers," I called to the footmen who stepped forward, "take the doctor up to the fort, please."

The doctor gave a few quick instructions to me and Bellweather about Graham's care, then grabbed his huge black case and followed Rogers from the room. I took one of the chairs and pushed it close to Graham. Then I took his hand again as he fell into a restful sleep.

Almost an hour later, the doctor came into my room once more and tended my now-swollen, aching feet. His gruff exclamations of horror about the morning's events awakened Graham. When he finished bandaging me, he turned to Graham.

"You will recover, Lord Darnley, but you must remain in bed. You have lost much blood and I would not have you reopening these wounds. Your cousin is another matter entirely. She is physically well. I removed the arrow from her shoulder. . . ."

Graham's eyes flew to mine and I nodded, then looked at the doctor.

"But she is very mentally disturbed. She raves on about a man named Charles. I gave her some laudanum to quiet her. But in my examination of her, I strongly suspect a disorder of the mind." He paused and looked meaningfully from Graham to me and back again.

"She suffers," Graham whispered with great difficulty, "from syphilitic dementia. I know the signs. I have seen it before, doctor. I want her taken care of for as long as . . ." Graham coughed and winced.

"Yes, Lord Darnley. I understand. That's all I wanted to know. I'll make the arrangements and have my man come round in the morning. In the meantime, she is rendered harmless by the strong dose of laudanum, ropes as restraints, and by two of your footmen whom I told to guard her. I gather from what I see here and what the servants have told me, she has caused quite a bit of trouble to you, my lord."

When Graham nodded, the man shook his head. "I'll see to it her last days are as comfortable as possible."

"Thank you, doctor. She is my cousin and I would see her treated as such, no matter what her malady or what she's done."

"Very well, my lord. I will return tomorrow."

As he left, Bellweather carried in a breakfast tray, ladened with every imaginable food.

"That's for both of you, and I expect no remains when I return." She smiled broadly at us. "Mr. Osgood has arrived, my lord, and waits in the drawing room. I hope you don't mind, my lord, but I told him about this morning's doings and . . . your wounds."

"Yes, thank you, Mrs. Bellweather. This will *must* be read this morning, no matter my condition."

"But, my lord, he wonders if Miss Helena can attend and says she must—if you can bear it, sir—because she is named in the will, too."

Graham sat still as stone for long moments. "Yes, Miss Helena will attend. Under armed guard, but she will be there. It's for the best. We'll see this thing through this morning, by God. And then, for once and for all, as Darian said the other day: The Chadwicks will finally be free."

Chapter Seventeen

The twenty people who assembled that morning in the drawing room of the Georgian wing were met and welcomed only by a stunned Forbisher.

He came to Graham as I entered from Jeremy's room at quarter of ten, and he told us how distant relatives and local notables took seats while the castle staff stood silently on the fringes of the room.

"My lord, everyone is accounted for, except, of course, yourself, Mrs. Chadwick, and Miss Helena."

Graham struggled up from his pillows. Very pale, he nonetheless displayed basic good health with his sure movements. At my insistence, he had remained in my room this morning, not only to rest but also to dress for the reading of the will. Meanwhile, I had gone into Jeremy's room to prepare, selecting the high-collared black silk mourning gown I had come to hate. Graham had had MacCarthy bring him the black suit I abhorred, but he found himself able to wear only the trousers because of his copious arm and shoulder bandages.

"I've got to see to Helena and speak with Darian before we start the reading. Help me up, will you, Mac?"

He needn't have asked. Both MacCarthy and Forbisher surged forward, one to grasp Graham about the waist, the other to support him under his good arm. Then, they put slippers on each foot and tried to arrange the black coat about his shoulders.

Graham shook his head. "Forget the formalities, men. This is a day for realities."

He glanced at my face.

"Wait there, Vanessa. Forbisher, get Lucile to help Mrs. Chadwick walk downstairs. She'll never be able to make it alone on those foot bandages."

I watched the two men navigate Graham out the door. Within seconds Lucile appeared, and we followed much more slowly because of my afflictions.

When we finally made the drawing room, I paused outside the double doors. This was the moment I'd waited for for almost two frightening weeks. This was the event I'd traveled thousands of miles to attend. This was the occasion I'd welcomed and feared—as had so many others. What happened here had such great bearing on my future and Jeremy's. Could our financial future be brighter than our present? More than that, could my reputation be restored? But could any money—large or small—buy me respectability? Then, could I ever forgive and forget the degradation that three Chadwicks had heaped on me?

I shuddered.

"Madam, are you cold?" Lucile asked. "I'll get you a lap cover as soon as I get you seated."

"Thank you, Lucile. I—I would like that." My teeth chattered, but I clamped them still and nodded toward the doors. "Open them. I'm ready."

But I was wrong.

I was not ready for the scene that awaited me. The drawing room had been transformed from a sitting room for polite conversation into an auditorium setting, with chairs of every shape and size from every part of the house lined up in rows before a deal table at their head. Behind the table stood Darian, mopping his brow with a white handkerchief and waving me into the room.

I scanned those arrayed before me. At my entrance, as if on cue, they all stood—and faced me! My heart hammered violently. What could they think? I paused.

Confusion wrinkled every brow. Astonishment widened every eye. Admiration—admiration?—melted every harsh feature.

To say I was confused and astonished myself would have been the grossest of understatements. Some one or two of the castle staff must have whispered words of this morning's events. Those words had traveled quickly, because here before me stood Chadwick aunts and uncles and cousins, Darnley villagers and castle servants. Here stood the cadre of those who mattered to Graham, to the Chadwick family, and to the Darnley estates.

I would see this through. I would!

I squared my shoulders, nodded politely to those whom I'd not seen prior to this, and murmured good morning to the others. They more than met me halfway in courtesy.

Suddenly, Graham's Uncle William—my father-in-law's only surviving brother—strode forward, his arms outstretched.

I balked. Lord William and his imperious wife Charlotte—both of them bastions of Victorian society—had been quick to sniff at my American "provinciality" six years ago.

"Vanessa!" Lord William took my stiff hands in his.

I pulled away, so terrified was I of another scandalous scene this morning.

Yet, he drew me into his embrace. "Vanessa. I'm delighted to see you up and about. We have heard, of course, of your travail." He patted my hands, and his black eyes actually glowed with friendly concern as he stepped back.

Stepping forward was his silver-haired wife, Charlotte.

"Yes, indeed, we have heard," echoed the woman who had served as one of Queen Victoria's ladies-in-waiting for over a decade. "Shameful, my dear. Shameful." She smiled consolingly as her eyes indicated a figure at the right side of the room.

My eyes followed hers, and immediately I understood the reasons for Charlotte's and William's reaction.

Against the wall sat Helena. With cords binding her ankles together and other cords securing her wrists to the armrests, she sat forward on a sturdy dining room chair, brought in for the very purpose of holding her. She, too, had a shoulder bandage that bulged her clothing in a grotesque fashion. I looked into her eyes.

"Come in, come in," she chanted in a voice that made my hair stand on end. "We need you here, but we don't want you here. No, we don't. No, we—"

"Helena!" Graham barked from the front. "I warn you. Be silent or be gagged!"

She jerked her head as if slapped. Her black eyes declared a thousand rabid things, but her voice went dead.

My head spun in the direction of Graham's voice.

He sat in a wing chair in the front row, befitting his place as closest living relative and heir presumptive to his father. Graham's dark eyes rested on mine a moment before they indicated a matching chair to his right.

"Come, Vanessa, sit with me."

Lord William and Charlotte nodded, urging me to Graham's side. "Go, my dear. Do go," they seemed to whisper in unison.

I checked Helena once more. She flared her nostrils at me and yanked at her restraints. But the Surrey brothers, who stood on either side of her, shook their heads at her in warning and she quieted again.

With my head held high, I made my way down the aisle toward Graham. Lucile fussed about me, arranging my somber black skirts and propping my feet on a stool before covering my lap with a cashmere throw. At my repose, Graham nodded at Darian, who cleared his throat.

"Ladies and gentlemen, good morning. As you know, we gather at long last today to hear the last will and testament of the tenth Earl of Darnley, Albert Charles Jeremy Chadwick. My lord the earl died May tenth, eighteen hundred and eighty-eight, having attained the age of sixty-seven. By your leave, if we are settled, I will begin."

He took his chair, removed spectacles from his inner coat pocket, straightened them on his nose, then pursed his lips. Peering over the rimless glasses, his blue eyes swept the room.

All fell silent.

I stared straight ahead. Before me sat a perspiring Darian. Looming over him was a glorious portrait by George Romney of the eighth earl, his black eyes shining down on this gathering. Beyond, a bleak September sun shed a few rays of light into the room, hushed and hot with human expectation.

Darian opened a leather portfolio.

Graham shifted in his chair so that his foot touched mine.

I glanced at him and expected a small smile, at the very least. What I saw there was sorrow and, perhaps, an apology.

I closed my eyes and Darian's mellifluous voice flowed over me.

"'I, Albert Charles Jeremy Chadwick, being of sound mind and body, do hereby make, publish, and declare this to be my Last Will and Testament, made by me this fifteenth day of February in the year of our Lord eighteen hundred and eighty-eight.'"

"Good God, man!" Lord William grumbled from his place in the front row across the aisle from us. "You mean to say he changed his will from what he wrote the previous month?"

Darian looked at Lord William with only a pittance of patience. "Yes, my lord, he did."

"But—but why? Once Charles was dead, the title went to his only surviving son, with allowances to the rest of us according to our station." William looked at his nephew and then at Darian. "Unless he changed that?"

"My lord, I know the earl's motivations will be evident as I read the document."

"But—but—" William was clearly afraid now. "I will protest. My brother was not himself after Charles died. He came to me—no, no, Charlotte, I will say this—my brother came to me in London one night, something he'd never done. He was, to be blunt, quite beside himself over things Charles revealed on his deathbed. I have never seen my brother so distressed, so unlike his natural composed self. If Albert wrote this afterward—and yes, I do believe from the date you just gave that he must have written this will one or two days after seeing me—my brother was definitely not himself."

People murmured to each other. I glanced at Graham from the corner of my eye. He stared blankly at Darian. Had Graham known this?

Darian shook his head at William.

"My lord, I am well aware of your brother the earl's state of mind after his oldest son's death and before his own. While Lord Albert was highly distressed by Charles's revelations, I assure you he was quite lucid until hours before his last breath. Therefore, I insist I be allowed to continue."

Charlotte put a hand to her husband's arm and whispered in his ear. Flustered but acquiescent, William nodded.

"Go on, Mr. Osgood. I wish to hear it all, sir."

Darian cleared his throat and let his eyes find the right spot on the page.

"'This will is dictated to Darian Osgood of Osgood and Mobrey, in the presence of the firm's young

258

assistant, Horatio Fenton. This document revokes any and all Wills and Codicils at any time heretofore made by me, specifically that of January fifteenth, eighteen hundred and eighty-eight and the first document of this nature, dated September fifth, eighteen hundred and eighty-two.

"'The reason for my first wills are obvious. At the marriage of my oldest son Charles, I bequeathed the title and estates of the Earl of Darnley to him and his legal heirs. At Charles's death, I bequeathed the title and estates to my only surviving son, my third living offspring—Graham McAllister Chadwick.

"'Since January sixteenth of this year, however, much information has come to light and I am forced to change my original bequests.'"

I purposely measured my breathing. I dared not look at Graham. Oh, what had my father-in-law learned?

"'To explain my recent actions, I now must commit the greatest of social improprieties: I will reveal the truths about my own past and thereby show their costly reverberations in others' lives. The tale is not pretty, but it must be told.

"'Reared strictly by a formidable father, an abrasive mother, and a tyrannical governess, my early years were a misery of endless duties and lessons. I was imbued virtually from the cradle with the import of being the oldest son who would one day inherit the illustrious earldom of Darnley and its estates. I was filled with awe at the prestige of a title and holdings worth more in legend than in fact. Nonetheless, as the heir presumptive, I was taught by my father to subjugate *all* to my future station in life: My taste for Irish whiskey was replaced by fine port; my desire for an education in Egyptology was replaced by a background in estate agronomy; my natural ebullience was replaced by a peer's superior demeanor.

"'Thus, I lived stoically, if not well. I treated my

two brothers with a disdain taught me by my father. I treated my blond, beautiful, affectionate wife with a benign neglect taught me by my friends. And finally, I treated my three sons with a haughty indifference taught me by my society.

"'I accepted all my lessons, learning too well. But I also learned too late the wages of my blind acceptance. My younger brother William learned to dislike and distrust me, so that he took himself and his family to London, from whence he has built a political career of which I am immensely proud. Yet, in twenty-five years, he has sought me out not once for advice or favor. Much like William, my youngest brother John learned to fear my wrath, so that he hid his fears in drink and died in disgrace, denied the financial aid he requested of me as well as my last respects.

"'But while my brothers avoided me, my wife merely tolerated me. She should have reviled me. Yes, for all she gave me—her love, her trust, her very essence to my keeping—I returned none of it. I responded to her avowals of love with smug acceptance. I took her trust and mocked it with scores of women, none as sweet or lovely, each more amoral than the last.

"'Even when she presented me with a son, I took her gift and cherished the child as if I alone had created him. I pampered him and coddled him. I personally supervised his nursery, his meals, his lessons. I taught him to command, to disdain, and to control. I was so successful and he was so impressionable that I could soon turn my attentions to his younger brothers. But Charles was not to be ignored. Ever.

"'And it soon became clear that my two younger sons were not of the same substance as the first. They, like their mother when we were first married, were more spontaneous with their joys, more effusive with their affections, and I, fool that I was, rued their shallowness. I concentrated more on Charles. Charles, whom I had created. Charles, whom I had molded. Charles, whom I could predict and control. Or so I thought.

"'I thought he bore my stamp, my mold, my imperator. What I did not know was that he bore it so well, I could neither predict nor control the thing he had become. Worse yet, I never knew the depths of his perversity until these past few weeks. I blame myself totally. I pay for my wickedness with the torment saved for the dying. For I am to die soon—within months, my doctors say. And I do know that most of the injustices of my behavior and Charles's cannot be rectified on earth or in heaven. However, in an attempt to mitigate some of them, I now reveal the magnitude of Charles's perversions and beg those assembled to forgive and forget them as best they can.

"'I think his character began to change at the tender age of five. That year, he suffered a terrible bout of cholera that rampaged through the village and the castle. Distraught lest I lose my heir, I frequented my wife's bed and begat another son for the Darnley family. Iselton was born nine months later, a healthy, happy boy who gurgled in joy at his birth.

"'Charles hated him. I could see it in his eyes. Shrewd child of my teachings, Charles knew Izzy was here to act as *the spare* should any mishap befall him. My wife spoke to me of her concern that Charles was unnaturally hateful toward Izzy, but I pooh-poohed her notions. Charles, I affirmed, was exhibiting those traits he should—pride, power, and aggressiveness. But when our third son was born and I saw Charles once more treat the infant with crass indifference, I knew in my heart my wife was right. No one should ever cross Charles. Increasingly, no one could.

"'His power increased apace with his brutality. He cursed a servant, he drowned a kitten, he lashed a stable boy. Yet, I turned my face away. He was

261

learning his place and position, I declared. When servants came to me with suspicions of Charles seducing the female staff, I sent the woman in question away and scolded him for improper behavior. When Charles was sent down from school for gaming, I promptly had him reinstated, claiming his natural boyish inclinations. Through all these ramblings of his youth, I found no great crimes, no perversities.'"

A hysterical laugh broke Darian's litany. The crowd muttered at the sound.

"Uncle Albert missed it all!" Helena cried. "Old fool—"

Graham spun in Helena's direction. One flick of his eyelashes at the Surrey brothers and a band of black cloth went about her mouth. Graham inhaled and sank back into his seat.

"Continue please, Darian."

"Yes, sir." Darian cleared his throat and mopped his brow. "'But now I know that I found none because I did not care to find any. I was blind. Blind to my own pride, but more blind to the wealth of pride my son possessed. So today, with the help of a London-based detective agency, I remove my blindfold and expose the vile actions of my firstborn son for all the world to see.

"'Since Charles slipped into a semiconscious state in early January of this year, I have been horrified by his hourly recitations of his misdeeds. In these baleful hours, Charles has told tales no man should tell. Certainly not with a smile on his lips and laughter in his eyes as my son, my sinister son, has told them. I recount them now, and as I do, I curse him and myself for all eternity.'"

I kneaded my hands and my eyes fell closed. Oh, no, no. How would he know what pain it was to hear these things retold? How could he possibly tell the world of hideous deeds best left buried?

"'The kitten he left to die I cannot resurrect nor

offer recompense in any kind to anyone. Uncivilized behavior toward the animals of the world is a beastly act unworthy of humans, yet worthy of condemnation. The servant whom Charles cursed has long since died and no apology, save to God, can correct the misdeed. The upstairs maid whom Charles mistreated and impregnated—"'

A hue and cry went up from the audience.

"Please, ladies and gentlemen," Darian pleaded feebly, "please." He returned to his papers.

"'The upstairs maid whom Charles abused and impregnated more than twenty-five years ago is an even sorrier tale. This maid—Mary Beth by name—endured years of lashings by Charles for the slightest of misdemeanors. Yet, when she came to me to reveal this, I upheld my son's right to discipline staff. Fully disheartened, she never came to me again and I, thinking the issue had resolved itself, thought no more of it. Until she came to me three years later and declared she was carrying Charles's child. Again, I took my son's part and sent her to a small fishing village along the Scottish coast. There, four months later, she was delivered of a boy. To hear Charles tell the story last month, one hears only how he inspired fear in the girl, how he cowed her, how he controlled her and got her with child. A child whom he thinks no more of than a trophy of his manhood.

"'Seeking verification of Charles's rantings, I asked the detectives to investigate this case. They report that a young woman named Mary Beth Higgins did indeed give birth to a boy in the village of Whitby many years ago. However, over the years, the hardship of making a wage for herself and her child led the woman to desperation. When the child was little more than three, she strangled him and hung herself.'"

I shook my head in grief.

"'But that is not the end of Charles's crimes, not by far. Amid his recent recitations, he has told a tale so

263

evil, even now I can scarcely believe it. It seems when he was but twelve and my brother John's daughter Helena but six, Charles took unto himself the opportunity to consort with the child as if she were his paramour.' "

Charlotte Chadwick gasped and in the next moment slumped over in a dead faint. Her husband caught her just before she slid to the floor with Forbisher on bended knee in front of her, smelling salts to her nose.

I ached for her mortification. She would think herself ruined by such revelations. But I began to feel something else. Some other sensation—amid the horror of it all—that I dared call hope. Some other one called freedom.

Charlotte blinked and sniffed. Thanking Forbisher and her husband, she waved off efforts to remove her from the room.

"No," I could hear her say to both men, "I will stay to hear the rest. Albert finally came to his senses and I wish to know firsthand how he came to such a state." She settled back in her chair and nodded toward Darian. "Mr. Osgood, forgive my intrusion. Pray, do continue."

" 'If Charles had taken his cousin's affections, turned them toward himself, and ruined her for any other man, he would burn in hell for that alone. Yet, God help us all, there is more. More, almost, than my diseased heart can stand to tell. Yet, I must and I will.

" 'Carrying on with Helena with every opportunity and in every locale, Charles should have known it would only be a matter of time before he was discovered. Still, he must have felt he could bully anyone who dared to counter the next Earl of Darnley. He never counted on having to bully his brother. The very person whom he had despised from the cradle became the very person who could ruin him in my eyes. Charles could not tolerate that. When Iselton discovered Charles and Helena at their play, it has been learned, Charles threatened Izzy. Izzy, who evidently never knew the playmate was his cousin Helena, did persist, however. For possessing such knowledge, Izzy suffered a terrible beating from which he barely recovered. And subsequently—according to the best that the detectives can reconstruct the incidents—Charles purposely lamed his brother's horse and left him to die in a terrible rainstorm.'"

Cries and moans and murmurs filled the room with such a din I thought we must be on the shores of hell. Even I writhed in my chair. To hear Charles's crime recited in the light of day before all these people was even more devastating than having heard it from Helena last night in the dark.

I felt Graham take my hand and I looked over at him. His black eyes met mine. Pain engulfed them.

"Oh, Vanessa," he whispered brokenly, "what have we Chadwicks done?"

"Not you, Graham. Not you."

"Ladies and gentlemen"—Darian was looking the very worst for wear now—"I know this is extraordinarily difficult for you. But I must continue." He swallowed a few times and, with weary eyes and sagging body, began once more.

"'Fratricide. Yes, Charles was guilty of it. Incest. Yes, Charles was guilty of it. Whoring. Guilty. Cheating. Guilty. Finally, there was not even a name for his crimes. So diverse, so inexplicable were they that they became merely occurrences in his day. Instances, with nothing to regret. Something to titillate and wile away the hours of one's useless life. Yet this man—whom I should have seen for what he truly was long before—this man I sent into the world to marry.'"

Darian paused and, beneath his lashes, looked at me.

I was so numb I could not move. Graham squeezed my hand. I remained frozen.

"'Here with this act—a sacrament, no less—begins a tale of yet another person sacrificed to my son's senseless cruelty. True, I sent him out to the world to bring back a wife of whom we might all be proud. A wife with a pedigree, a presence, a dowry. Charles, true to his upbringing, did as he was told. He brought us back the loveliest, most charming woman ever. In fact, had he been less wedded to his licentiousness, Charles might have found in his darling wife the very reason to wed himself to normality. Still, I believe he was too far gone by then to reform. Even the loveliness of his bride could not lure him from his ways. Instead, he chose—and Helena, too, it appears—to try to seduce Vanessa to join him in his escapades. When that did not work, he and Helena not only sought each other's company once more, but also indulged themselves with others. Charles proceeded once again to take up with actresses and barmaids and ladies of the blood while he continued to cavort with his cousin.

"'Then in a fit I can compare to that of a mad dog, he and Helena decided to wreak vengeance on Charles's wife. According to my detectives, my innocent daughter-in-law Vanessa had by that time lost most hope of saving her marriage. Whether at that point she truly did seek comfort in the arms of another man is something my men cannot prove or disprove. What they can prove is that George Hayden, the man in question, did receive from Charles an exoneration of his gambling debts soon after the man and Vanessa were accused by Charles of adultery. For whatever reason, the man merely states he was caught in the act of seduction with the viscountess and refuses to discuss his actions with her . . .'"

I shuddered in revulsion, remembering how Hayden had asked me to his room at the Ascot Inn on the pretense of meeting others after the races. How he lured me in, declaring Charles was to follow soon.

How he assured me other chaperones would soon present themselves. How he poured me a scotch whiskey, bade me drink it while I worried over Charles's whereabouts. How he urged another drink upon me and I refused. How he attacked me, backed me up against a wall, then carried me to the bed. How Charles burst in upon us. How my husband blanched and then ridiculed me, pointing at me, my skirts above my waist, George in a hideous state of nakedness. And me, frightened and quaking beyond my wits. How Charles roughly pulled me from beneath the man and hurled me toward the door. Ohhh, God. How I cried. How I hurt. How I hurt even more now to hear it all retold—and yet not retold with any accuracy.

I moaned.

"'. . . and therefore, we can only conjecture as to the true paternity of her son whom she calls Jeremy Charles Chadwick. Even my investigation of the child's paternity by my men in the city of New York has yielded no substantial proof. This is the remaining unanswered question of my men's search. Above all other facts, this is the one piece of information I do fervently wish they had found.'"

So Graham was to be the next earl, not Jeremy. Still, I knew—and what's more, Graham knew—Jeremy was the rightful heir. How could I claim an inherited trait so minor that only a few—perhaps only Graham—knew of its importance? How could I when I had no money for lawyers. More than that, I had no stomach for a fight.

"'Therefore, of this crime of cruel mental abuse, I accuse my son, Charles. To Vanessa publicly today, I can give only my abject apologies, my unwavering admiration for her courage, and the sum of money equal to her dowry. It was with this sum she came to us, bringing us the ability to rebuild and prosper. It is only right and fit that I now return it to her in her hour of need. I pray that one day she may find it in

267

her heart to forgive a blind, proud man who admired her when he should have loved her without question.

"'To my niece, Helena Louise Chadwick, only offspring of my youngest brother John, I leave my pity . . .'"

The sounds of a struggle met our ears. Graham and I turned. Helena had jerked free of her gag and, eyes wide, now yelled.

"Pity! I want none of his pity!"

Graham gave a nod and the Surrey brothers had her under the arms, hauling her away through the doors.

"He owes me more! I had the Darnley heir! I had Charles's true son!" She was yelling as the footmen practically lifted her under the arms.

Darian stared at Graham. "I would read this to her and then she may go if you wish it, my lord?"

Graham waved a hand. Disgust lined every feature of his face.

Darian bent to his task. "'For her travail throughout her life, Helena has received too much and too little. Too little love. Too little affection. Too much sordidness. Too much perversion. Too much compensation. Therefore, as of the day this will is read, I rescind her monthly allowance, confiscate her house, and dismiss her servants. The house and the servants were paid for with Chadwick estate money from her father's trust, which I administered. As of this date, all revert to the estate. Also, as of this date, I hereby order my solicitor Darian Osgood and my son Graham to commit her to the York House for the Incurably Insane, where she will occupy the left wing at Chadwick expense until her demise. There, like Charles, she will see her end soon from this insidious disease that has rightly afflicted them both.'"

"Thief!" she was shouting. "Take my house, my property, my pride! Fool! Fool! He cleans *his* house too late!" She ranted on.

But Graham sent a fierce look to Darian.

"My lord, that is all."

Graham spun his head round to look at the Surrey boys. "Take her away, men." And the double doors closed on the wreckage of her life.

Those assembled sat stock-still, white with shock. Even Charlotte sat openmouthed.

My eyes fell closed. Oh when would this end?

"'To my only remaining brother William, I leave my love, which in my lifetime he never saw but always had. I leave him his regular estate allowance and our mother's hunting lodge in north York, which he and his wife Charlotte always enjoyed. Most of all, I leave him my apologies—my heartfelt apologies—for years when I neglected him in the service of my pride of place.

"'To my only remaining son Graham, I leave all other worldly goods, including my title, the estates of the earldom, as well as the sole proprietorship of the family shipping company Darnley and Sons.

"'I have already given Graham in March of this year the authority to sell Chadwick House in London. That property had a buyer whose offer would allow Graham to fund Darnley and Sons for a very wise, very necessary major expansion. That property, I hope by this time, is sold and its proceeds serving you well, my son. You had the best head of all three boys for logic—and for business—and I know you will enjoy great rewards from your endeavors.

"'As for the rest, my dear boy, may you use all my worldly goods in better service and to greater glory than I ever did. I knew not how. Much to your innate goodness, I believe you do. I bid you use them both in love and joy for yourself and your family, as yet unformed.'"

I could not help myself; I glanced at Graham. He sat, his fingers pinching the bridge of his nose, his eyes covered. He was swallowing hard. I was recoiling with the events of the day. All I could do now was gaze at Darian, who now read the end of the text with various small sums bequeathed to villagers, the Preservation Society, and to servants.

I sat, hearing none if it. Finally, I saw Darian close the portfolio and stand.

"Ladies and gentlemen, thank you very much for your forbearance this morning. I do appreciate it. With the assistance of Mr. Fenton, I will now begin the dispersals. Please remain here in this room. Mr. Fenton will call you into me in the withdrawing room. Thank you."

To discreet murmurs of appreciation, Darian bowed slightly and made his way to the door leading to a small sitting room we'd always called the withdrawing room.

No sooner was he gone than people—masses of people—descended on me and Graham.

"Congratulations, sir!"

"My pleasure to know you're next in line, milord."

"I'll be proud to serve you, sir, I will."

"Vanessa—?"

Charlotte Chadwick bent toward me.

"My dear, may I say I always thought the Chadwicks had done you a disservice. Forgive me for being so forward but—but . . . well, I could tell by looking at you that you were not the sort of lady who—"

"Aunt Charlotte," Graham intruded, "thank you. I value your words." He glanced at me and I saw he fought tears as I did. "Vanessa has had rather a bad time of it these last two weeks and—"

"I know, dearest. I know. It's Helena. Terrible, Graham darling. We shall never forget the sight of her here." She reached to squeeze my hands, knit tightly in my lap. "But you are so strong, Vanessa. I commend you, my dear."

Darian's tall thin assistant, Horatio Fenton, suddenly appeared at my side.

"Ma'am, Mr. Osgood wishes to see you."

I rose from my chair on unsteady legs. A clucking

Lucile was right behind me, though. As I turned to go, I glanced down at Graham. Relief, joy, anguish, all played within his ebony eyes.

What could I say? The torment was finished.

I turned and allowed Fenton and Lucile to lead me away. With mincing steps, I made the withdrawing room.

Here, amid the sumptuous red Rococo room, Darian sat at a small writing desk but rose to help me take a chair before him. When I was situated, he smiled sadly and took from the table a long yellow slip of paper.

"Vanessa, this is a bank cheque made over to you. You may cash it in York or London whenever you wish."

I bit my lip to stop the sobs that suddenly welled up and threatened to wrack my body. Darian placed a white linen handkerchief between my clenching fingers and I dabbed at my tears.

"You knew, Darian, that the earl had investigated—?"

"Yes, I knew, my dear. Toward the end of his life, Charles began to have hallucinatory periods. At first, we made no sense of his ramblings. But some statements recurred with an exactness and then with a perverse logic that set the old earl reeling.

"'Could Charles be so malicious?' the earl asked me one night last January. I could only tell my lord what I knew from rumors of Charles's behavior over the decades. And, of course, I could tell him what I knew of your true character. Lord Albert could not accept it merely at face value. Charles's ravings about you and then Helena and others frankly frightened the old man. He'd just learned he was dying, that he had only a few months to live, and he wanted things settled. That's when he bade me hire the two detectives from London.

"When they returned with evidence—sworn statements from credible sources—that matched Charles's ravings, Lord Albert was wild with fury. He employed them to investigate Helena, Margaret Hamilton-Fyfe, some actress Charles had taken up with—in fact, anyone Charles named in his daily rants.

"Within days, my lord had enough evidence to substantiate Charles's worst claims. He even had me set the detectives on George Hayden, as you heard. We didn't get as much there as we would have hoped. But then, there was enough to convince Lord Albert that Charles was a spawn of hell. The old man died quite beside himself. At his end, I daresay he was tormented most by what the future held for you, my dear. He knew of no way to totally recompense you, and so he made the codicil that all named must attend. He counted on your goodness to come forward."

"Did he know I was penniless?"

"Yes, he knew what had happened to your father's business. He thought you'd come forward to provide for your son. He was right. He would be very happy to know you have this money in hand, my dear. He told me himself he would rather see the earldom of Darnley destroyed for all time than to see the wrong done you not rectified in any small way. For him, for Jeremy, for yourself, I bid you to use that money to make a better life for yourself and your son beginning now."

"Thank you, Darian." I clutched the check to my chest. "What of Graham? With all the dispensations of money today, I wonder—I know I overstep my bounds—but I must ask: Does he have enough capital to run the estate and save his business?"

Darian raised his brows and shook his head. "You know I can't reveal that, my dear." Yet, his lax countenance told me there was little hope.

Blanche. Blanche, with her dower and her virtue and her unsullied love, was Graham's only hope.

I could not bear to think of it.

I stood and he did, too.

"Thank you, Darian."

He took my hand and kissed it. "You deserve more, my dear. I always thought you would become a most impressive countess, madam."

My arms went round him and I wept softly as he kissed my hair.

"After today, there will be no more tears," he crooned. "I must dispense their due to others now, but I will see you with Graham afterward."

I nodded and wiped the tears from my cheeks. Unable to look at him, I left the room by the hall doors.

I waved away any assistance from Lucile or footmen, then descended the stairs and traversed the length of the castle to my apartment. Gaining courage and speed as I went, I knew I must leave here immediately before I lost whatever dignity had been returned to me.

In Eliza's wing, I thrust open Jeremy's door, to find him and Miss Simpson playing chess in the nursery.

"Hello, darling." I ran my fingers through his glorious blond hair. Hair like my mother's, not George Hayden's.

"Hello, Miss Simpson. I hate to interrupt your game, but we are going to leave now. Miss Simpson, please order my trunks back in the carriage. Jeremy and I leave for the York train station immediately."

"But, ma'am, the will . . . and I . . . Am I to go with you?"

I stared at her. Over the past two weeks, she had softened. She had become more likeable, more the type of governess I would have wanted for Jeremy—or any child. I would hate to leave her. But leave her and everyone and everything I would.

"The will is read, Miss Simpson. And no, you are the earl's employee and remain here. Whereas Jeremy and I are going home."

Chapter Eighteen

Dusk fell as Jeremy and I sat in our compartment awaiting the departure of the London-bound train. Rain beat upon the metal roof, creating a tattoo that matched the tone and cadence of my sorrow. I hadn't stopped weeping since Graham's carriage took us down the Darnley road toward York.

Jeremy, never having seen me in such a state, had the natural reaction of a little child: He was frightened. He huddled into one corner near the window, looking at me now and again through black lashes. The toy soldier he held lay between limp fingers.

Attempting valiance, I straightened my spine and wiped my eyes once more.

The train whistle blew. The engine hissed. I felt the wheels churn along the tracks, taking me away, far away. Away from sorrow and defeat, away from poverty. Taking me into financial security that offered me some dignity, some hope. But no great love.

I clutched my arms more tightly about me. Fresh hot tears traveled my cheeks. With Darian's ravaged handkerchief, I wiped them away.

The compartment doors suddenly slung open with a bang!

I jumped.

Jeremy squealed.

Then he was out of his seat, throwing his arms about a tall, blond-haired handsome man with an arm sling.

"Graham!"

"Yes, by God! Graham!" He sat down with a thud in the seat across from me, his one arm full of a delighted Jeremy, his relentlessly probing eyes full of anger.

"You left me!" he was gasping for breath, shaking his head in disbelief. "You left me! Without a word . . ."

"I left a letter."

"Don't lift your chin to me. A letter? A damned letter! Jeremy, I am sorry, son, but could you wait right there in the corridor while your mother and I talk? We must speak of adult matters. Be a good boy, will you? You can watch us through the glass door, you see." He slid open the compartment door and handed a happy Jeremy into the corridor. Then he shut it with another vicious clang.

"Graham, please—"

"No! I came here for you to hear me out!"

I turned my face to the window. Outside, the countryside, dappled by the dying sun and drenched by a steady rain, sped past my eyes.

"I must leave, Graham."

"You must leave," he echoed my tone. "Again, eh? Well, this time before you go, I will give you two things *I* want you to have. This time, both are due you. Unlike the divorce papers . . ."

"I—"

"Listen to me, Vanessa. You must, you see, because I am on this train till London, too. Now, look at me. Please. Thank you. First, I will give you an explanation coupled with an apology."

"No." I shook my head. God, I could barely stand to look at him, so near, so very dear to me he was. How could I stand for more senseless, pointless *talk?* "I don't want—"

"I know what you want and don't. This conversation is what *I* want. And I will have some of what I want, by God! First, I want to give you an apology for my failure to protect you from Helena and my reasons, weak as they are, for my failure."

"You owe me no apology, Graham. She is ill, devious. You could not know what her mind could concoct."

"True. But nonetheless, I did try to stop whatever evil befell you and Jeremy."

"I know you did."

"No, you don't. You have difficulty trusting people, particularly men. Particularly me, my darling. And I have sought to remedy that. I failed. No, no, it's true. I failed to protect you.

"Last week, when we arrived in London, I hired the same detectives my father engaged to investigate Charles's background."

I gaped at him. "You knew—before this morning's reading—what they had discovered for your father?"

"No. Their work for him was confidential. In fact, I never knew my father hired a firm. It was Darian who referred me to them when I asked him for advice that first day we arrived in London. Darian told me they had done some work for my father and he had been well pleased with their thoroughness. I can't say I have been pleased with their thoroughness or promptness for me. On the contrary, if they'd worked harder and faster, much of your misery might have been avoided." He sighed.

"But I will say that what they found did leave an impression on my father. Before he died, I suspected by his behavior that he had learned a good deal of how devilish Charles had become. In those few months we spent together, Father was kinder, gentler with me than I had ever known him. When he passed away, I mourned his loss. I think he tried to make up for all those years he had favored Charles. And, I must say, to a great extent, he did make up for them.

But I wish to tell you of what work the detectives did for me."

He glanced out the window. "I told them to investigate the clippings and the note you received in Southampton. With every new threat, I kept them informed, and with every event, they followed new clues. They seemed to find as many confusing ones as we did.

"Margaret Hamilton-Fyfe was our first suspect, naturally. She was there in the hotel and she had motive. I told my men that I questioned if she would know you would be there at that date and time, and if she would have on her person clippings six years old. It seemed a far stretch of logic. But we could not find the source of the notes, only how they were delivered.

"The detectives checked the hotel staff. That revealed that a young boy had asked for the whereabouts of your rooms that afternoon. The detectives could not find the boy. A shop boy was the description we got. Someone who had been hired just for the delivery. He had disappeared, of course, into thin air.

"In London, my men followed up on the man in the Mews who attacked you. That, as Helena revealed last night, was a dead end because she had not hired him. My men certainly could find no links to you. If the man in the Mews was a madman—this Jack the Ripper—or if he was the Duke of Clarence or someone impersonating him, we had no idea. We did conclude that the man had simply disappeared.

"Then, of course, came the second note, delivered by post. There, my men could merely conclude that whoever was sending these notes knew quite a bit about us. Well, we knew that from the very start! You would not let me see it and so I could not have them analyze the handwriting. We were stuck on that one.

"Finally, we left London and I honestly believed we had escaped the clutches of whoever was pursuing you. Days went by, days of peace—" he searched my eyes and I closed them to shut away the memories in my heart—"days of joy and nothing threatening happened."

"You thought the menace gone. I did, too."

He nodded. "But we were so wrong. I was so damn shortsighted!" He pounded his hand with his fist and raked his hair. "I should have *seen*. But I was so involved in the shipping disaster and so very engrossed in you, I saw nothing . . . nothing but the opportunity to show you how I cared. I let the detectives do their work and I . . . well, I only wanted to be with you. How could I know my own cousin would follow us?"

"She didn't have to follow us, Graham. She overheard us one night talking in the hallway. I know now Helena was not jealous as much of our relationship as she was of the fact that you and I could find happiness together and she and Charles never could."

Graham looked at his hands. "After that, Samantha was found dead. In that morning's conversations, I was doubly shocked. Not only was an innocent animal brutally murdered, but Helena revealed her knowledge of Atherton's employ by the Hamilton-Fyfes. That afternoon, I cabled my men, of course. They went to my house and questioned Atherton, then later, the Gwynns.

"Atherton told them that she had certainly been employed by the Hamilton-Fyfes, and that at the interview Helena thought that a plus. Evidently, Helena hoped you'd discover the fact and find it frightening. The Gwynns told my men that Helena decided on Atherton the moment she heard she'd once been part of their staff. Coincidence again. But a coincidence that Helena turned to her advantage."

"And so Atherton's snooping in my trunks—?"

"Was merely that. She did so out of curiosity, not maliciousness. She claims Helena never gave her any instructions to snoop or act against you in any way.

278

She knew of no notes, either."

"Yes, I have both locked away safely in my diary. No one has taken them."

"The death of Samantha was quite another matter, however. Shocking as it was, we could find no clues other than what I told you. The deed had been committed outside the staircase door. Whoever did it knew the castle well and also had to know how and when I arrived and left that night. Whoever did it had wanted to throw suspicion on me, I knew. And while that might have been anyone, I knew of no one of my staff with such a vicious streak. I concluded and told my detectives that whoever killed Samantha was probably the same person who sent the notes. That person had to know not only the castle but also your whereabouts.

"I went to York that day, not only to cable my office in London about my ships off Madras, but also to give instructions to the detectives. I returned late the next morning to find the portrait slashed, the pony's straps tampered with—and you and Jeremy gone.

"I went mad trying to find you. Forbisher and MacCarthy helped as much as they could. But you were clever, darling. Never did I think you would remain for the reading of the will."

"But I knew what would happen if the will could not be read because not everyone was in attendance. I couldn't let you lose everything, Graham. Not when we'd all come so far."

"But your life was at risk . . ."

"And your heritage."

His eyes caressed mine. "You are a unique woman."

I took my eyes from his.

He continued. "You managed to slip away from me. We had a devil of a time tracing your actions. But Helena had better sources. My two detectives reported to me this morning—too late to save us any torment—but nonetheless, they did discover that it was Helena who hired the two highwaymen who attacked your carriage. She took the gold sovereigns from Father's collections and paid them to fall upon you and Jeremy. I thank God they found you in a storm and I am grateful they are dead. We brought you home, of course. You were so ill, my darling . . ."

His voice broke and he squinted out the window. "I feared you had left me forever. But you are strong and you recovered. Recovered just in time to be attacked by her. She came in through the secret stairs in Jeremy's room. She must have hidden there before I put up the guard."

"Thank God you were there to help me."

He snorted. "Help you! Like hell I did!"

"If you had not intervened, heaven only knows how far she may have gotten with her plan."

"She was far more demented than anyone—anyone!—could conceive!"

"But she didn't win."

"No, she could not. Not against you." He inhaled deeply. "Now—now for the second thing I promised you."

He reached inside his coat pocket and extracted a fat white envelope.

"Take it."

I would not.

He laid it in my lap.

I stared at him.

"Not like the divorce papers I gave you at your departure years ago. Far better. Open it."

I could not move.

"I had Darian draw these up last week on the day we had the discussion of evidence of Jeremy's paternity. You remember it. The conversation in the library."

I nodded. How could I forget?

"Please note the date on the documents. You were in our presence when I handed them over to Darian. There are three copies—one for me, one for Darian.

This is yours. Read it."

I broke the seal—Darian's solicitor's seal and that of the Earl of Darnley. I opened the legal papers and began to read the finely scripted words.

My mind registered only the basics of the legal verbiage. I frowned and had to read the words once more.

The papers drifted from my fingers. My eyes sought Graham's.

"Why?" I whispered.

"Freedom. Justice."

"This freedom binds me. This justice limits me. There is no need."

"I need this!" He thundered and pounded his chest with his fist. *"I* need to do this!"

"I do not want it!"

"You are not given it! Jeremy is."

I trembled in agony. "I will take him back to New York."

"Wherever he goes, wherever he lives, he is the eleventh Earl of Darnley."

"You cannot break your father's will!"

"Oh? Who says I do? Not Darian. No one else has the right to challenge my decision. And I now know after this morning's reading that had my father lived to ever see what I saw in Jeremy—the mark of the Chadwicks—he would have made Jeremy heir, not me. I do my father's will here by passing to the rightful heir his due. No matter where you go, Jeremy has inherited the estates and title, Vanessa. Would you, as dowager countess and regent of his inheritance, administer it from near or far?"

I closed my eyes and fought the urge to cry or scream or both. But I recovered myself when I heard Graham rise.

He was leaving?

"Inheriting the earldom is a dubious honor," I said in a calm voice as I watched his hands grasp the door handle.

"Isn't it, though?"

"I know not how to administer it."

"You are brilliant. You will learn."

"I cannot do it alone."

"Darian will help."

"May I also count on you?"

His eyes fell closed. "I hoped you would."

"Even from afar?"

"From anywhere."

From the shelter of Blanche's arms?

His body convulsed as if he'd heard me! As if I'd wounded him mortally! Yet his next words came out almost breathlessly.

"I am sailing for India next Tuesday. I must see to my ships and my crew."

"What will you use for capital if—if you have now given Jeremy and me all rights to the estates? How can I help y—?"

"I have borrowed money from Nathan Rothschild. He knows me, trusts me."

I opened my mouth and shut it quickly. Silence divided us. Beyond the divide, I saw years of loneliness and sorrow loom before us.

"Ask it!" he seethed, his back still to me. "Ask the question that burns in your brain!"

I shook my head and gulped audibly.

"Ahh, my darling Vanessa." He rested his forehead against the glass and closed his eyes. "Pride prohibits you. Haven't we learned, today of all days, how pride can kill? You will not ask about my marriage, so I will tell you. I am not capable of marrying for anything less than love. I would have tried. Over a year ago, I had progressed to the point where I had forgotten you—or so I thought—enough to consider another woman. Enough to consider Blanche Margrave. But that was before events drew you to me. Before Charles died and Father wrote this will. Before you returned and I held you in my arms. Before I knew the sublime joy of making love to you. After that, do you honestly believe I could take another woman to my bed? No. I will walk this earth, and perhaps heaven as well, requiring no other woman except you."

I stood and in the tiny confines of the compartment, I reached out and easily encircled him with my arms. My cheek to his strong back, I twined my fingers together at his waist.

He shuddered.

"My sweet man, I love you."

"I love you, too, Vanessa." He declared it as bald fact.

Then he turned the handle of the door.

"No! Don't go!"

"The very thing I begged of you! Yet, you leave me every time!"

"I won't leave you! I swear I won't!"

He pivoted. His eyes pillaged mine. A question rose there and I . . .

I stood emotionally naked. Minus every ounce of pride, I declared now one glaring fact.

"I want you to marry me."

He narrowed his eyes at me.

"I love you, Graham. I have never loved another man. Never. And I—I know I have much to learn in the way of trust, but I will never learn trust without you. I need you, darling." I spread my hands wide and told him with my eyes, my heart, my soul, how much I cared. "Won't you please marry me and help make me whole?"

He groaned and captured me with one sweeping arm about my waist. His moist lips seized mine in a barrage of sweet, savage kisses.

"Promise me," he urged, his one good hand thrusting into my hair.

"Anything!"

"You will never leave me!"

"Not on earth or in God's heaven."

Epilogue

September annually arrives in Darnley with the fading glories of the midnight sun. Over the past six years, I have come to know this, enjoy this, and revel in this time of year. It is the anniversary month of my return to England.

I write here in my diary in my sitting room off Graham's and my bedroom. Occasionally, I raise my head and watch the autumn roses in the garden below sway in the offshore breeze. I feel my baby kick and place my palm over my rounded form. Once again, I am startled by this baby's power and his urge to life. If, indeed, this baby is a boy.

Our two older children have been boys. Sons, full of vigor and curiosity. Sons with blond hair, one bronze like Graham's, one platinum like mine. Sons whose hair is sun-streaked and whose complexions are tanned from hours of playing with their older brother, Jeremy. Sons who play well together and whose arguments are minor and quickly patched. Sons who show no signs of meanness or envy, no deference to one alone.

Jeremy is Earl of Darnley, yet to himself he is Graham's and my son. He calls his uncle *father* and Graham returns the name of *son*. They are well-pleased with each other and I am well pleased with both.

With all my life, in fact.

No one is more astonished than I at my good fortune. No one is more grateful, except perhaps my darling husband. With his help, I have learned much. How to trust a man, how to love a man. But with Graham, the task was so easy. With Graham, from the moment of my surrender on the train, my life has been so full.

Within minutes, Graham had taken me and Jeremy off the train at the first stop and led us back to York and Darnley the next morning. Nothing would do but that I marry him within days.

"Before I sail," he said.

And so we did in a small ceremony with Jeremy, Uncle William and Aunt Charlotte, Darian, and the household staff in attendance.

When Graham left for Madras a few days later, I was not only the Dowager Countess of Darnley, but also Lord Graham Chadwick's wife. Whatever anyone called me, I could not care. I knew only that I loved, completely, and was loved, totally.

By the time Graham returned two months later, I knew I was with child. This first baby we named Austin. Not a family name. Simply a name we liked. For a baby we had created in utter ecstasy. Austin looks like Graham. With bronze hair and black bold eyes, he is an imp. Like his older brother Jeremy, whom he shadows night and day, Austin is a joy. As is his younger brother Peter, who at age three has not yet developed a characteristic by which we might measure his future.

With this new baby, Graham and I wish for a girl. Yet, Graham says it matters not because if I want a girl, we will just try until we are granted one. My husband is funny and dear.

And hardworking. He has, single-handedly, rebuilt Darnley and Sons to become one of the biggest, most profitable shipping companies in Britain. He has been so successful that rumors in London abound that he will be asked to join the home ministry to advise on trade issues. Graham considers it, particularly because his uncle William—who is now Foreign Minister—says there is no authority equal to Graham. It is a measure of how well Graham has done, but also a measure of how society has forgotten my plight, that he is now considered for such an honor.

Still, the thing that makes him balk is how much time it would require away from me. He has been away often and we have spent innumerable lonely nights these past six years. But when he returns, he comes first to me. And I welcome him with open arms.

"It matters not where you go or for how long," I told him just last night when the subject resurfaced. "I will always be here waiting for you, my love."

He had urged me closer. "I never want to lose you."

"You couldn't if you tried."

He slept instantly after that, but rose early to take Jeremy with him to the villagers' harvest meeting. Because of Graham's business interests, we live mostly in London rather than in Darnley. Yet, Graham and Jeremy return often for similar meetings or other events. And Graham and I always return for the birthing of each baby and the coming of September. This year, both are simultaneous.

Yet, this year we came for another reason. A sadder one. Helena began to slip away yesterday morning. She died within hours.

The disease that destroyed her left her strangely calm just before the end. No more did she chant and hiss at me and Graham. No more did she need to be chained to her bed at the sight of us.

No. She lay there on her bed, blind and almost deaf, but peaceful. Serene.

"Vanessa and Graham, how nice of you to come. You come for tea, I presume?"

Graham and I had looked at each other. "I—I can't remember what you like in your tea, Vanessa? Did you pour the milk or sugar in before it was poured or afterward? Silly, silly, what we remember and forget. How is Charles? Have you seen him? He was by the other day, you know. Yes, he was. Brought me carnations. I always liked carnations. Red ones." She started to weep then. Without a sound, the tears filled her sightless eyes and coursed down her sunken cheeks. "He loved me, you know."

I almost cried with her. "Yes, I know," I told her.

For hours, she went on about Charles. Lovely stories of how he had cared for her and been kind to her. Sweet stories of their childhood, of sharing cookies, romping in meadows, riding in forests. Nothing sordid, nothing unseemly. Just the memories of one child caring for a smaller one.

It broke my heart. I sat there with Graham's strong arms about me until she sighed her last breath. As she expired, I felt the vestiges of all horrors drain from me. I could forgive. I can forget.

This afternoon, when we bury her, I will inter all my awful memories with her.

I wish all might do the same.

Indeed, yesterday, as we stood on the front steps of the hospital where Helena had lived these last years, I heard one nurse speak to an attendant.

"Those are the Chadwicks, aren't they?"

"Yes, that's that famous Chadwick woman. That cousin wot's locked up in there, and the old viscount tried to say this one 'ere was a harlot. But Lord Graham there, 'e brought 'er back so's 'e could make it right."

I checked Graham's eyes to see if he'd heard. He smiled sadly and hugged me close. The carriage drew up to the steps, and with difficulty, I settled my girth into the seat.

He climbed in beside me and shut the door on the world.

"But more than that," he drew me close and whispered against my temple, "he wanted her back so that he could love her in spite of the evil done her and adore her for all she truly is."